BOY AND THE BEETLE

A catalogue record for this
book is available from the
National Library of Australia

Thank you Plume Editing Services
and Seth Mao at Mao Illustration
All illustrations by Seth Mao

Other works by Mick J. Adams
see on Instagram @mickjadams

Linellen Press
265 Boomerang Road
Oldbury, Western Australia
www.linellenpress.com.au

Contents

1

Boy sat below a crude shelter, hiding from the rain. The incoming downpour found its way through the branches and leaves he had wedged above him, which were balancing in the crevice of two boulders. Water pooled in the dirt around his feet, finding its lowest point. He leaned back on his heels, wrapped his arms around his knees, and took a moment to rest. He was still only a child, thirteen summers old, on the brink of adolescence. He had childish looks, except for a nose racing ahead to be an adult, none of his remaining features expelled a sense of urgency. His fluffy brown hair curled in the drips of rain, clumping to his forehead as he struggled to keep his feet dry. It was not cold, but the forest was darkening as the storm system moved across the sky. His ankles and knees began to tire, and shuffling around in between the granite boulders was not going to be comfortable for long. This was Boy's first day waiting alone, precious time he would one day look back and appreciate: time with himself to think, reflect, comply, conspire, devise, and do nothing. Boy, under his leaking roof of scrap, was lost, and this was his blunder. He would remember this wet day, for it would be one of only two times it rained in his story.

~

A few days before, Boy had been playing with his younger brother and sister amongst the dark boulders that lay by the river. He had always called the river 'Tree Deep Trundle', even though, in their ancient land, it was known as the Hew River. Smooth boulders rested at the base of Tree Deep Trundle's waterfall. The forty-foot fall lay upstream from Boy's home, and it was a destination for fun, to chase and play amongst the sandy shores with his brother and sister. Boy, Tilly and Armue ran through the boulder maze, which was lined with sandy paths, wet from the river. They laughed and teased, playing their game of tag, as they would until tiredness forced one of them to decide the game was over. Usually, Tilly was the timer for the finish; Armue and Boy knew this from experience. But, this day, it was Boy who stopped running, allowing Tilly and Armue to catch up to him. Panting for air, he curled his feet back and forth through sand while he caught his breath.

The shadow of Boy's stance disappeared as a large flock of birds flew high above: so large a flock that it blocked out the sun for some time like a thick storm cloud would. The three siblings watched the flock fly over the top of the waterfall and beyond.

'Boy! I'm thirsty,' said Armue.

'Yeah, me too,' said Tilly.

'Tree Deep Trundle is just there. Go and drink that.'

'Mum told me you were the only one allowed to go close to the water,' said Armue.

The Hew River was not to be trusted. It changed faster than the weather and had more power than a storm, and somehow it reacted differently to each person. The river was alive, dangerous, yet Boy was the only one who had positive reactions from it: The water regarded him as a friend.

'Boy, just get me some water. I'll let you go and hunt with Kie-hep,' said Armue.

Kie-hep was Armue's pet: he had found him lying in between jagged rocks alongside Tree Deep Trundle's shores. He was much like a hunting bird – a strong bird of prey – but neither a falcon nor a hawk, his father had told him. Kie-hep's talent as a hunter didn't come from camouflage or stealth but from the vibrant colour emanating from his magnificent feathers as they caught the sunlight. His prey would be oddly mesmerised when approached, as the colour of his feathers would change rapidly before the final strike. Kie-hep was a master hunter and a great friend to Armue and their family. He was the only one of his kind they had ever seen, but he was growing old and slow. Their father would soon have to revert to catching rabbits with the old wooden traps, unused for a long time and stored at the back of their barn.

Boy left his brother and sister where the sandy riverbank met the grassy earth. He climbed down the familiar granite boulders towards the water as he had done many times before. Using one arm to balance and holding a wooden scoop in the other, he fell, tumbling down the rock and falling into the shallow water. He jumped up, splashing in anger.

'Armue, you idiot! Next time get your own damned water.'

The river began to ripple and move around Boy as if it felt his anger. Tilly ran back home, but Armue slowly backed away to the trees, keeping one eye on the close water.

'And what do you want, Tree Deep? Stop swirling!'

Boy waded through the water, around the boulders to a small sandy part of the shore. Tree Deep Trundle began to settle down. Its surface became smooth, and it regained its slower current, winding through the lands to the southeast of their farm.

All Boy knew was within the realms of his birthplace. He thought it had everything: a great forest to the west, and his family house built between the forest and the great River Hew. When Boy was growing in his mother's womb, his dad built the home using the forest and the river, clay and wood. He had to kiln the bricks in a large stone fireplace and weaved an intricate thatched roof cover supplied by the forest on his land.

The farm was peaceful, and the days of happiness were all he knew: from working hard in the fields with his father, to long walks with his mother. She and his siblings would roam along the edge of the forest, gathering baskets of horn berries. Then his mother, Leesiele, helped by Tilly, would make jams and sauces for gifts and sparse trade. Boy had no extended family living nearby, only friendly neighbours to the north, at least a three-day hike along the edge of the forest. The neighbours were of similar age to his mother and father and had two girls of Armue and Tilly's ages. Boy had not seen the girls since last harvest season when they had met in the forest to trade minor delicacies, before farewelling their fathers who traded their grain further away from their families.

The light began to fade in the river's valley. Boy gathered buckets of water from Tree Deep Trundle when he heard his mother call.

'Boy, come inside. Dinner is almost ready, and we need more water.'

Boy jogged back to the house, arms stretched out, challenging his muscles to keep the water calm. Despite his efforts, half the amount he'd begun with bounced back and forth and hauled itself over the rim. He slowed to a walk and let the delicious smell of roast chicken coming from the house draw him closer. His mother stood hunched over the stove, stirring a large cauldron full of floating vegetables.

'Mum, how come we haven't seen our neighbours lately?'

'Well, they're busy, Boy. We'll have to go and see them soon, though. We discussed having a large dinner at their place with all their family some time, so you'll see them soon.'

'Great! I want to show them the new cubby house I've built.'

'What cubby house, Boy?'

'I started building a little wooden hut down near Tree Deep Trundle.'

'Why in all the land would you build it there? You know I don't want you taking anyone to the water. You'll have to enjoy it on your own, and don't you go taking Tilly or Armue down there.'

'But, mum, it's really great, and they'll be fine. They're

always down there with me.'

'Too bad. Why did you start building it there in the first place? There's enough work for you to do here. You should be fishing if you're down there. It's getting harder for your father.'

'Tree Deep told me to.'

'What? That bloody river made you build it there? Don't listen to it then. I don't want any of my children being taken downstream.'

'But, mum!'

'Just take it down, and move all the wood to the edge of the forest, but not too deep.' She turned her attention back to the cauldron.

'Ohhh, okay.'

Armue sat quietly facing the stone hearth in the middle of the room, throwing sticks and woodchips, and barely stoking the flames. Boy tiptoed across the floorboards towards Armue and dropped himself down beside his brother with a dramatic huff. Armue twitched in surprise and shuffled away.

'Armue, where are you going to build your house when you grow up?'

'I don't know. I'd like to build it just in the woods behind our house, I suppose,' he said, stripping bark off a stick and throwing the flakes into the embers.

'You can't live that close to mum and dad's.'

'Why not? I want to live next to mum and dad. Forever.' He scowled.

'Because it's not normal. Did our mum and dad build next to their parents?'

'Be quiet, Boy. I want to live here.'

'Well, too bad. No one can get you water, especially when I'm not here.'

'Where will you be?'

'Somewhere. I dunno, but you need to fend for yourself and not live off Mum and Dad.'

Leesiele overheard this and was not happy.

'Boy, don't say that. Armue and Tilly can live wherever they want, and I want them to live close.'

Armue poked his tongue out at Boy.

'Okay, Armue, how are you going to find water? You're already nine summers old, and you still can't find water.'

'The spring in the woods is my water. I don't need your stupid river.'

'Yeah, only 'cause he doesn't like you.' Boy pushed his bottom lip out with his tongue.

Silence hung in the air, and Armue turned away. Boy began to think he could easily live away in a house he would build himself. He would be free to joke and fart and play whenever he wanted.

~

Later that evening, Boy climbed into bed. He tucked himself under the cool, soft blankets and stared at the roof beams. Lost in the grain of the timber, he began imagining what lay beyond the forest and the hills. He could start to build a home amongst sheltered boulders in the forest, and he could invite the family over for boiled tea and berries ... at a time *he* deemed fit to see them, he thought. Soon he was asleep.

Boy dreamt of clouds suffocating the stars in a clear sky. The grey developed into darkness, then rain. The clouds began to drop sheets of water like the sky was collapsing into the sea and becoming one. He awoke to the first light of dawn shining through his bedroom window, the sound of water still echoing in his head. Like a happy childhood memory, he felt a warm cloak of contentment.

Boy poured himself a drink of water from the chipped pitcher in the kitchen. A large pot was boiling over a small fire, but no one was there. His mother and father were outside yelling at Tilly about her chores. He suddenly remembered the work his father expected from him that day and immediately felt aggrieved at the torment of everyday chores that hampered his own wants. Annoyed, he crept out the front door and ran from tree to tree, down towards the river. With one last frantic dash, he reached the boulders nestled in the banks. He peered out from behind a tree, looking towards the farm, but it did not appear anyone had seen him.

As he ran from the tree to tree, Armue and Tilly carried firewood into the house, his father chopped wood and his mother picked fresh herbs from the garden. No one seemed to have noticed him. He'd do his chores after midday when he returned. There'd be enough time.

As soon as Boy was under cover of the boulders, he could pick his way upstream towards the falls. His siblings wouldn't dare to go there alone, not without him protecting them from the river. Boy thought himself a genius for getting out of today's work. Obviously, he knew he would have to help out eventually, but not this morning. This bright cool morning was for him to get away for a moment of solitude, to sit in peace and dream of the future: where he would live, what his wife would be like, what kind of family they'd be, and how he would make friends with everyone who lived nearby. He would make lots of friends when he became a man, more than just his little brother and sister on an isolated farm. It was a day to dream.

Boy clambered amongst the boulders as he made his way upstream. This side of the river slowly ascended a thick, forested slope that met the top of the falls. The water dived high off the stage and thundered into the deep pool. The far side of the river was never ventured to, not even by his father or mother, he'd once been told. Its bank rose steeply – practically a cliff – covered in green moss that flourished in the afternoon shadows and spray from the falls. The river had carved an ancient groove through the cliffs, exposing the grey rocks wedged in the earth of the northern bank. From Boy's one-sided view of the far cliff, it was a shrub-laden horizon that had no large trees and little birdlife, as far as he had noticed.

Out of boredom, he began shouting at the river to see if he had the power to make Tree Deep stop the waterfall. But the river flowed as usual, and the sarcastic tone in Boy's voice probably hinted it was only a test. It appeared Tree Deep's mind was way off in different waters, but if Boy spoke with authority, maybe it would listen.

His mother and father did not trust the river, and they forbade him to go any great distance up or downstream where they could not hear or see him. His mother knew he had an uncanny relationship with the river, which had a life of its own, but her worst fear was to have one of her children lured away in false trust and taken from her. Boy knew this, but he still wanted to explore further upstream. *What's there? More boulders? More fishing pools?* he wondered.

He looked up to the cliffs on the far side of the falls and saw movement, something like a large fox pacing back and forth, as if it were a human waiting impatiently for friends. As he moved further upstream, he could no longer see the cliff-loitering creature, so he ignored it and pushed on to reach the waterfall. This was the furthest point of the river he had explored. The banks grew thicker, with fallen trees and splintered boulders to climb over as he approached the rocky foot of the falls. The sound was deafening – *perfect for his dad's hunting*, he thought. As the hot sun neared its zenith, the rocks heated up and the clean water invited him to cool off.

As he sat in the shallows shielding his eyes from the hot sun, he noticed, high in the sky flying upstream, the largest bird he'd ever seen. When it flew closer, Boy realised it only looked enormous because it was carrying something. *A large animal, maybe?*

He hid in the shade of a boulder as the bird turned its giant head to look his way. He was sure the large beast had seen him. Gliding lower on the wind, the bird settled itself on the clifftop, where the pacing creature had just been. It dropped what it had been carrying and immediately flew back in the opposite direction. *That's weird,* he thought. Curiosity grew like tomatoes in turds: it was his nature. He quickly put his clothes back on his wet body, soaking them through, and began to pick his way through the thickening bush along the riverbank.

Eventually, Boy reached the top of the falls. The view was spectacular. He had never seen this far in his life. The view of his house and the forest beyond reminded him that it may take quite some time to walk back. *Dad's going to be so angry. It'll take me until late afternoon to get back home.* The cliff across the river was not far away and, sitting on the smooth surface, was a large basket made of thick cane.

At the top of the falls, the river ran fast, and Boy sensed it had a different energy. Luckily, at this time of year, Tree Deep was shallow enough to allow rocks to protrude out of the water. Boy began to jump delicately from rock to rock; he knew if Tree Deep really wanted to kill him, it just needed to rise a little and he would be taken over the falls. It must have sensed his fear as a request because the water began to rise, flowing fast. The rock he was balancing on almost went underwater, so he jumped from one to another, then onto a split boulder jutting high above the surface.

'Tree Deep! What are you doing? Calm down. I'm not joking! I'm only crossing for a second,' he shouted vehemently.

The water began to calm its current and retreated lower than before, leaving Boy with a safe passage to the other side. As he reached the far bank, he climbed the granite boulders. The view to the north was like nothing he'd ever seen before. While his farm was surrounded by healthy forest and meadows, from the north's horizon erupted jagged boulders, dry shrubs and salt bushes as far as he could see. Upon the distant horizon, looking northwest rose giant mountain peaks that vanished into the clouds.

Boy stepped carefully across the flat granite path high above the river. A rustle sounded in the bushes ahead, and he carefully edged past the basket and looked over the long drop to the water. *What was that?* The bushes ahead shook from side to side as he listened and waited. He carefully picked up a stone and threw it towards the sounds. A large black tail appeared. The beast it belonged to moved through the undergrowth away from him, then around in a wide loop. Then it headed straight for him.

Boy looked over the cliff's edge; saw the river's surface glimmering in the sunlight far below. The rustling drew closer and his skin began to crawl. It did not feel right to be there. He turned and ran, skipping onto a flat boulder and launching himself into the basket.

'Squeeeeak!'

Boy landed on something that wriggled. A furry little ground pig shuffled around by his feet, desperately trying to find something to bury its head under.

'Sorry, little guy. I didn't see you there.'

Boy pulled himself up to look back over the edge of the basket. He locked his arms over the rim and into position so he could have a good look around. Nothing moved, and silence reigned. He waited and watched until he had exhausted his strength, then he slid back into the basket.

'Are you all right, little pig? I hope I didn't hurt you.' He held out a hand, attempting to show he was a gentle creature himself.

The pig ruffled its hair and ran around, trying to find somewhere to hide.

'It's okay. I'm not here to hurt you.' He softly patted the fluffy piglet, and within a few moments, it calmed down.

'See, I'm no threat to you. How did you get in here?' The pig whistled a sad tone.

'Were you captured for dinner? I hope not. You're just a cute little guy.' The furry pig squeaked and ran around Boy's feet. Boy looked up to the high walls of the basket, then bent his knees and jumped high to grasp the top of the rim. With all his effort, he pulled himself up to hook his elbows over the edge. The pig squealed a sad tone: *Don't leave me here.*

'Sorry, little guy. I just wanted to see if I could get out, but I won't leave you here.'

Again, more rustling from the bushes. Boy felt the hairs on the back of his neck stand up, and a cold shiver ran down his spine. The black tail flicked up out of the shrubs as it moved closer, then Boy saw the large head of a dark wolf. It had large pink eyes, rife with infection, and its teeth were stained with black and red slime. A putrid, damp smell emanated from its mouth and skin. It crouched aggressively and growled. Boy looked into its glassy eyes and read its desire – *it needs to sink its fangs into warm flesh.*

'Give him to me!' sounded the wolf in Boy's mind. Boy was shocked and fell back into the basket in surprise. He could hear its voice as painful vibrations in his head. He shivered and wanted his dad. The wolf's voice was deep and as gravelly as a granite landslide. His head began to throb just hearing it. He jumped back up to the rim.

Keep your eyes on him. Don't let your enemy disappear, sounded in his head, but this time it was his own voice.

'No! Back off! Go back to where you came from. I've never seen you before and this is my land,' growled Boy. 'Back off!'

The wolf watched with unblinking eyes.

'I don't like your flesh, but I'll take it anyway. Give the little one to me,' said the black wolf.

Boy dropped back down into the basket, his arms exhausted. A few river stones lay in one corner. He placed them into his pocket and pulled himself up to the basket's edge again.

Where the hell did he go? He looked left and right, his neck working frantically. The wolf appeared again, camouflaged by the black granite steeped in shadow. Boy held his hand up to shield the glare of the sun.

'Give him to me!' The voice ached around his tender skull.

'He's under my protection now and the protection of the mighty Tree Deep Trundle, my thunderous river.' A poor attempt to sound like an authority of the territory.

'He's not yours for the keeping.'

'Leave us be!' Boy threw a stone at the wolf, which he easily sidestepped.

Thunder sounded in the clear afternoon sky, closer and louder at every beat. Appearing in the south sky, an enormous winged creature flew towards them. The wolf rustled back behind the bushes, then suddenly leapt at the basket, almost slamming into Boy's face.

Boy was knocked backwards, landing next to the piglet, who again squealed in fear. Boy carefully grasped the pig and froze, cowering at the base and hoping time would speed the moment past.

The wolf snarled as it paced outside the cane wall. It began to scratch violently at the basket's edge. Boy watched as the cane strips began to move back and forth, but the cane held firm. The thunder of the winged creature drew closer, like slow tribal war drums.

Boy grabbed another rock and jumped up to the basket's rim, looked down to where the wolf was snarling and foaming at the mouth. He ditched the rock hard, but the wolf dodged the clumsy throw and leapt again at the basket. Boy threw himself backwards without any hesitation. Two paws and a black head came over the basket's edge, the foul stench clinging to Boy's nostrils.

The swoop of thunder sounded even closer, and the black wolf swept straight over the top of them. Boy closed his eyes in fear, waiting for sharp teeth to sink into his shielding arms. But the wolf was gone.

Boy pulled himself back up to the basket's edge in time to see the flying beast carrying the black mass tight in his talons. It banked and circled around, flying over Tree Deep's wide waterfall. It swept lower and threw the wolf from a great height into the waterfall before circling back for another pass over the basket.

At close glance, the creature was a large bird with raptor-like talons and a body the size of a barn. The beast had fine yellow feathers showing underneath its black wings, and a yellow streak underneath its long black tail. Never had a creature of this size ever flown in his family's sky, Boy realised.

With one loud swoop, the great golden talons clawed the twined basket and swept them off into the sky. Boy panicked – they were being flown away from his farm and up high … very high.

'No! Put me down! You stupid bird! Put me down!'

No reaction came from the beast, and he screamed louder and louder until his throat was raw.

Then it hit him like a wall of cold water: *this thing is going to drop me and eat my corpse.* He put his head between his knees and wanted to weep. He felt helpless.

The pig ran around his feet, squeaking about the rough flight.

As a tear ran down his cheek, he summoned the courage to climb up to the basket's rim. Carefully clinging to the top, the air rushing by, he didn't recognise the lands. He couldn't even see Tree Deep's waterfall.

They were heading roughly north, upstream. Tree Deep was hard to see, except for the green tree-lined banks. To the south, nothing was familiar any more: his farm was out of sight, no fields of barley, not even a wisp of smoke from his mother's burnt cooking. He felt odd smiling at the memory at that moment, but she always burnt the meat, and dad would always complain. He liked his meat red on the inside, almost bleeding, he would joke. She liked it with a crisp blackened exterior, knowing that the animal was sure to be dead.

Get out of here now. His voice ran the words over in his mind. The pig wasn't helping much, running around his legs in a panic. *Maybe I can jump into Tree Deep and it'll help me with a safe landing.* But the creature had veered off the river's line, and now headed further north past the wild forests. *Dead end. Think, Boy, think.*

He dropped his centre of gravity in furious hopelessness, lying on the base with the hard cane pressing into his shoulder blades. He noticed how sharp the talons above him really were, how very easily they could slice through flesh.

The cold frosty air of the spring night set in and the open sky let the chilly depths of space into his world. It pierced Boy's skin and chilled him to the bone, almost as a deliberate action from some past sin to the night air. He hunkered down to stay out of the wind, brought his knees to his chest and cradled the shaking pig like a baby. As he hugged the little creature, he lay on his side, and his last thoughts were of its puny heart beating against his hand.

The basket crashing hard into the ground startled Boy; the impact bounced him mid-air, and his legs flipped sideways into the hard cane wall. The piglet flew out of his hands and he lost it momentarily. The winged creature had plummeted to the ground and now dragged the basket along in its talons, flapping and struggling to launch itself back into the air. It began to tire in its efforts, and the loud painful shrieks it made horrified Boy.

He gripped the cane floor of the basket as it bounced

violently around, the creature dragging it over logs and uneven land. Finally, it came to a halt on a large rocky outcrop surrounded by flat granite boulders. The massive creature stopped, weakened – it could not lift its feet off the ground. It squawked in pain, crying for help. Then it started to breathe deeply and thrash its head back and forth.

Boy grabbed the pig and held onto the sides of the basket. Without waiting and missing the opportunity, he flung himself out of the basket, fell a few metres onto his hip and skidded down the side of a rock shelf.

'Argh!' he shouted in pain. 'You okay, little guy? I hope I didn't squeeze you too hard?'

The pig whistled a high-pitched tune: a squeak of thanks, he assumed.

The boom of drums – of wings, large wings – sounded again in the sky. But it was not their black and yellow captor. It was another behemoth, bigger than the other, with brown speckled skin that shone with an oily sweat from its pores. It dropped down onto their struggling captor, clamped its huge talons into the other's neck, ripping it from side to side. This strange creature had leathery scales rather than feathers and it smelt disgusting. There was an odour of filth before it was even close, as if every living thing had deposited its bowels before fleeing the area.

The basket, now free, was kicked away in the struggle. Boy froze in terror at the sight of the creature being torn to pieces. He began to retreat, slowly, moving backwards towards low shrubs which grew implausibly out of a rocky crevice. He didn't make any sounds or large movements, yet the big scaly creature lifted its wings and turned toward him. Its footsteps rumbled through the rock, its golden eyes those of a hunter, a predator like none he had ever heard of.

Boy bolted, sprinting and jumping from flat boulder to boulder, over pockets of moss and little streams on the sloping rock face. He risked a look back to surmise his impending doom. The creature had its teeth buried in the basket, which it then flung away. Boy just ran and ran. He didn't have a better idea, not that he had time to sum up his creative options.

A giant beat of thunder shot at his back and loose foliage dropped from the dusty air as the beast leapt to take flight. Boy surprised himself by running this fast until he realised how steep the rocks had become. His momentum headed downhill, and he no longer had a choice of direction. Rocks shone and sparkled with water in the morning light. The thunderous beats of air sounded closer and the stench of the thing filled his nostrils, like opening a door to spoilt meat. Two finely-sharpened talons dripping with blood swooped down from above.

The boulders were now too steep to run on; it had become a cliff. Boy could not see the bottom, only the forest beyond. He slipped, landing on his bum, and slid along the steep moss. As the shadow of the creature loomed overhead, the cliff met the roof of the forest and they slid hopelessly into the vine-laden treetops.

The creature banked its wings and turned from the thick treetop canopy. It screeched a long raw note, sickening to the ears, and beat its mighty wings to gain height.

Boy careered through branches and vines and hit the soft ground. The rock face had immediately met a sludgy, mossy and moist slime-bog hollow. It was the beginning of the forest, where the stubborn rock forbade the vines and their seeds any immediate life, yet in return, helped gather much-desired water for the green tangle of the jungle. Boy lay on the moist ground, happy to rest for a moment.

A frog hopped away from its new downward arrival.

Groaning in pain, Boy softly rubbed his freshly-bruised hip. Luckily the skin had not broken, but the bruise appeared and would long be with him. He lay on his side and leant the side of his cheek against the cool smooth rock, slurping the fresh water that trickled down the granite slope. He picked up the piglet and shoved its face towards the water.

'You'd better just come with me. You'll probably get eaten out here alone. We'll look for a new family for you. If you smell some little furry guys like you, start whistling. I don't have a good sense of smell like you. You just seem to sniff constantly.'

The pig whistled a high note as if to agree with him.

The surrounding vegetation grew wide along the wall, and tall trees entangled with vines and creepers stretched far across the roof of the vast bushland.

The distant thunder of the beast's wings returned to echo along the treetops. Birds squawked and flew away to their hiding places. Boy stayed still and did not move as the forest fell silent. A shadow passed above them. Then a giant rock, more like a boulder, crashed through the treetops, thumping into the muddy ground. Mud splattered the tree trunks and splintered branches came crashing down. The shadow of the winged creature began to circle above, surveying its damage.

'Come on, let's get out of here.'

Boy ran fast through the forest, attempting to stay closer to the wider, taller trees until tiredness forced him to stop and crouch in a low gully. He watched the sky. The creature still circled above, another boulder in its talons. Boy left the low gully, keeping one eye on the sky. He picked up his pace, but it was difficult to keep watching the beast as he climbed over fallen logs and avoided the tangle of reaching vines. He let his ears hear what his eyes could not account for, as the sounds in the air told him how close the beast was coming.

'It can get to me here. The forest canopy is not too thick for it to penetrate,' Boy whispered to himself.

Ahead, a huge ancient tree lay fallen over a flowing gully. Boy climbed underneath, drank some more water and lay still. The drumbeat in the air sounded further away. As he waited and waited, the adrenaline left him, and his hip began to burn.

He spoke slowly, forcing his breathe out for the pig to hear.

'I don't know if its right, but I think we should keep moving, little piglet. And don't whistle. Shhhh.'

He crawled out from under the shelter of the monstrous fallen tree: a sight to behold on its own. When standing, it must have been over one hundred feet tall, but now the wise old man of the forest lay sleeping.

Boy headed along the side of the fallen tree, staying hidden in its shadows. He dragged his tired legs through the dense bracken until he reached the gigantic root system that had lifted high in the air, leaving a crater in the soil where it had stood for thousands of years. The forest was now mainly giant trees with a blanket of bracken on the ground. The shadow passed over, scything the air above, and the forest again went still. Boy lay down, hidden by the curling prongs that inhabited the forest floor. He held the shivering piglet against his chest and listened beyond his breath and the irregular beat of his heart. He did not move, but waited, watching the beams of light that penetrated through the forest canopy and flickered on the bark of the trunks.

Carrying another boulder in its talons, the beast above circled for another pass and released it. Splintered shards of timber cracked and shattered as the boulder burst through the trees, the granite projectile landing with a heavy thud close to Boy, its impact vibrating through his body.

He covered his head with his arms, shielding himself, and waited as the branches dropped around him. Then he lay on his back and felt blood trickling down his arm. He hoped the forest would become silent again, but the thunder of wings vibrated through his head as the creature flew by, dropping another boulder from a mighty height.

Boy watched this time as the granite appeared to fall in slow motion. It would be a direct hit. Immediately, he rolled like a cut log along the ground, flattening the bracken. The boulder landed inches away. Scrambling, he climbed inside the end of a hollowed-out fallen tree, the piglet in one hand. Knees and stomach scraping on the surface, he crawled deeper inside, shuddering: *a perfect home for bugs and worms.*

The sound of branches snapping and falling to the ground, the brush of wings stripping the trees echoed through the forest, and then came a thud. *It's on the ground.* Boy could hear it struggling over the logs and broken bushes. It was sniffing and crunching, wood breaking around it and a deep throaty grumble came from its stinking belly. It was no more a bird than a giant lizard – some kind of flying mutant griffin goanna.

Maybe I can outrun it on the forest floor. The thing won't be able to fly unless it's above the treetops.

But he was too scared. Indeed, fear wrapped around him like a blanket, strangling his very essence; he couldn't move; he couldn't breathe. A spider crawled up his leg, and he quietly flicked it off, sending it further into the hollow log. He waited and listened, without any other option evident to him.

A heavy foot landed close. The thing was waddling slowly through the bracken. Without Boy realising, the little piglet was slipping out of his hands. With a little hop, it jumped off his leg, squeaked and ran through the hollow log. The beast turned and sniffed, put its foot on the log and pushed the trunk over. Boy rolled with it, bouncing and tumbling off the insides; he tried not to cry out with the pain. He was upside down and could hear the little piglet running off into the bush, squeaking loudly. The beast screeched high, then growled low, and then followed. The furry pig shuffled his little legs fast through the leaves, zig-zagging across the forest floor, while the fat beast waddled slowly after it, breaking through the bushes at a slow pace and snapping at the ground with its long jaw.

You silly little guy. What are you doing? He's going to eat you.

Blood still ran down Boy's arm. He wiped his face and climbed out of the log to the sight of broken branches and dropped boulders. He moved carefully from tree to tree, hearing in the distance the snapping of wood further away. He ran and ran until his muscles ached like fire and his veins pumped with what felt like lava.

Ahead, the forest changed, and a grassy clearing emerged that signalled the end of the tall timbers. Boy circled its border until he reached the other side. It was a perfect hunting zone for flying creatures to get any ground-dwelling animals leaving the blanketed forest. On the far side, a small stream babbled. He approached it cautiously and drank more water than he should have, causing his bloated stomach to ache. He panted for breath and thanked the little piglet for the diversion. *I hope he finds his home,* he thought, even though he doubted it very much.

Boy knew he had to find shelter and move further away from the stream. *Water will always attract creatures, and maybe even that beast.*

He moved through the land into the late afternoon and eventually found a safe shelter amongst a rocky outcrop with a large overhang that was not quite a cave. He wanted to avoid logs again, to stay away from insects, but also find shelter in case the spring rains hadn't finished for the season. The rocky overhang was somewhat protected from the rain or anything that may be lurking in the night. The crack of thunder sounded above, and the forest grew dark. He lay down, nestled between the join of two resting boulders and shivered through the night.

~

Boy woke, confused and sore. He rolled onto his knees and surveyed the forest looking at him, but there was nothing unusual to be seen. He waited and watched, finally calming himself in the knowledge that he'd been woken by the end of sleep, not by a watching danger. His muscles ached and he noticed he was bruised all over. A jagged lumpy mass of blood gurgled on his hip. He walked back to the stream he had passed the day before.

I have to find some kind of water skin. Boy didn't like the idea of wasting all his energy trying to catch an animal just to skin it to make a water flask.

I have to find Tree Deep. He can lead me home and probably help me get food. Again he drank more from the stream than he probably should have; he felt sick but full. He looked to the sky. *Okay, if the sun is setting over there, then home must be that way ... or is it that way?*

Overhead, birds watched the young lost human waving his arms around in the air as he tried to find his way.

So, Tree Deep should be to the south of me ... or maybe over there. He had never needed to be directed by the sun, but he was no idiot. It was common sense for anyone who was lost and uninjured, with working neck muscles.

Boy forced himself to march that day, bustling his way through the thickening forest that slowly transformed into a vine-laden jungle. The air grew thicker and more humid. Strange forest clearings began to appear along his path, where the air was cool and crisp, and the light was clear and sharp. These areas didn't seem to be trapped in the humid jungle, but rather enigmatic pockets of air and space, too stubborn to leave with the passing weather. There were many he came to, and the air was revitalising.

Now starving, he stumbled, tired and cautious, through the trees. Ahead, another air pocket appeared and, standing in all its glory in the centre of the grassy area, was a single impressive olive tree. Hesitant of the food source that would see him vulnerable to predators, Boy crouched low and threw a rock to the far side. Nothing moved. Birds chirped happily. Butterflies flew in the warm sun. He jogged to the tree and started eating the olives fervently until his teeth were stained a dark maroon. He thanked the olive tree and the fresh air for this sudden gift. Then he filled his pockets until they overflowed and reentered the cover of the forest's thick canopy. Energy returned to his aching body, his cramping stomach levelled itself to contentment, and he began to walk taller, quicker and stronger than before.

More and more clearings came and went before the jungle spread thin again. The land dried and the vegetation adapted amongst the gravel, and shards of broken boulders protruded from the earth. He noticed a group of foreign trees ahead in the sunlight. *They don't look native to this part of the forest. Maybe there's a village or farm nearby ...*

Beyond them, he sighted a tree with light grey bark and small white flowers standing healthily on the banks of a dry gully. As he approached it, he noted its branches were laden with hundreds of almonds. He stopped, stared momentarily, and smiled at his own luck, then he climbed the tree and again ate long, crushing the shells carefully between stones. His pockets overflowed and, as he left the area, the precious nuts tumbled out along the forest trail behind him – a sign that a hungry man had once been here.

Past the almond tree, growing tall and old, stood other flora not native to the area. *Possible civilisation, a farm of some kind,* Boy hoped. But his hopes were not granted. He stopped for a rest and began to think more clearly about the events of days passed.

I hope the little furry pig is safe and finds a little clan to join. He really did save my life, and I his. I wonder if, in his little piggy brain, it was a deliberate move to be the decoy so I could get away. So small and so fluffy, so cute with so much courage. I hope he's okay.

It became clear to Boy that the size of the creature did not reflect the amount of courage they had. *And that little guy had the most. I believe he is okay. Yeah, I have a feeling he is.* He smiled to himself and let the moment leave.

As the sun hung low in the sky, Boy's energy began to deplete. He had covered a significant distance that afternoon, stopping regularly to gorge on olives and almonds and to drink at every stream, spring and water source – although he did let some old murky puddles pass. The land ahead began to slope downhill, and Boy could hear the deep rumble of a broad river running across rapids. Laughing with a limp breath, he leaned forward and let gravity take him downhill. He just needed to lift each heavy leg in front of the other and he would soon reach the river.

Was the water his old dangerous friend Tree Deep Trundle? *It better be Tree Deep.* The gravel underfoot turned into a floor of needles caught from thick pine trees, and in the fading light, the air grew cold. The darkness began to merge with the shadows of the forest. He heard the noise of rapids, the cascading thickness of water flowing fast amongst the rocks and echoing across the steep valley. Boy quickened his steps again in the hope that his friend Tree Deep could take him home. He imagined floating through the night and making it into his own bed before his family awoke the next morning. His mum and dad would be furious. He would be in for a lot of questions and the wooden spoon across his backside.

'Hey, Tree Deep, stop your moving. I want to cross safely!' Boy yelled at the water. He watched its flow and waited for a response. He ran his hand under the cool falls, but there was nothing. The water was water, with no signs of life. It was not the great River Hew.

As Boy washed his face in the cool water, a fateful sound made its ultimate intrusion: the roll of a rock on rock. Downstream on the far bank of the river, a large shape moved slowly in the shadows. Boy dried himself off and crouched behind a tree, wary of giving himself away. He squinted in the dusk and blinked in amazement. There were four giant half-moon-shaped creatures like nothing Boy had ever seen before. They were well over his head in height and longer than a warrior's horse. They looked to be giant insects – beetles, to be exact –two large shells and two smaller ones. They drank from the water and rummaged around on the ground together. Their backs had a brownish tinge, with flecks of silvery green. *They must be a family; they look so peaceful and content.*

He found a soft clump of earth covered in pine needles to sit his sore behind on. And leaned against a pine trunk to watch the beetles rummaging through the foliage gathered along the banks. Upstream, the thick waterfall thundered into a pool hugged with rocks. Downstream, the forest river ran faster, returning to a much more normal-looking river. On the northern shore, stunted great pines cast blackening shadows while the southern bank was scattered with tall timbers and rocks that looked like baby beetles.

He leaned against the tree, eyes half-closed, enjoying a moment of relaxation. He would soon be needing to cross the falls and find a place to shelter for the cold night. Luckily, it was leading towards summer, and spring had come early this year. He took a deep breath and opened his eyes. *Did something just move, or was it the low branches? Was it the wind?*

Two dark figures moved through the pines ahead of Boy. They crept slowly downstream, further away from him. *Great! People! There's two of them, and they can show me how to get home.* He stood, brushed the pine needles from his behind and watched the two hooded men crouch low, each behind a pine. Both retrieved an arrow from their quivers and notched them into small hunting bows. They both drew and launched their evil tips across the river. The largest beetle was pierced in the head. It screeched in agony, only faintly heard over the river, then it twitched and began to spasm. Boy could see its pain clearly. Its two children began fussing around their father, twitching, little legs flailing in fear.

'No,' he said, watching the hooded men each notching another arrow. The remaining large beetle herded the two small ones up the sloping riverbank. Boy watched, not knowing what to do. Arrows whistled through the air and struck the massive male again. Its legs withdrew into its shell. The giant creature tumbled down the riverbank, wedging its large shell against a falling tree leaning off the bank. The men notched more arrows.

The remaining beetles scurried to the water's edge as

arrows finished off the father, hitting where his head had been. The river began to flow faster. A whirlpool flowed down the rapids from nowhere.

The hooded men jumped across submerged rocks and waded through the stream as the beetles began to surround the injured beast in the shallows.

Boy ran to the waters' edge. 'Get out of the water. Stay on this side of the bank!' He hoped the other creatures would run away when they heard him yelling. Startled, the men turned around. One slipped and fell over; the other reached for an arrow.

'Who's there? Get out of here, kid. He's ours – we caught him.'

Boy waded into the water.

'What are you doing? Get out of here! It's not our fault if you get in the way.' One man notched an arrow in honest threat. Boy stopped and held his hands up in the air. He had no idea where he was and what type of people they were – he came from a part of the land that worked with all animals – his people wouldn't want them for breakfast. He didn't like to see a strange creature slaughtered by men. *Who would want to eat a beetle anyway? Not me.*

The second man also aimed his arrow at Boy. 'I'm warning you, kid. Go home.'

Go home? Boy was furious at hearing those words from a stranger who would never help him anyway.

'I'm not here for your kill. Get out of the water,' he shouted. The men still held their aim towards him.

'Help!' he yelled to the river on the off-chance it was Tree Deep, which had just not reacted to him before. The water moved quickly, not just from upstream but from down and from below. The men began to yell, losing their balance. An arrow shot up into the sky. The river picked up the dead beetle and flung it downstream into the men, who tumbled down the rapids and around the river's bend. The river flowed into the far bank, flooding the area and sweeping the three remaining creatures off the banks and into the rising water.

'Stop this! Water, stop it! Leave them alone … I command you.'

The stubborn river ebbed with vicious currents, washing the beetles downstream; it did not adhere to Boy's commands. He dived into the waves, surfing them downstream to save whoever he could catch. He struggled to keep his head above water as he shouted desperately. But to no avail: the river did not listen.

Boy managed to cling onto one of the smaller beetles – still ten times his size – and float down the river with it.

'Tree Deep, stop this inferno of water! Stop it now.'

But no command was heard. The strange river continued its vicious swell. Boy was tossed into a fallen log and lost his grip on the creature's shell. He grabbed and held onto branches protruding from the surface and pulled himself up to the bank. Boy could see a calm cove at the next bend in the river where the other smaller beetle was struggling on the muddy bank. He climbed onto a log and ran to the drowning beetle, and dragged the creature ashore. Puffing, he collapsed, gasping for air. The beetle did the same, twitching its two tentacles madly in what Boy thought was exhaustion.

The beetle, giant as it was, crawled up the bank and scuttled downstream. Boy could only assume it was looking for its family that had continued down the river. No one was in sight – no other giant beetles – no hooded hunters – and the river's fury kept going around the distant bend.

As exhausted as Boy was, he followed the beetle, realising that its family had probably all been killed by the river. He caught up to the beast to make sure it didn't get taken by the water again. It was now close to full darkness. Nothing could be seen in the rapids. Boy kept his distance from the creature now it was back on dry land, watched as the beetle stopped and let out a high whimpering cry of sadness. It lay on the grass bank and watched the water.

Beneath the stars, Boy watched the beetle for a long time. The night was clear and cold, but there was no sign of rain, and the beetle didn't appear to be going anywhere. He searched the surrounding area in vain, hoping to stumble across food, but he only found firewood. He built a fire up to sustain a larger log that could burn deep into the night, and curled up near the warmth. He watched the beetle's shell glistening in the bouncing light until the arms of sleep welcomed him.

Boy woke to the first light of morning, not knowing if the beetle would still be there. It was, although standing now, still watching the water. Its tentacles moved in slow circles of curious hope while birds danced and chirped on the branches above. Boy stood and began a long stretch which triggered his stomach muscles; they clenched and grumbled. He remembered the olives and almonds, but only a few stubborn ones stuck to the bottom of the pockets – the rest had been washed away by the river. Boy made a small amount of noise at the fire to deliberately warn the large creature before slowly approaching it.

'I'm sorry, big guy. I tried to save them, but water doesn't always do what you want it to do. This isn't a friendly river, but I tried.'

The beetle turned to look at Boy and responded with a 'chicha-chicha' sound as his tentacles moved freely around his head.

'Well, if it means anything, I've also lost my family and home. They didn't get swept away by the river, but I got swept further away from them. Now I just may be lost. I'm looking for a bigger river than this. It runs straight past my home. I just don't know where to go.'

Boy and the beetle continued to look at one another, not knowing what the other would do.

'Do you have any other family, Beetie?'

It just looked at the ground in a melancholy way.

'Sorry, dumb question. Maybe you can help me out. Do you know this land quite well? Because I don't.'

The beetle looked up, waving his tentacles around.

'I can help you too when you need water from the river, or fruit from trees.' Boy waited a moment for an answer.

'Chik-chik,' the beetle finally responded.

'Okay … well, I have to keep travelling, otherwise, I'll be lost out here forever. Come with me, if you want. I'll keep an eye out for those hunters, but beware, I must find people who can help me. They'd better not all hunt your kind.'

Boy couldn't read the beetle's reaction.

'Your tentacles are just moving from side to side, Beetie. I don't know what that means, but I want to try.'

Boy stepped closer to it and held his hand out to show the beetle his caring intent. Its tentacles stopped moving, and its black eyes turned away from him to again watch the water flow by. Boy placed his hand softly on the smooth shell and held it there for a moment.

'Let's get away from this cursed river. Follow me.'

To Boy's surprise, the giant beetle appeared happy to follow him. Occasionally, in the thicker parts of the forest where it would get jammed in between trees, Boy would have to wait for the beetle to catch up.

All morning they picked their way through the changing forest, over streams and through minor clearings. All the time, Boy was telling his new friend about his family and his home, where he loved to play and the types of trees he loved to climb. The subject started to ebb towards his favourite food: the soups his mother would cook, the fresh herb potatoes and roast chicken. The smells engulfed his nostrils as if the smoky charcoal cooker ran hot before him. Boy could taste the salty chicken skin in the waters of his mouth, the crisp crackle of tearing the first bite, and the texture of the bone on his teeth as he sucked the last of the flavours. He talked of this topic over and over that morning, changing it to introduce toasted bread drowned in glorious cow's butter – the mopping tool for the dish's heart and soul.

The giant creature had no idea what he was describing, but responded with the occasional 'chika-chika' as if to advise his new friend that he was still listening.

They stopped for a rest at the top of a hill before they began their descent across a low valley. Boy sat on a log and peeled out the last of the olives stuck to the bottom of his pocket. He threw an olive to the beetle, whose head slowly moved closer to inspect the squashed fruit. It just nuzzled the olive with its head and then left it alone.

'Don't you like olives, Beetie? That's okay. We'll head off soon, and at our next stop, I'll leave you to find your own food ... whatever it is that you eat.' Boy shrugged at his own lack of knowledge.

He then noticed smoke rising above the treetops and into the clear sky across the valley. He stood and held his hand to his forehead, shielding the glare. *Possibly a small campfire or a farmer burning off the weeds of spring?* Whoever it was, dangerous or not, Boy decided he would follow the smoke. The chance was an obvious gamble to make.

Boy and the beetle walked directly through the forest as there were no trails in the valley. The trees in this immediate area were spaced close together – a hindrance to the large shell of the Beetle. They soon entered the vicinity of the fire maker. Boy stopped and watched the smoke rise vertically; it was a strange grey colour, and did not appear to be moving with the wind. He paused a distance away and held his hand above Beetie's head, placing his palm down on the hard shell before he spoke to the beetle.

'Beetie, I don't know what or who is ahead, but I am so hungry, and we need to know where we are going. If it's more of those bad men, I truly am sorry. Maybe you should only come a little way further, and I'll see who it is. If I don't return, then just run away, far away from here and hide, always hide. I can talk my way out of things if need be. No one is going to eat me – I'm too skinny.'

Boy smiled as the beetle's tentacles waved in response. He left his friend alone and approached the fire slowly, carefully choosing where to place his feet. Without much noise, he moved from tree to tree.

A jingle of riding tack sounded. Boy picked up a rock for protection, holding it behind his back. A tethered mule swung its head up to watch him. Considering this stranger to be no threat, it ignored him and went back to eating the grass. A hunched figure stepped forward from behind the mule's tree, dark and hooded in the heat of the day.

'Good morning, young man,' he said with a cheery wave. 'Sorry if I frightened you. Did you seek out the smoke?' asked the figure.

'Yes, yes, I did.' Boy kept his eyes fixed on the man.

'What brings you to these parts? And where are you from?' asked Boy, attempting to sound like he wasn't lost.

'Questions like that make this place sound treacherous. I am neither a scholar on these parts nor well-travelled in these lands. I am after information on the land, though,' said the figure.

'If that's what you're looking for, then I may only be of limited help. Where are you trying to go?' asked Boy.

'You sound like a smart young man. Would you like me to start a pot of tea? The fire's almost bloody well gone out,' said the stranger.

'You're not dangerous, are you?' He didn't know why he even said it … just to be on guard … to show that he was on guard.

'No, I am dangerous to no man or to no creatures of land, sea or air … well, some would argue that statement.' The man smiled.

'Can you please step forward and take the hood off. I am only being cautious, for men and creatures of this land have been dangerous and foreign to me.'

The figure stepped forward. He was an older man, of regular build and height, but not a race of human Boy had seen or heard of before. He had no hair. Instead, the lumpy jagged surface of his bald head changed colour depending on how it caught the light, reflecting browns, reds, greys and earthy tones. His maroon eyes should have run a shiver down Boy's spine, yet they radiated wonder and warm curiosity. He looked peculiar enough to stay on guard, but his mannerisms and gestures were the gentlest of any Boy had come across.

The man sat down, looked at the fire which danced brighter under his gaze, poured a skin of water into a pot, and sat it over the old charred coals.

'Now, don't be alarmed.' The stranger grasped his hands together and tapped his chest, throat and head. He cupped his hands over the fire, like they were filled with invisible water, then opened them apart, and, with a gentle flicker, flames fell from his hands and caught the warm charcoal. He placed a handful of dried twigs on the fire and, within a brief moment, it was roaring with life. Boy had been read tales but had never seen anyone wield fire before.

'I'm sorry if I startled you. I should have at least introduced myself first. I am Glohring, romancer and pyromancer of the east. Well, east of here, I think. And that is my true name, and the truth is held always through one's connection to a true name freely given. At least that's what it's like for my people, where I come from.'

Glohring smiled, then rummaged through one of several ground packs that allowed his mule to rest. He eventually pulled out a small pot, enough to boil two small cups of water and some herbs for a tea.

'You must be pretty bold to travel the woods and give your

name up that easily to anyone?' enquired Boy, hoping his question would get the stranger talking again.

'No, not to anyone. I just saw the look on your face.' He went back to preparing the cups of herbal tea.

Boy now felt uneasy. This stranger had trusted him so easily and was so nice, he felt he needed to test the situation.

'Without sounding rude, aren't you a little decrepit to be a romancer?'

Glohring laughed. 'Well, yes, the long years of my life have certainly taken a toll. But the knowledge is the reason for the title. However, the lack of practice does fade the skill. A dying art, and I'm probably the only one left in these lands.'

'Why is an older man lost in the woods then? I assume you are lost. It's dangerous. I have already been attacked twice in the last few days. It's been the worst few days of my life. So, excuse me if I'm on guard.'

'I am sorry to hear that. One most probably would be on guard when coming across a strange race so close to your own. But, believe me, I am no threat. There are some out there, though, ones that endeavour to destroy my studies and my surroundings. They are my only real threat. I still have my life, but my purpose is now driven by what has been taken, and that I will definitely not share.'

Glohring looked into the fire. He seemed to draw back warmth and energy from it through his eyes, and his rough head changed colour slightly.

'I understand. The purpose for what drives me now has not been taken, but given … and I don't know where to go. I'm lost,' Boy replied hesitantly, pursing his lips together.

'Very well said. So, you are not from these lands, just like me. But what is a young boy – motherless and fatherless, alone in the woods, far from his home – doing here?' Glohring raised a cheeky eyebrow.

Boy fidgeted in annoyance at the reminder of being lost.

He felt ashamed. 'I can confirm that I am lost and trying to find my home.' Boy spoke loudly, proudly and bordering on sarcasm.

'How long have you been lost for?'

'Three days now, I think. I hope someone can help me find my way. I just want to go home.'

Boy appeared sad for a second, before his eyes caught the movement of vegetables being taken out of a bag. Glohring grinned and, taking out a knife from his bag, he began to slice up carrot, potato, parsnip and fennel. He placed each individual piece in a random order down a long steel skewer.

'And I never caught your name, young man,' Glohring said, head down as he prepared the food.

'It's Boy.'

Glohring placed the vegetable skewer over the fire. The flames reacted to him and adjusted their height underneath the warming vegetables. He finally looked up and caught Boy's eye.

'It's very nice to meet you, Boy. Are you hungry?'

'I am at that, very much so.' Boy's mouth began to water.

'Then, you shall have some. And what of your sleepy beast?' Glohring pointed to the trees. The beetle had quietly followed Boy and failed in his attempts to try to stay hidden. A giant beetle shell sat in the middle of the narrow track, his head, legs and tentacles all tucked inside his shell. Boy guessed this was the first hiding spot he could think of.

'Beetie!' Boy stood up and walked over to him. 'What are you doing? I was going to come back in a moment for you. It's okay, you can come on over.'

The beetle's head and legs slowly emerged from the shell, accepting that he had now been found in his hiding spot. He followed Boy over towards the camp and scuffled around through the foliage.

Boy quickly sat back down near the fire, trying politely not to give away his detailed tracking of the cooking process.

'So, that's Beetie. He's my friend. His family was killed, and he doesn't have a home now. I'm not too sure if he'll eat cooked vegetables, but I can share some of mine with him. From what I have seen, though, he likes to scratch around in the dirt for food.'

'Are you sure?'

'From all my observations, yes. Why do you ask? Do you know of these beetles?'

'I have heard of them on my journeys. In my years of study, I have read old books about them doing remarkable things. But it does baffle me to think they just scratch in the dirt for herbs and bugs. They're huge things.'

'You sound curious about their behaviour. I don't want my friend being an experiment for you to study.'

'If he is your friend, as you say, wouldn't you allow some friendly study?'

'No! For all I know, these extraordinary things you speak of may just be a ruse to spark my curiosity so that I give you free rein over him, for whatever actions you see fit. So, it's a no. I have seen nothing from this creature but helplessness. I saw his family drown by the river. I see sadness and feel the warmth he shows from knowing someone needs him. He's just an animal – let him live.' Boy felt bad for sounding so rude to a stranger … after all, the man was about to feed him.

'I am no demon. I speak the truth, and I mean no harm to anyone.'

Glohring passed a cup of tea across to Boy, fresh and steaming from the fire.

'I'm sorry. I didn't mean to be impolite. I just cannot tell who's dangerous. Thank you so much for the food and tea.' Boy paused, thinking how much he should say to this stranger, but he conceded. He was still lost and any information to help him get home was a gamble he was willing to try.

'Fair enough,' Glohring replied. 'But in truth, you are making a mistake if you are alone. It's very dangerous out there, and a man of my skills always comes in handy. I only need to travel a short while.'

'Where?'

'To a town, village, castle. I've never been there, but the description of the place may fit my expectations. What I want is there. I seek knowledge, to wield and to teach. I'm too old now not to teach what I have learned.'

'Your strange skills … do you have any others who know of them … you know, rivals?'

'I speak no more of these things. Hold out your hand.'

Boy stretched his arms out in front of him, ready to receive anything remotely edible. Glohring slid hot portions of food off the end of the skewer onto Boy's flat hands. He waited for Glohring to eat first, then began the most delicious meal he had eaten since home.

After their meal, Glohring rummaged through his belongings and found Boy a water skin, some cheese and a generous portion of assorted vegetables, all wrapped in a small cloth sack. Boy accepted everything with a great many thanks and a bow. *Why did I bow? People don't bow.* He felt self-conscious.

The giant beetle grazed with the mule and scuffled around in the dirt under rotting logs, nibbling on what it could find. It had no interest in the pieces of cooked carrot Boy held out on his hand, yet nuzzled his nose in the leaves at Boy's feet.

Glohring busily packed his mule, and tossed Boy a length of spare leather reins.

'Take this. You may want to use your friend to carry some packs if you have a long journey ahead of you.'

Boy examined the reins: a quality cut of leather at that.

'Thank you, Glohring. I will be able to use this,' he said, without bowing. Boy decided that he would carry the new gear for the time being, and his new cloth sack was bound up and tossed over his shoulder, hanging by the overlapped length of leather.

'So, Beetie, do you trust him?'

The beetle turned his head towards Boy. 'Tch-tch-tck-tck,' he chirped.

'Yeah, I think we should just be wary, that's all. But, if you think he's fine, I trust you. Are you thirsty?' Boy poured the water skin above Beetie's mouth. He didn't know if any reached him or just trickled on by, but it was better than nothing.

Glohring soon approached them with his pack mule in tow, whistling a joyful melody he pitched with ease.

'Well, I'm ready. It was very nice to meet you, Boy, and good luck on your journey.'

Glohring walked a few paces then stopped. Letting out a sigh of breath, he turned his head. His wrinkled skin folded and gathered lines up his neck before his feet turned to follow, unravelling the tight folds. His eyes shrunk, confused about where they should look, but his face shone relief, and then he dimly smiled, a bare twitch across his face.

'Would you like to join me riding for the day? I don't think I will be reaching my destination for at least two nights … wherever it may be in that direction.' He pointed roughly northwest, waving his hand in the general direction.

'We are also leaving now, probably in that direction.' Boy pointed to what he thought was west, his arm stiff and straight.

'Well, ensure that food lasts a long time if you are heading deeper into the wilderness. I'd suggest buying a flint if you ever come across a town or any coins.'

It dawned on Boy that this man had fed them and helped him out. Why not have safety in numbers? Just until he found his way and possibly reached Tree Deep Trundle. A farewell then would be the same as now. *Trust your instincts*, he told himself. His quick character assessment of Glohring had reported no ill intentions.

'Thank you so much for the food and the supplies. You are welcome to come with us until we reach a town. I have changed my mind, but on one condition: we choose the path and you stay in front and in sight at all times.'

'It sounds like a prisoners' march, but very well. I don't mind if it's still in the direction I want to be heading. One last question: do you have a sword?' Glohring noticed Boy went still. 'I'm only asking as I know nothing of your past, and you do not look well-equipped or prepared. I have a large dagger – it's more like a small sword – you can have. I never use it anyway, only sometimes for cheese. If we both come across danger, I will not need it; better in your hands than mine.'

Glohring handed Boy the sheathed dagger. Boy tied the leather strips to the side of his belt and felt like he had become a dangerous warrior.

'Thank you, it will come in handy. I did have an idea to make a forest javelin, but it wouldn't be weighted properly, only sharp.' He smiled, holding the pommel of the dagger.

Their journey under the sunny, cloudless sky demanded walking long stints through varying terrain. Wooded forests quickly transformed into clear areas sparse of trees and wild underbrush before returning to winding animal trails, then shrinking down and darkening into thick moist jungle-like vines with intruding thorns and leaves. Then they faced an insurmountable wall of pollen seasonally feeding the natural fields, where granite outcrops hindered the earthy root systems of little seeds desperate for a chance where they fell. Up and then down, out and then back into the unforgiving sunshine of late spring they went.

Suddenly, they found themselves alongside a steep ridge, which appeared so quickly it confused Boy and Glohring.

Heading away from the ridge, they walked into a small clearing from where they could see the horizon all around them. They had inadvertently found the peak of a good-sized hill. The view didn't stretch very far, but it was good enough to take in the approaching landscape.

'We have to keep looking at every opportunity for the River Hew. Do you know of it or where it may be?' Boy was annoyed that he hadn't asked this question earlier.

'Well, it's easy. We're on top of a large hill, so if we head straight down the other side, there should be a river. If there is a good-sized river, then there will be people, and probably a village too. However, it may be too dangerous for the animals to head straight down this slope. I suggest we keep to the flatter side and work our way down. And, no, I've never heard of this River Hew.'

'If what you say is true about a river and we have a good chance of finding a town for help, then let's go the steep way and get down there quicker,' Boy suggested, not willing to go the safer route because Glohring had suggested it. His distrust would still ebb and flow, teasing his own judgement that a trap was imminent. *I cannot keep up this defiance. Who could? If he is up to no good, I will be able to see through it.*

'You are most definitely right. It's no use breaking our legs and not being able to get home altogether. But, we'll take the steeper route anyway,' Boy stubbornly touted. Glohring chuckled aloud at the regal demand and changed direction towards the valley's depths.

The path remained surprisingly easy as the natural layout of the rocks and dead logs created a chance staircase. They crept further down into the shadowed valley, stopping at a large tree that grew lushly from a natural spring. Small frogs jumped back and forth and burrowed into tiny mud holes at their sudden approach. Beetie watched them jumping.

'Chicka chika,' the beetle chirped playfully.

'With all these springs around, they must be feeding a large river. We are close, aren't we?' Boy asked as he crouched down to fill up his water skin.

'We most certainly are descending quickly. It may flatten out, so hopefully, we can find a nice place to camp tonight. I don't know how far. I can't see through the trees. And it's a no if you thought I had special eyesight.'

Boy looked disappointed. He had hoped Glohring might have some extra information. But if he couldn't see anything, how else could another? He felt like a fool for no reason, and for the rest of the day, he tried to shake the dull feeling away.

'Hopefully, we can find a sheltered spot to camp, but not too close to the river. Not on its edge if it is the River Hew,' Boy said.

'It's funny you should say that. I have more experience with lakes, but I swear these rivers changed more rapidly when I approached them. I've never seen that before. I was quite bemused.'

'Well, you are right. Here they are strange. Some rivers are dangerous. The one I'm talking about – the Hew – is extremely old and grumpy. We … my family and I … call it Tree Deep Trundle. Do not trust the River Hew if you ever come across it.'

'You live near a beautiful river, and yet you cannot trust it? No wonder you don't trust me if rivers are committing crimes in your neck of the woods.'

'It is a beautiful part of the world … the most beautiful.' Boy's voice softened.

'How can you say it's the most beautiful in the world when you haven't seen the whole world?'

'The most beautiful that I have seen. Out of the world I have seen, it is the prettiest.' Boy grinned, attempting to mask his ignorance.

'Well, I have not been to your part of the world, but there are many wonderful places that I have lived. Places that would bring you to tears at their beauty, breathtaking and bemusing all at once,' Glohring recalled, lost in memory and looking at nothing.

'Yes.' Boy did want to see these places. Glohring's descriptions would plant a seed in his imagination that would one day intertwine itself through different pools of his soul.

The afternoon sun that warmed the valley began to lose its heat, and a cool breath sent far from the ocean careered through the trees, creaking and stretching their elastic branches. Brown leaves drifted, and dried nuts fell from their open pods onto a flat blanket of ground that ran all the way to the river's bank a hundred yards or so away. Few trees remained in between. It was an overflow area from floods of the past, but this flat ground had not flooded in a long time. The sound of trickling water grew louder, a slow-moving river through a rock-laden crossing.

Boy ran to the river's edge and shouted at the water, but it did not respond. Nothing. He was disappointed that it was not Tree Deep Trundle. He threw a rock at the water in anger and turned back.

Glohring was setting up a small camp and fire pit about hundred yards back from the water's edge and way off the path they had come down on.

'So, is it the river you spoke of?'

'No, it looks just the same as the river where I met Beetie. I wonder if it is the same river? If it is, I am extremely lost.'

'We'll try to find you a map then, eh? From the next town or next people, we'll get information. Not everyone's lost.' He smiled to lift Boy's spirits, and Boy nodded sulkily.

'I'll fetch us water,' he said.

Glohring collected firewood and began chopping vegetables for an early evening meal. Boy found Beetie a small place to forage for food, but he didn't look interested; he looked tired. Once the beetle was watered, he appeared to be content with resting his tiny legs. Boy wished him pleasant dreams and found a small cushion of leaves to sit down on by the fire. Today he felt bad eating someone else's food, but he was just so hungry. He'd had the idea to get up early in the morning and spear something in the river – freshwater trout, or possibly a much more elusive crustacean – at least something he could, in turn, feed Glohring and fill both their morning bellies.

The last of the day's light began to be replaced by the crisp bite of cold air. Even though the spring nights should have been getting warmer, that night it returned to winter. The sky was open and the depths of night felt closer than usual. The four of them sat around a small fire in silence: Boy shivered, the mule and the beetle slept, and Glohring carved. Boy wrapped himself in Glohring's spare blanket and watched him pare away at a small wax tablet for several moments. Boy couldn't see what Glohring was carving, but noticed he would shave, then stop and consider what he had done, look further at it, figure it out, then rub it until it disappeared. He did this until he smiled with satisfaction. Glohring finally packed his wax tablet away and started to walk around the camp. Boy was curious: Glohring did not seem to be affected by the cold. Maybe the pyromancer fire in his soul, or the overly large cloak he wore on his body, kept him warm.

'Boy, come here. I see something.'

'What is it? People?'

Boy stood up and made his way, shivering, through the trees. Glohring was crouched behind a pine. He pointed across the river's valley.

'Do you see what I see?' whispered Glohring.

Across the valley, a group of small fires burned. Shadows would pass momentarily: figures holding what looked like weapons. *They are sallying in the night,* Boy thought.

'We have got to put our fire out!' Boy jumped up, but Glohring grabbed his arm tight.

'Leave it. They already know we're here.'

'Let's put the fire out and leave. I can lead Beetie at night. Once we're over the hills, you can make fire and light the way.'

'No.'

'Then what the hell is going on? Do you know them? Have you set this all up to capture us?'

'You wanted to come this way, and I advised against it. I thought you wanted to find people?'

'A safe township of folk in the daylight … not bandits in the night.'

'I do agree – they don't appear to be your normal traveller, but bandits they are not.'

'Are you being followed? Have you put us in danger?'

'I know they have been coming. I sensed their fires. If it's who it should be, then we are perfectly safe.'

'Well … are they dangerous? What are we going to do?'

'Go to sleep. We continue your path in the morning as planned.'

'But I can't sleep now.'

'Look, you seem to be panicking. Forget all your questions. You are not in danger, and they are just a troop of travellers. You are under my protection.' Glohring winked. His calm composure in the face of an imminent threat annoyed Boy.

As paranoid and distrusting as Boy was after the last few days of danger, he did believe him and surprisingly fell asleep straight away. He did have dreams, though, of them being tied up in the bushes and left for dead. *Why would my brain insert such horrible images for me to fret on?*

Boy awoke to the sound of a raven cawing in the trees. It perched on a branch observing the large shiny-shelled beetle. Beetie, in return, watched the crow hop along its perch. The smell of warm bread and pine needles assaulted Boy's senses, and his body sprung awake. His muscles ached as he stood and stretched, groaning.

Glohring sat resting against a pine tree. He was busy slicing cheese in one hand for the light breakfast he was preparing for Boy. *So much for the trout.* Beetie ignored the crow and rummaged around his area, finding his own breakfast.

'You slept in,' said Glohring.

'I was thinking …' Boy's mind trailed off, his thoughts not connecting. He turned back and packed up his bedroll.

'You appear to have many a question for me?' Glohring waited patiently, even though he was keen to leave.

'I do, but I'll see to Beetie first.' Boy turned in a huff and watered his giant friend, hydrating him for the day.

'You can ask away whenever you want, but we should leave. It's later than usual. Your breakfast is waiting here for you.' Glohring put out the remaining embers with a wave of his hand.

In the morning light, they could see further up the valley. It was surrounded by a beautiful and widely-spaced pine forest, rocky, with large valley clearings among the rivers. Perfect for hunting. They headed upstream and found an accessible shallow bend in the river where the beetle and mule could cross without trepidation. The water swirled in annoyance around Glohring's legs, however, but he sensed this and danced through the water quickly to the safety of dry forest where he felt more comfortable.

For such a tall timber area, a surprising amount of light reached the pine needles on the forest floor. Usually, areas like this were dark and gloomy, but this forest welcomed the light.

They began the steep ascent to the hill's summit, Boy walking slowly, leading Beetie with his reins. The path was vague and picked by Glohring, who led the way. Boy was happy to just follow someone this day and let his mind rest. The only problem was the gas the mule expelled downwind straight into Boy's face. Climbing the hill and panting for air, a full breath of surprise mule fart was sucked down his dry throat, thickening his lungs, causing him to cough and stumble, searching for air. Even Beetie didn't like it and made the odd complaint when it happened.

'Chica-chica...eea.' His tentacles oscillated.

'You had questions, Master Boy?'

He nodded. 'Do you know those men?'

'Not personally.'

'But, you know where they came from?'

'Yes, the same city I did pass through from the north.'

'And what is this place?'

'A city.'

'I've never seen a city. I've only heard my father read about their grand scales and large archways in books. Is it a great city?'

'The city is a wonder – a beauty that stretches on throughout the ages without a hint of stress.'

Boy walked with his head down, watching the ground, daydreaming of a grand city … many stalls and market places, musicians, storytellers, warriors, pretty girls, and jesters. *A wonder to be seen … sometime before I finish living.*

'Do you have more questions, Boy?'

'Yes, lots.'

'I thought you did. I sensed it.' Glohring laughed.

'Why are those people following you? Or better, who are they following and why?'

'They are heading to the same place I am trying to get to.'

Boy didn't fully understand.

'What have you done? What laws have you broken?'

'I haven't broken any law, but if I tell you, you must promise not to tell another soul. I thought you a smart young man who would ask the right questions.' Glohring stopped the procession and looked around. The area was quite open, and it appeared no one was close. Boy held his right hand to his chest.

'I promise on the light of the day and the dark of the night, across my heart and across my soul.'

'Hmm … okay. Well, I have led them here under false pretences. See, they are travelling to make a trade with me. We must meet and trade. I'm giving them a precious fire-stone gem, but I cannot divulge any information on the stone.'

'So, why don't you just go and meet them to swap the stone for … what are you trading it for?'

'Well, that is a secret. A book of secrets, actually, and something that I once studied myself long ago. I cannot remember most of the bits and pieces, and I really need to study up on the knowledge if I am to teach the craft. I need these ancient pages that the daft owners care nothing for. They have no idea what lurks beneath the pages and probably now use it as a window jam. I was once a mere apprentice in the subject of romancing.

'My master at the time used his skills in service of the then prince, to align a marriage with a chosen woman of a powerful clan. But, how should I say …? The prince, for all his royalty, was not the most handsome of men. With five sisters, the bloodline had to go on and become stronger than it had once been. The prince did become king and went on to have an heir to the throne. However, my apprenticeship was cut short when my master was sent away. The new king refused to have that power used to aid anyone else. 'Until now, I have not passed on the teachings. But, a person I shall not name has propositioned me to teach someone of keen interest: an offer I am most unlikely to refuse. But, I lack the knowledge.'

'Was this a long time ago? You seem quite wise now.'

'And who will tell who is wise and who is daft?'

'I dunno.'

'So, since I stupidly came out in the open seeking the book, they have an idea of its worth. How naive I was. So, now *they* want this stone because *I* want the book.'

'And is it a good trade?'

'Well, it is, and it isn't. Both could bring harm or create marvels, in either the future or the present.'

'Well, I hope you create marvels with this book.'

'That is the dream, but there is a lot of work ahead. A lot.'

Beetie seemed to listen in with curiosity, agreeing with a 'chichica' or whistling in surprise every now and again. Boy sometimes thought Beetie understood everything they were saying, then he'd brush the idea off.

'May I see the gem?'

'I thought you may ask. You're quite bright and observant. Do not change and you will go a long way in life. But, I do not have the gem.'

'Why not? What are you going to trade? I hope you are not going to steal the book. Is that why you have led them out into the wilderness?'

'No, the fire-stone gem is what I have to steal. And you mustn't tell anyone this, remember you promised. Where the gem lies, it may be near suicide to try and steal it. The guards will run you down and capture you, if you even made it into the forest. I cannot defend myself against a dozen armed swordsmen. I will need to make the trade straight away, so I am luring this pack of men in. They will get their trade, but only once I have escaped with the stone.'

'You can't put these men in danger unbeknownst to them.'

'Hey, I won't steal it. The warriors will.'

'No, you're going to steal it.'

'But that's not what the castle guards will think. They are hardened warriors, and their master's use for this gem is not a tasteful thing. You do not want to know its use.'

'You know of this gem and its surroundings? You told me that you know nothing of this place?'

'I don't. I know who holds it and the fortress castle it resides in, as I have read about it. But, I don't know how to get to the bloody place!'

'A fortress? Are we going to run into trouble?'

'So long as I don't reveal my true self until the trade.'

'And who is your real self?' Boy stopped walking and looked him in the eye. Glohring seemed happy to have the examination. 'Are you a hermit, a councillor, a master of the spirit arts, or a rogue wanderer most likely?'

'You are most correct with one. But, alas, I have taken up the rogue wanderer as my character for this journey.'

'I don't want to go to this fortress, and I must protect my beetle. Some men killed its family, and I don't know if this is common practice in these parts. You can find your way and I will go my own.'

'That is fine with me.'

'Hang on, why don't you just follow these men? They'll lead you straight to this fortress.'

'Because they have never been there either, and I am meant to meet them on arrival for the trade. I'd better hurry up. You are right as a backup plan, to just follow their tracks, but I'd rather get there earlier than later.'

'You don't have much time before they get there. Don't you need weeks to plan your entrance and escape with the stone?'

'I have seen a map of the palace, detailed with outbuildings. I have a plan. Sadly, the map is only of the fortress and not how to get there, but I have an idea of the general direction which was verbally given to me. This castle has a grand library, so I will find some maps for you if I have the chance. I can't promise anything. If you wish to stay with me on the way to this place, at least you will be safe, and hopefully, I'll get you some helpful information.'

'Well, let's hope the guards are not expecting a thief. And whatever the plan is, I hope it's well-thought-out.' *But it doesn't sound like it*, Boy thought.

Glohring looked his way. 'The plan will succeed. The book

has been rotting under dust for too long, and I need to continue to work.' He smiled and kept walking; the mood now that of no more talking.

Late in the morning sun, they rested their tired legs beside a noisy stream that meandered through the pines. Boy left his companions and walked towards the sounds of water. He found a small pool that was deep enough to dunk his entire head in. He leant forward against a flat boulder, submerged his face up to his chin, while the current forced itself up his nasal cavity. Boy wrenched himself up straight, snorting out the sharp backflow of river water. He filled up Glohring's and his own water skins, and returned to relax leaning up against Beetie's hard shell.

'I've just had an idea since you are pressed for time,' Boy said, handing the full water skin to Glohring.

'Let's hear it.'

'Do you have any extra leather or rope I can use for a bridle so I can ride Beetie? Well … if he lets me.'

'I do have a small amount, but I cannot ride my pack mule. All I can do is keep a steady march and we'll get there before those men.'

The old mule barked its thanks. It had long ago had its last human rider and didn't want its spine harassed again.

Glohring threw Boy some rope, and the large, shiny beetle curiously looked his way.

'Hey, Beetie, I'm not sure how to do this, but if you don't like it, tell me.'

'Chicka-chripa-chik,' Beetie appeared to agree.

Boy set up a makeshift bridle but struggled to climb high onto Beetie's back; numerous times he slid down the smooth shell.

'Are you okay? Am I too heavy?' Boy asked.

'Chicka-cckhickachika,' Beetie said happily.

So, they set off further into the forest, with the stream to their right and the strange warriors nowhere to be seen. Because the beetle had six legs, it was surprisingly smooth to ride, unlike a horse or mule. The only problem was that Beetie thought he was leading and, not being used to the bridle and only recently the lead, he would wander off the path at times to wherever he wanted. Glohring marched peacefully behind, amused at Boy's attempt to control his strange steed.

'No, Beetie! Left … around that tree,' Boy grumbled.

The distracted beetle often left Boy's desired path and headed into lower scrub near the flowing stream.

'No, not that way! You can't go near the water. There are too many rocks. Stupid beetle.'

'Chik-ccerchrru,' the angry beetle sounded.

'Sorry, Beetie, you're not stupid. I love you,' Boy whispered.

Boy was having difficulty ducking branches and twigs as Beetie veered off the path. Left, then right, his neck contorted past the low branches and sharp twigs. A clearing finally appeared ahead; Boy spotted a group of rectangular stones which looked like a possible fireplace, and timber logs with angles cut by men.

'Glohring! Look ahead.'

'I see it.'

But, it was nothing – a very old camp. A few stones remained stacked: maybe once an old wall, or perhaps bored children. On the grass lay old timber logs, well-cut as if they were going to be used for the structural supports of a farmhouse.

They ambled on past the rubble, but there were no recent signs of life. Then they came across a peculiar straight stick nestled between two of the cut timbers. It had a long shiny strip of material hanging off the end, like an old lord's crest. Because of its peculiar appearance in the middle of the wilderness, Boy stopped, slid down the shell and grabbed it. Then he had an idea. Perfectly weighted, Boy began dangling the shiny cloth in front of Beetie's eyes. It went left, the beetle went left. It instinctively followed the shiny material: a never-ending curiosity of dangling shininess.

'Glohring! Look at this. It's perfect. He follows it wherever it goes. Well, that was a stroke of luck.'

'Yes, very good. But don't rely on luck; it will always abandon you. Rely on yourself.' Glohring spoke loudly as if he lectured in a great hall.

Boy was busy swaying the material in front of Beetie's head.

'Left, he goes left. Right, he goes right,' he chuckled.

Boy happily steered the way through the trees until they came across a stone pillar and the beginning of a road. The stone said nothing on their side, but where the road would have stopped for someone going in the opposite direction, the stone read: BEWARE ARTEM CHAROI / HAUNTED TRIPARTITE / BEWARE.

Boy eyeballed Glohring for answers.

'Well, I think the people in these parts still believe in old fanciful stories,' said Glohring.

A cold shiver went down Boy's spine as he read the sign again. *But I believe in old fanciful stories*, he thought. Glohring must have picked up on his mood.

'You just went through there. We camped in the darkness, and there was nothing to worry about. It's all fancy tales for fools.'

'You're probably right, but it still scares me reading the sign.'

'Well, you never have to go back through there. I do, but it'll be fine.'

Boy still felt uneasy, and he reluctantly looked back, expecting to see spirits and headless haunts, but the forest seemed ordinary enough.

As the afternoon sun shone in the sky, they came upon a small farm. Chickens darted off the roadway and, beyond a splintered fence, an old farmer tended his hogs. Glohring turned off the road and waved for attention. The old man was too busy and didn't see them approach the muddy sty.

'Good morrow, my esteemed hog owner. May you be of some service to me?' asked Glohring.

Startled, the old man looked up. Two brown hogs came to his sides like protective hounds and began rubbing their muddy hides back and forth along his legs. He patted them kindly on their heads, stood up straight and stern, tall and thin – expelling venerable farming experience – hands on his hips.

'And what do you want, strange traveller?' His voice was gravelly and unwelcoming from the rear of his throat.

'Just some information, and maybe some herbs if you can spare them.'

'Herbs? You just walked through the bloody forest. Shoulda picked 'em yourselves.'

'My begging your pardon, but I forgot to do so. Pressing matters were at hand.'

'Hmph! Strange you are, strange traveller. What information do you want? Probably something strange.' The old farmer's right eye began to twitch and close over. Glohring glanced at Boy, confused by the farmer's ill-temper.

'Well, if I had the information, I wouldn't be asking. Would you mind answering a few questions for me?'

The man stood silent and motionless for a moment, except for the continuous twitch of his eye.

'Well, ask the damn questions. I got a hog that needs tending too.'

'Maybe that's his wife he meant,' Boy whispered to Glohring. Glohring smiled with a twitch of his mouth.

'I come from a land far away. I am to deliver something to

the mysterious fortress west of here. Do you know of its name?'

'No name!'

'Do you know where it is?'

'No clue.'

'Okay, thank you for your time. I'll let you get back to your duties.'

'I do know the next town will have that information. There are men there that trade and owe fealty to the lord of the area. This fortress you speak of is probably his giant stone home. But I don't know where it is, or why it needs to be so big … who knows what he keeps inside. Very strange.' He picked up his rake and went back to his hog pit.

'Thank you for this information. How far to this town?'

The farmer let out a huff of annoyance.

'Keep heading up this road, across the river and then turn inland on the only road.'

'Your time has been most valuable to my apprentice and I. Thank you.'

'I'd be careful with that beetle,' said the farmer with a grim face.

'Pardon me?' Boy said, halting his mount.

'The cursed thing you sit on. That beast will only attract more beasts, the ones you don't want.' He leant on his rake with a frown, but Boy ignored him and turned back to Beetie.

'Don't worry about him. He doesn't know anything, and you are my friend. I'll take care of you.'

Beetie's tentacles darted in agreement.

~

The road widened and slowly became a smooth clay highway. More crossroads formed junctions to unknown places which Boy wondered about. His back was now getting used to riding on a giant shell, the leather reins to support himself and help balance, and the stick and material to help him steer. It all became quite natural to him. His muscles were not paining sharp daggers like before, but his spine still felt like a crooked swamp tree.

The road ran alongside open paddocks, some vacant, bounded by thin conifers, and others with farmhouses and barns littering the horizon. Fresh wagon tracks moulded into the clay showed the direction to the local village. Soon enough, the road was full of people; farmers and local villagers passed by. They looked bemused at the sight of someone riding a shelled beast yet carried on quietly with their own business.

Boy grew unsettled deep in his gut; he went on guard as they approached the town. A large stone wall surrounded the village. There was a high wooden spiked gate, left open for everyone to come and go in the safety of daylight. No guards were there to intimidate and enforce local decree. One would assume by this the promise of a beautiful culture, but the townsfolk looked scared. Grim stares towards strangers in their own land reflected an unsettled history. Boy felt this everywhere: on the faces of the people and the buildings of the town, scars laden below a transparent hopeful mask.

Boy and the beetle slowly scuttled through the muddy streets, staying close and following Glohring. Boy didn't feel welcome in this dark town and stopped Beetie when the street was clear of people.

'Glohring, I don't like this place. I need to get home. This is wasting my time.'

'And how do you know where you are going? Do you have food? Water? Shelter? Tools?'

'Well, no. And I have no money to buy anything.'

'I'll always have spare. I have never hoarded coins, and I am happy to purchase items of need. You'll need food enough for some parts of your journey. If you travel with me a little further, we'll load up your pack and you can get moving south.'

'Okay, but I don't want to dawdle.'

'We may even find you a map. Wouldn't that be nice?' Glohring's red eyes shone.

Boy smiled at the prospect of finding a map, but his cheeks soon sagged, and tension started along his jaw. His teeth ground as he reflected on speaking quite rudely and unfairly to Glohring. He shouldn't have to apologise, though, for not wanting to saunter through the town without urgency. He was aware he was impatient – mainly because his mother always told him so – but he could not see it until its inherent quality lowered his mood.

'Come here, weird rider!' an old man shouted. He sat on a barrel of ale squeezed between two houses. He wore a black cape and a leather battle vest.

Boy ignored him and kept Beetie walking forward. They looked back to see if the man had started to follow, which he had not.

A weather-beaten sign swung from an old timber building, held on by one rusty chain and a piece of rope on the other side. The sign said BAWN'S BARREL and had a crudely painted barrel of ale and what appeared to be a roast leg of ham sitting steaming on top. It could only be an inn, however poorly signed it was. The smell hit them as they approached the side of the building: greasy fat smoking over hot coals, stale beer, and long-overdue cleaning needed in the stables. Boy was hesitant to leave the beetle outside overnight. Beetie was too cumbersome to fit in the rickety stables, and Boy didn't want to go anywhere near their stench anyway.

'I'll stay out in the hayloft with Beetie. It's the only place he can fit.'

'Fair enough. I'll get a room with a view over the sheds. If there is trouble, I want to be close at hand. But don't worry yourself. Get the beetle settled if you can, then at least come and have a bath and a warm meal.'

'That sounds splendid.'

~

The night had little wind and the sounds of the inn could be heard as clearly as if Boy were inside. The cackling laughter of a crowd and the occasional stomping of floorboards as men and women drunkenly assembled their dance procession to a fiddler's tune.

Meanwhile, just outside, a giant beetle and a child wished they could drift off to sleep.

Boy's wish was granted, but soon he woke to darkness with no drunken noise coming from the inn. The sounds of the night seemed louder than before, yet everyone was at home or asleep. The wind had picked up, scattering leaves and hay around the shed. Branches dragged along the side of the loft, like rats scratching to enter. An owl swooped on the night's adventuring mice, and the beetle clicked in response every time a horse neighed. Everything seemed to ring in Boy's ears and made it harder to sleep again. Although the slow dark night drifted by without trouble, Boy woke shivering. He'd been leaning close to Beetie all night, but these giant beasts do not expel much warmth from their hard shell. Glohring entered and found Boy shivering curled up on the ground.

'Oh dear, you'll catch a death of cold. Come here.' Glohring helped him up. He placed his hands on Boy's shoulders and breathed in and out, sounding quiet tones. His hands moved to Boy's head then his spine. 'Just breath and let the warmth flow through you. Imagine it is extending through your extremities.'

Glohring transferred warmth to Boy's icy body, then pulled his hands off and stepped back to observe him.

'I feel great now, like I've slept all night.'

'In a way, you have, but I can't do that every night. You need to get yourself some blankets.'

'Can we leave this place today?'

'Yes. We will grab some supplies for both of our journeys and leave this village.'

'Great, let's get moving. Come on, Beetie, let's go. You can find breakfast later in the forest.'

'Chika chika,' Beetie accepted.

'It may be easier to leave him here. I don't think a giant creature blocking the stalls in the market will make us any friends when haggling.'

'Okay, but let's be quick. I don't want to leave him here long.'

'He's under the protection of the innkeeper, as is the mule and our baggage. He is responsible for all his guests' stabled beasts … even beetles, I guess.'

'But I can't just go and get another beetle, like you can a horse.'

Boy whispered something to his friend, who responded 'Chok chok chik.' The shiny shell slowly dropped on to the ground and tiny legs pulled back underneath, then Glohring slid the barn door closed.

In the main square of town, the stall owners were more than happy to see strange travellers. The market was full of colours and smells that were new to Boy. Everyone seemed to move from place to place in a flurry of speech and hand gestures. Chickens, breads, cheese-wheels, ribbons, armour, weapons, clothes, saddles, riding-tack, pumpkins, potatoes, fresh berries, mead, wine, flour, seeds, sugar, herbs, spices, nuts, dried fish, jewellery, water Skins, hats … everything could be found and everything was eagerly for sale.

Glohring managed to buy a large quantity of supplies for himself and Boy. First, they bought two leather bags for their separate long-distance journeys. After traversing the market stalls from one end to the other, each of their bags was fully-loaded with the most important items they believed they would need.

They left the diminishing crowd and markets behind. Boy

scurried behind Glohring, thanking him profusely for his generosity. By now, Boy completely trusted Glohring and considered him a friend. He thought it was probably about time to be open with him about how he got lost. Glohring may have some answers to explain the strange events before Boy met him.

They arrived back at the inn to find a large mob arguing outside the sheds. Boy dropped his new provisions at Glohring's feet and barged through the crowd. A man in a long robe and a strange folded hat was arguing with the innkeeper. The large crowd listened while some added their advice, insults or agreement.

'You priests can't come down here yelling sacrilege and gods-know-what-else at me and my guests,' the innkeeper nervously explained to the priest, hoping the crowd wouldn't turn on him.

The beetle backed away slowly into the corner of the shed. He shook, his hard shell rattling against the wood panels while the ensuing mob stepped closer towards his corner.

'You and your heresy shall be banished from this town for harbouring ungodly beasts, hiding this abomination of nature. This creature is evil. The haunted woods on our border have long since brewed in these dark demons of an ancient kind, and you think you can sneak it under the townsmen's eyes? The nerve of you!' The priest directed his speech straight at the innkeeper, confident his people would agree with him.

The crowd yelled and hooted in return. The priest held his hands in the air, acknowledging his support to the gods. He began to chant and sing to the sky, raising his voice over the commotion. As a clear tenor note projected out of his open mouth, a handful of pig turd splattered into his face, pitched from the crowd. Boy pushed his way through the people, who were bending over in fits of laughter. He jumped up onto a hay bale.

'This weak man speaks pig turd, and you are all receiving

an ear full of it. The creature is mine. He is not evil, and we are leaving this town now. Go back to your homes.'

The priest ran off to clean the faeces out of his teeth. Boy felt like an adult; he couldn't believe he had disrupted the mob. He was getting older, but he had never before experienced that kind of reception, not on his farm anyway. *Maybe these people listen to the youngsters, not like in our land.*

Boy stepped down off the hay bale, and the people began to quieten down and disperse without the priest's incitement.

A large, hairy brute of a man stumbled between the townsfolk, careering off others to keep him from falling. He was inebriated and stinking and, having just drained the ale stocks at the inn, he'd decided to find out what the yelling was about.

'And what if that bumbling priest is right? It can't stay in our town if it's evil. Let's burn it!' slurred the drunk.

'No!' Boy stepped down and held up his arms in protest. The boozed man stumbled towards Boy.

'Get out of the way, kid. He's mine now.'

'No!' Boy screamed. 'Help! You can't do this.' He burst into tears.

The drunk man unsheathed his dagger.

'Get out of my way! Someone grab him for me.'

Boy held his arms out to shield Beetie's shell, but was pulled away and pushed to the ground.

Beetie turned his enormous behind towards the drunk man and kicked him backwards.

'You bloody bug! We're going to burn you!' He looked up at the crowd, but they weren't actively participating any more.

The large man crouched to attack, just as two armed men marched in and disarmed him. They grabbed him by his arms and legs as if he was as light as a feather, and threw him out through the barn door, without as much as a word. Boy ran back to Beetie and wiped away his tears, ready to defend his friend. A small band of warriors, clad in leather and without crests, marched in and fully dispersed the crowd.

'Go home, you dogs! I didn't see one of you even attempt to help this young man – all just wanting to have some part in the mob. It's cowardly,' said the older of the men.

Glohring suddenly appeared carrying Boy's pack. He looked to have retrieved all their gear from the inn and had packed his mule and now dragged it behind him on leather reins.

'Come along, Boy. We must get out of here … now.'

'Where were you? They were going to kill Beetie.' Boy wiped the snot from his running nose.

'I would have stopped them. Let's go. We must leave this instant.' Glohring kept his back to the band of warriors.

Boy readied the beetle and pulled himself up onto the smooth shell. Balancing his hips, he secured the stick and guiding ribbon in his right hand and left the inn's yard. At the back of the hayloft, a small alley led straight into a scant forest.

They picked themselves a quick path through the remaining onlookers who were now gossiping amongst themselves. In attempting to clear the area to the road, the pack of warriors had surrounded the exits. A group stepped out into the middle of their path.

'Now, stop right there! Who are you? And what was that all about?' A tall bearded man stood in their path, a sword on his belt and a thin leather pack strapped to the middle of his back.

Glohring didn't respond.

'Young man, what was that all about? I see your mute servant is of no use with answers.'

'He's my friend … the beetle, I mean. The town's priest believed he was an abomination of nature and should be destroyed. So, I threw some pig turd at him. It was all he deserved for spreading lies so easily. They have no right to kill a friend of mine through their fanciful beliefs. What is wrong with the people of this town?' Boy didn't realise how the words growled from his mouth.

'Well said, and I agree. You appear to be travelling the road. Which way are you heading? We are also journeying through this land. You may need further protection through the forests, seeing you are small.'

'We are heading to a large town, over the hills that way. I know nothing of its name or environment, but we will be okay.' Boy dropped his head and kicked the shell to move forward, although Beetie did not appreciate the boot. They moved past the watching men.

'Well, as a captain of the north, I freely give my services not only to my king, but to the weak and vulnerable. You may travel with us for a while if you wish? We are on foot for the time being, but we are seeking mounts to hurry us along.'

Boy didn't know what to say; he glanced at Glohring for guidance, but Glohring was quiet.

'If these lands are anything like our own, you know nothing of the bandits that converge in the forests. Not to mention the hungry beasts of the skies, men travelling to war across the warmer months, and the haunted shores of rivers, lakes and swamps. So, I bid you good luck. You're braver than most,' said the grim warrior. 'The offer still stands.'

Boy was intimidated by his brutish appearance, but he smiled and kept Beetie moving forwards. The armed men parted the way.

'We'll be fine, thank you. Bye,' Boy eventually said. The warrior seemed disrespected and annoyed at the young man's dismissal of a proud warrior. *Little turd*, he thought, *who would turn down my protection?*

Boy and Glohring walked by their last man, passing a young scrappier warrior who smiled awkwardly.

'We saw you camping in the haunted forest two nights ago. It was very brave,' shouted the captain.

Boy looked back over his shoulder. *Were they to travel the same path as their own?* A few of the warriors stood with their hands resting comfortably on the hilts of their swords. They watched him, but they did not follow.

Later that morning, Boy and Glohring were far from the village, walking through an area of dry bushland blanketed with tinder, devoid of greenery so early in the summer. The tree-line finished like a wall, and cleared land opened to a wide view of low-lying hills – farming country with very few sheds and no people in sight, but the sniff of a town within a day's march, one could assume. Since leaving the town and the morning's ordeal, Boy and Glohring had travelled mostly in silence, the sunshine of the open road warming their moods.

Glohring began: 'So, tell me … how did you manage to get into this predicament? And how did you stray so far away from home to become lost?'

Now feeling completely comfortable opening up to his strange travelling companion, Boy stared ahead down the road and recounted his harrowing tale up until the moment he saw Glohring's campfire. Only then did Boy turn and look across at Glohring, whose eyes were glazed red with a shiny discharge and whose mouth was half-open. Boy's self-awareness of his circumstances, now vocalised, bore a hole through his layers of confidence and arrogance. His self-belief was now gravely and duly injected with trepidation.

'This news is very grave. Very. The beasts of the air are moving, and this basket you speak of … hearing that a beast carried it and made an unexpected landing is very, very odd. It makes no sense whatsoever. It's almost like your flying beast has nothing to do with the ones I'm talking about.

'Maybe it's a different kind from a distant mountain range, very far away. What you have experienced has not happened in a very long time … from my studies, I think maybe fifty years before I was born. You said you had never seen these beasts before?'

'No, never. As far as I know it, my mum and dad have never seen one either. We live in peace. Well, except for Tree Deep annoying everyone.' He smiled at the memory.

'Your ability to control this mighty river is truly fascinating. Have you ever felt like something strange has passed through your lands before? Even in your dreams? Or tried to seduce you further away from your home?'

'I can't recall. But I am always exploring and going further and further away to see things. I just never meant to be taken this far without control.'

'Interesting. And yes, it's very sad to have no control. For anyone.'

Glohring looked up towards the clouds, stared for a long time and finished with a deep breath. Boy didn't have the heart to ask what he was doing so changed the subject back to the present.

'How far did the innkeeper say this city was?'

'Three days' ride to the south-west.'

'And how far are we going to the west, do you think? I don't want to travel too far from where Tree Deep Trundle may be.'

'We are actually heading south. If you say your river also runs south, then we should be parallel to the river. Each day you are getting closer and closer to home, my young friend.' Not really knowing where the young man's river lay, he mumbled under his breath, 'Or further away.'

'Can you hear that?' Boy asked.

'Yes. Horses galloping, a lot of them. Get off the road. Farmers don't gallop in groups.'

The land had all been cleared for farming, so there were not many trees or bushes to hide in. The dust rising from hooves gave the riders' distance away. Boy and Glohring halted, moved off the road into a field, and decided to have a quick break for lunch. They were sitting down relaxing, trying to act as if a contingent of mounted horses meant nothing to them and their motives.

While they snacked on a hunk of salted pork, cheese and fresh bread, the troop of twenty-five or so armed warriors – who they had met that morning – arrived on horseback and slowly formed a ring around them. Their horses were of a hodgepodge mix: some battle-bred, some small farming breeds, and one pony that an embarrassed warrior was struggling with. Glohring stood up and approached the bearded man who had previously spoken to them, assuming he was the captain. Cheese in hand, he casually signalled for him to get down off his mount and approach.

The captain did so obligingly, thinking this mute was a humble servant of the young boy. The captain moved closer and stared Glohring in the eye.

It's intimidating, Boy thought.

But Glohring didn't move; just casually finished his cheese and dusted his hands together.

'You managed to find horses. But not all the most desirable breeds … ugghh, look at that one.'

'So, you're not the mute servant we all thought you were?'

'I never said I was.' Glohring and the captain kept their eyes on each other.

'What can we do for you today? My journeyman and I may not be of help as we are foreign to these lands, as you have also mentioned yourself, but we will help if possible,' said Glohring.

'Thank you. We are heading to the Manne castle, the fortress to the west. Do you know of this place?'

'I'm afraid we have only heard of its existence from farmers. We are travelling beyond this Manne, but through it we must go. Am I able to assist you with anything else, good captain?'

'Can you read, Master?'

'Glohring is my name, and my friend is Boy.'

The captain bowed. 'I am honoured to formally meet you. I am Gruldarht, the captain of this pack of dogs. Now, can you read, Master Glohring? There are peculiar symbols across this map. They are of a different kind to what I have seen before.'

'Why didn't you ask the man you bought it from what they meant?'

'Well, the man we are supposed to meet at this castle gave my overlord the map, so I was never able to question him. It appeared to be sufficient until now. We believe we are getting closer, and further details would be of some use now that we have horses. We must be there by summer solstice at least. None of the people in these towns can read or write, especially the tavern drunks who usually keep us company at the inns.'

The captain rolled the map out on the ground. It was old and deteriorated with three types of language scribbled in random spaces, each one pertaining to a different key. Glohring scrutinized the map.

'I'm sorry, but I am unable to read this script and its symbols.' A blatant lie. 'But I think I may be able to translate the geographical sketching as we make our way across the land.'

Gruldarht looked disappointed. 'Well, not to fear, troop. Just because we're no pack of bumbling scholars, we do know the forests and the ways of the hunting lords. We'll make it to this fortress, good and proper.'

The troop cheered their captain.

'And, Master Glohring, I will offer as a courtesy for the second time – there won't be a third – would you like to join us on our journey as far as Manne castle? Your map-deciphering skills may come in handy, and we'll provide the food, shelter and safety for you and your small friend.'

'And my friend!' Boy's hands propped on his hips as he scowled at the warrior troop. 'In no circumstances are any of you allowed to touch my beetle. You cannot go near him, and there will be no exceptions. Do you understand?' Boy looked around at all the men.

'Ummmm, yep, ummm … yes,' fumbled the large swordsman. Boy was shocked that they'd even listened.

'A tough young fellow. I like that,' the captain said to Glohring, who nodded.

Boy nodded in acceptance of their word, turned on his heel, and marched away to finish his food with his friend.

'Chickachickchk.'

'Yeah, I'm quite surprised it worked. I never thought they would listen, but they seem to believe in some type of honour. I wouldn't be too hasty with judgement though, Beetie.'

Boy began to clean the mud and clay from Beetie's legs and feet. 'Chick chika chika.' The beetle enjoyed the leg-tickling game.

'At least we'll be safe for part of our journey and can hopefully get a long peaceful sleep. I hadn't thought about it until now, but having all these big people around … I really do miss my little brother and sister.'

'Chick-chikaa?'

'Their names are Tilly and Armue, Beetie. I do miss them, and they would love you, especially Armue. Tilly may be scared, but she'd warm to you in the end. I'm sorry, I know you lost your family. I wish you could have them back too, but maybe I can give you a better life, or a different one at least. You can join my family one day as the sixth member – the largest, shiniest, greatest ground-twiddling, dirt-scattering, tentacle-twirling one of us all!'

The beetle turned its head away, gazing into a possible future.

Boy and the beetle furtively assumed the front of the pack and led the small troop along the gravel road. Glohring walked behind them, ensuring he lead his own mule and kept his belongings close to him. Casually, he gave directions at each crossroads as he read the captain's map, pretending to be unsure of certain symbols and letters. They stayed on the road all day until it again became a thick forest that led down into a valley. As the light faded in the west, the darkness held its warmth and they stopped to camp before crossing the water at the bottom of the long valley.

Boy sat down and leaned against Beetie's shell, watching the troop of warriors set up their camp. He was very impressed at their efficient structure, and the roles each person played. *Very well-practised*, he assumed. A hasty camp may be needed in a retreat or chase against enemies across the land, but they were in no rush. Their work was executed with precision, very little talk, and only minor grumbles.

Boy began removing the reins from his mount. A young warrior watched and strode over to lend a hand. This man always appeared to be alone, Boy had noticed, and clearly wasn't one of the captain's close men riding up the front. *Maybe he is looking for something to do; he doesn't seem to have an important role.* He was below-average height for a warrior and looked to be the youngest, with a stubbly beard and scraggly brown hair that added shape to his nearly invisible head.

'Can I help with your makeshift saddle there?' The man pointed to the reins.

'No, that's okay. I'd prefer to do it myself.' Boy shrunk into himself, and the man looked disappointed.

'May I help in any way? I can wipe down your ride. I'm sure your pet's colour would look great once cleaned. He doesn't appear to have ever been cleaned.'

He's not my pet; he's my friend, Boy scowled internally. 'Hmm, okay. But be careful. If he doesn't like it, just stop and slowly back away. Otherwise, bad things could happen.'

'I understand. I've had many a steed in my life.'

'But your horse at the moment looks like it's losing its hair.'

'I guess it is. I've only had it a day. Not like the grand steeds

I once had back home … now they truly were great.'

'How long have you been away from your village? I mean, with this band of warriors?'

'I left my home a long while ago in search of adventure. My family would rather have me stay to protect them, but I am searching for a grander life than they will never know. The captain sought me out to join the group. I am the only young man from my town to be hand-picked for this kind of duty to the sovereign. I will have a grand position in life.'

'Wow, that's very exciting. I could never imagine that happening where I am from.'

'Well, my decision was better for everyone. I may return one day, and I will be richer than all of them. That is, if I ever want to see a village estranged from royalty again.'

'It sounds like a great opportunity … you know, for adventure. I'm far away from my family, but they will welcome me back with open arms.'

The young warrior looked off into the distance as if he hadn't heard what Boy had said.

'I'm Boy of the lower Marithijseon forest.' Boy didn't know why he lied.

'I am Tendai, of nowhere for the time being. Soon it shall be Tendai of the grand palace.' Again, he grinned to himself.

Tendai wiped down Beetie's dusty shell until the colours gleamed in the last of the day's sunlight. Boy kept one eye on him, but thought it safe enough to leave them be and to set up his bedroll for the night at his modest camp.

Just as Tendai had finished cleaning down the shell, his captain called to him, screaming his name over the noise of the other men. He ran to the shouts of his captain and disappeared without another word to Boy.

Later that evening, Glohring and Boy shared a fire together away from the soldiers, where the laughing and singing ebbed and flowed as they bonded with a drink of ale.

'Glohring, I was thinking today ... I know you can read the map Gruldarht has ... I want to know how far away my home is. He said it had other symbols and languages on it, so maybe I can decipher where exactly I have to go.'

'I will most certainly try to show you the map when the captain hands it to me next. But when I looked at it earlier, it was quite small and mainly ran east to west. I don't think your farm or the great river you speak of is marked on it. I'm thinking it's further south. If that is the case, you were surely taken a long way north, but I'll have a closer look.'

'I was thinking ... if there is a roundabout way from this fortress, maybe I don't have to get tangled up in this trade thing.'

Glohring cut him off. 'Hush, not another word. It would be most unwise to head off into forests close to cities and castles. That's where the worst people lurk. They like to stay close to large towns but not connected to their society. The space they are in lends itself to their forbidden deeds in a secret lifestyle. It's cheaper and easier to rob people and to remain hidden. I think it would be safer if you stayed close to me. But I'll ask for the map from the captain this instant.'

'Before you go, do you think these men ill-omened? I mean, should we be travelling with them?'

'I can't see anything wrong with it, and they've been quite pleasant.'

'But, what if they're not? What if they want to take Beetie back to their home to sell and ... I don't know ... perform evil experiments on, or whatever bad people do?'

'Boy, it's okay to not believe where your mind likes to wander. Don't let your judgement and actions respond to what you cannot account for,' Glohring sighed. 'It's actually a great and wonderful thing to trust someone. I know you have had bad experiences since your debacle, and some people have not been very nice at all, but that doesn't mean everyone out there is like that. Just reach to your gut feelings and they'll guide you. Some people may help you in small ways on your journey home, as I'd like to think I am doing.'

'You are helping me the most, and I promise to think about what you said.' Boy snapped a twig and threw it into the fire.

'Good. I'll go and speak to the captain about looking further at the map.'

As Glohring left the fire, Tendai appeared from the shadows and sat down without being asked.

'Hello, Tendai, have you eaten? I have more cheese and bread than I can manage in one sitting,' Boy offered politely.

'No, thank you. I've just come to sit with different company. And there is no one more different than you and Master Glohring. Tell me, is he your uncle or some relation? You don't look related.'

Boy reminded himself of Glohring's advice to trust. But he decided to do the complete opposite, to make sure the advice was thoroughly tested.

'He is no relation of mine. I am trying to get home to my family, and he has accompanied me on this part of my journey. Why are you asking?'

'Oh, I didn't mean to pry. He just, well, errrr, appears to be from the far north, that's all. They can be dangerous.' There was a pause between them. 'Just making sure you're safe,' said Tendai, leaning back and pretending to relax.

Boy had by now spent long enough with Glohring to know when someone was scared of him. He thought he should oblige by backing up their original judgement.

'He is frightening,' Boy whispered.

Tendai didn't know what to say; he looked around, hoping Glohring had not overheard. Boy did think Tendai was a trustworthy man, but he was just over-cautious, for caution's sake. He reminded Boy a little of his dad: caring, helpful, detailed in his application to work. He decided to break the current mood.

'Why would anyone want to become a soldier? Getting stabbed all the time. Is it what you wanted to do? Or did you have some skills as a youngster?' Boy broke the awkward silence at their fire.

Tendai slowly raised his chin in the air. 'Yes. I've always been good at it. But I am a trained swordsman. I worked hard for the skill.'

'Really? That must have been very dangerous, training for such a long time with weapons. It would have been nice to have those options where I am from.'

'In truth, I would have liked to become a bard. I'd like to have been trained in singing the great tales of the kingdom.' Tendai poked the glowing coals with a stick. 'Are you also trained at singing?'

'No, no. I thought better of it and stopped when I was really young, like most should. I have only had a bit of sword training and some in cheese making. My parents couldn't stand the sound of me singing. The cheese gurgles better than you sing, my father used to say.'

'Who cares what he says? You shouldn't have given up.'

'There was no bard where I came from, no grand palaces. There were plenty of other things to do on the farm. Maybe one day there'll be things to do in the surrounding towns.' Boy thought of all the things he wished he were better at. There was a long moment of silence as he reflected on his lack of talents. He was thankful he didn't have pressure and insults from his parents.

'Did your parents send you on this journey? As like a coming-of-age trip?' asked Tendai.

'No. My parents would never send me away. They are perfect. Well, kind of. We all worked hard on the farm, and they taught us with many a book at night, stories about the joy of the outside world. I've now seen it's a different place to what was read to my brother, sister and me. It's very different … our way of life. We have no religion or coming-of-age rituals. We do not have large temples or gold statues of perceived gods. We do have common beliefs that are passed down, but it's our choice to discard them if we wish.

'My dad read one over and over like this: 'We are born into this world to experience happiness, sadness and everything in-between. The gift taken of life is to be innocent, a child. The gift given of life is to be a guardian, a parent. All elements of happiness and peace shall be in the life of a child. All elements of caring and love shall be given by a parent.' I really don't know why I remember that. I think he would say it sometimes to distract us from fighting, booming his voice because it probably sounded like we were being told off. What of your world?'

'I don't know. My world is very different to yours, Boy. Your home sounds like a nice place. I can see your friend coming this way. We shall speak again. I'm tired, and I am going. Enjoy the fire.'

'Thank you. You are always welcome at our fire.'

Tendai hurried off, head tilted to the ground, while Glohring curiously stared at him as he passed. Glohring sat down next to Boy, handing him a fresh apple.

'What is that young warrior's name?'

'Tendai.'

'He was asking questions about us, was he?'

'No, he was just lonely, I think. He appears quite new to their troop, and I don't think many of them have really taken him in yet.'

'I thought the same myself. Now, I've been talking to the captain and we have sighted a good path through the back roads. That should get us to the castle in three days' ride. He says they would much prefer to go unnoticed when arriving in the town. Large amounts of warriors are not the most welcomed guests, especially if they are not expected or invited. I have informed him that the day before they arrive, we will be departing on our own separate route. The map Gruldarht showed me extends quite far in the direction of where you believe your home to be. When I pointed out our route to the captain, he shook his head. A man at the town's inn had said he knew of someone to explain about that area to him, and he'd brought over a shabby mute. The mute pointed to this area on the map and then to his mouth. His tongue was missing. All that was left was a stumpy bit of flesh where it should have been. I don't want to scare you, but the captain believed the fear in this man's eyes.

'So, my point is, you should be thinking of going a roundabout way or heading straight back to the river once we part ways. I do believe it is best for you to stay with me and the warriors for as long as possible for protection. It's the unknown land I'd be worried about, but I know you might reason *if I don't know what's out there, then why should I fear it?*'

'I do fear it. I just want to be at home now. Did the map show the Great River Hew?'

'Possibly. It showed two major rivers. One leading south and the other west, and there is only forest on the map where both of them head – no mountains or oceans.'

'Before we leave the troop, do you think the captain will let me have the map? I mean, they would already be so close to their destination.'

'We'll just have to ask him when the times comes. It may be worth a lot where he is from. Off to bed now. We have a long day of riding tomorrow, and, yes, we will be riding. The captain is lending me their packhorse so we can make more speed.'

While Boy made one last check on Beetie, a wolf howled in the distance, its eerie tone echoing through the valley and bouncing off the tall timbers. Beetie didn't flinch; he just tucked his legs in beneath his shell. One of the night guards moved past slowly, watching the edge of the night.

'Go to sleep. They're too far away,' the dark warrior said. Boy climbed into his bedroll. He could feel his stiff spine mould back into its proper shape. It was only then that he realised how riding Beetie slowly curled him over; he may need to adjust his riding style. With that last thought, he slept. A long night followed, dreaming of tumbling boulders, trees crashing to the ground and the creepy feeling of being incessantly chased.

When Boy awoke, the camp was still asleep; the fires were dying embers, and the first of the day's light was dim in the east. The cold pressure in his bladder demanded he go to relieve himself away from the camp. Wrapped in a blanket, he put his boots on and headed quietly towards the trees. When he turned back, he couldn't see any guards amongst the camp. He headed towards the forest. Then he noticed a figure leaning against a tree, flipping a blade. The man put the blade away and moved towards Boy. It was still too dark to see.

'It's okay, it's only me. If you needed to go away from camp, you should have found me first.' It was Tendai.

'Sorry, I just thought I'd go by myself. I need to pee. Where are the other guards?'

'They always put me on alone, which is fine by me. I can handle the entire watch. Don't go too far.'

Boy re-wrapped the blanket around him and walked into the forest, trying to find a tree big enough to hide behind. He turned and looked back to camp, but Tendai was gone. As he finished relieving himself, movement in the darkness caught his eye. A shadow moved behind low bushes. Boy slowly stepped back, tempted to call for Tendai. Behind the bush, big red eyes opened, glowing in the blackened morning light. Boy froze.

'Boy, come here. I'll show you something. It will be something you need. Come here if you want to live,' a deep gravelly voice echoed through Boy's head.

'Tendai!' Boy screamed. Just then an arrow sped past him and into a branch. A large fat black wolf growled and moved away, slowly, sluggishly. It looked like a half-walrus, half-wolf.

Boy stood frozen, shaking, as Tendai came running up behind him.

'It's gone off that way,' shivered Boy.

'That's okay. I'll track him down before breakfast.'

Tendai went running in the direction of the wolf, which had literally disappeared. Boy couldn't see the thing.

The camp awoke, the troops all pulling on boots to see what had alarmed the young man. The captain jogged toward him, his sword drawn.

'What happened? Where's Tendai? He's meant to be on patrol.'

'It was a large wolf. It spoke to me. Tendai went after it.'

'A talking wolf?' Gruldarht scoffed with disbelief.

Boy nodded.

'Ha! You were probably still dreaming. Children and their fantasies. Well, it looks like no harm was done. That lout had better be back before we ride. Come along; we'll be setting off early today.'

'But what about Tendai?'

'Who cares? If he's worthy of our pack, he'll be fine against a lone beast, and he owes me a wolf pelt. That young bastard's been eating for free for too long.' Gruldarht sheathed his sword and made his way back to his fire.

Boy drew the distinct impression that the troops really didn't like Tendai or were impartial to his fate. The morning darkness had lifted and the easterly breeze began to blow hard that morning. The dark pines sprung to life in the wind as if discussing the day ahead, swaying and caressing each other, while the birds of the forest whistled to their hypnotic creak. Boy jogged back to camp looking for Glohring and found him quickly packing his mule.

'Glohring!'

'Yes? What was that yelling about? Get your bedroll and load up the Beetle.'

'I forgot to tell you that near my home before I got taken away, I had an encounter with a giant black wolf that spoke to me.'

'My god! This is serious. Why are you only telling me now?'

'Because I just saw another one, that's why. I shouted for Tendai because he was on guard duty. But this wolf also spoke to me. It was a lot bigger, though, and fat, really fat … like a slug. The captain thought I was dreaming it.'

The look on Glohring's face scared Boy. It appeared his skull was moving around under his skin; his skin became translucent and crisp as his body reacted to this news.

'If you trust me, Boy, don't ever talk back to these beasts. If you come across any on the rest of our journey, get away from them and don't talk back. Don't trust anyone who says they know them. We'll talk soon. There are things you must know about where I am from.'

This new cryptic information scared the hell out of Boy. He wanted to scream aloud for someone to tell him the truth about what to expect in the forests when he was alone. Fear sank into his mind – he wouldn't have this surrounding protection forever. He was learning the world was a much more dangerous place than in his father's books.

The troop mounted to begin the day's ride as Tendai returned to camp. The men ignored him, passing him by without a glance. They hadn't bothered to pack up his remaining gear, which was laid out by the fire the way he'd left it. The captain gave him a few stern words as they left him to pack up and steered their horses through the crisp air of the forest shadows. Glohring and Boy fell into line, choosing to ride towards the back of the line, out of earshot of the other riders.

'Where did Tendai go?' whispered Glohring.

'To hunt down the wolf.'

Glohring immediately pulled on the reins. Stopping, he turned around to see if Tendai was approaching them from the campsite.

'Boy, you have to be extra careful. I'll tell you something quickly, and I'll embellish later. In my part of the world, there are some people or creatures that work evil. They can change into the image of some of their gods, one being their god of temptation: a large black wolf. Only the masters can turn into this god. You have encountered two, and they don't just make this transformation for fun. Something else is on their minds. I've never heard of them travelling this far from the homelands. They are my natural enemies, and I really do hate them. They try to undo the work my followers and I create in our lifetimes. Don't go near anyone who leaves the camp, disappears, for a time. These wolves can steal the souls of the weak and inhabit their bodies for a while. Disgusting creatures. Go and ride with the troop. I have to stop and check Tendai before he rejoins us.'

Glohring kicked his horse and rode back to camp. Boy hoped the situation wouldn't turn bad; he was just regaining some sense of peace. Beetie stopped and turned back to see Glohring go.

'Chickchickchachickah!' he said frantically.

Glohring broke through the low branches of the forest, his heels kicking his horse into a gallop, straight towards Tendai. Glohring swung down gracefully from the saddle at speed, blocking Tendai's way, his hands clasped together above his head until they began to glow red.

Tendai's horse reared, and Tendai leapt off to calm it down. Both he and the horse reeled in shock, and Glohring knew instantly that the wolf master had not enslaved his soul. He thrust his hands in his pockets, hiding his powers, and acted as if nothing was wrong.

'Master Glohring, what is it? Is there something wrong?'

'No, my young warrior, I just wanted to see if you were alright.'

Tendai was too shocked to ask about his glowing red

hands. It was magic, but he dared not ask – it would be easier to go along with Glohring's act and pretend nothing was out of the ordinary.

'Okay, Glohring, I'm fine. I'll just calm my horse down and we'll be on our way.'

'Wait. Come here for a second.'

Tendai waited, unmoving as Glohring approached and peered into his eyes. He was frozen still. He had thought himself a hardened, battle-gloried warrior, but now compared his courage to a cook battling with a wedding feast.

'Good news, Tendai. Your soul hasn't been enslaved by the demon wolf. Mount up, and let's go,' he said, cheerfully stepped back into the saddle.

Tendai peered behind him into the forest. Then he vaulted onto his horse and galloped straight for the troop, a cold shiver running up his spine. *He is just jesting with me*, Tendai thought, trying to calm himself.

Glohring chuckled lightly to himself. Tendai was as frightened as a newborn, but he had to know if those wolves were lurking about. Were they following him? Or did they have a vested interest in Boy and his surprising talents? 'Let's hope he doesn't have to chase another one,' Glohring said to his horse.

2

Tilly and Armue began the long and arduous task of roping buckets of water from the river. Since Boy's disappearance, the river had become angrier and quickly vengeful of the family's attempts to take water from its shore. As summer approached, the natural spring and stone well had a limited supply, and the River Hew became more important to the farm. It was now an everyday chore and, without Boy to keep an eye on the river, it was a dangerous task to survive near Tree Deep Trundle's malevolent life force. It had become more alive.

'One more bucket, Tilly. Keep pulling,' said Armue.

'I wish Boy were here to do this like before, without this silly rope. My hands are red and sore.'

Aged seven, and with one less member of the family at home, there were no more excuses for Tilly not to help out.

'Well, we don't know where he is. Like mum says, *soup and baths go on, Tilly*. If you complain about fetching the water, you can swap places with mum if you want … you can do all the cooking and all the cleaning!' he laughed.

'I'll just help with the water,' scowled Tilly.

'Good. I don't want to be eating your cooking anyway. Probably just be mud cakes with worms and sand. That's what you made when you were young.' He scrunched his face up at her. Tilly couldn't remember if she'd done that or not when she was young, but she scowled back anyway.

Armue dragged the last of the water into the house. Their home seemed smaller and emptier: less wood, less colours, less songs, and less warmth. Their mother was chopping carrots and sorting herbs at the kitchen bench under a dull natural light.

'Armue, make sure it all goes through the strainer this time. And Tilly, be careful. Watch out you don't burn yourself.' Tilly picked up a bucket of water, ready to pour it into the already steaming cauldron.

'I can't reach. That's why I burnt myself before,' whined Tilly.

'Oh, you can too reach. You did it last night, so you can do it again. You just don't want to do it,' Armue replied.

Their mother kept silent, with one eye on them. Armue took control as the water filled the cauldron to an acceptable level. Armue had stepped up to a role he was too young for, the responsibilities thrust upon him. Boy had now been away long enough for Armue to realise their home wasn't going to run itself, especially without Boy, and with their father away for long periods. The standard of housework and jobs on the farm had been deteriorating each day, affecting their health and relationships.

If only my son were home, Leesiele would think. Her baby Boy was gone, lost and forsaken in a dangerous world, without her to protect him and hold him in her motherly arms. She dreamed of ruffling his hair and watching his beautiful smile in return. She thought it was totally inconceivable that something so beautiful came from her body. She was lost in that thought when the door flung open.

'Dad!' Tilly yelled, running up to hug his dirty legs.

'Ah-ha, Tilly. Look at you. My silly Tilly.' George wrapped his large arms tightly around his little daughter.

'Hi, dad. Did you find anything?' Armue asked with clear worry.

'Let's all sit down first. Your father is wretchedly tired.'

George pulled out his familiar wooden chair from the head of the table and groaned as he sat down. He untied his boots and tucked them under the table out of the way. When he looked up, he saw his wife shedding a tear.

'Mum, don't cry,' said Tilly, peering around the cauldron's edge.

Leesiele stepped forward to hug her husband, who stood tall and embraced her gently.

'It's okay. Please don't cry. I don't need it,' George whispered into her hair.

'Well, dinner won't take care of itself if I'm a blubbering mess.' She smiled and pulled herself away. Armue watched them with one eye as he began dropping vegetables into the cauldron.

'I'm sorry, but it's just a vegetable soup. We ran out of rabbit,' she said.

'That's okay. All I've had for the last week has been rabbit. Vegetables are all I'm after,' George smiled wearily.

'Dad, I tried to go hunting with a spear I made, but the critters are too quick. I couldn't get close,' said Armue.

'You'd be better off with a small trap. Let them catch themselves. I'll show you how to make one, one day.'

'Not any time soon. We have too much to do around here,' snapped Leesiele.

'We sure do. There is too much to do around the farm. I'll show you another time, when you are older.'

When you are older, when you are older … Armue hated hearing that. Boy got to do everything when he was here. *So, why can't I now?*

Once the soup was ladled into wooden bowls and served, George dragged the dining table further away from the heat of the cauldron and the family each took their usual seats. Summer was close, and the kitchen heat became irritating.

George went through the details of his journey briefly. Armue listened intently, paying attention to descriptions of the living and dead creatures his dad had seen, and the various landscapes that were unfamiliar to him. His father described how their neighbours were faring and the rough terrain he had encountered on his journey far to the south. He had followed the river as far downstream as any of them had ever visited, and the land had grown vibrant, with strange new flowers and fauna. Large birds circled the skies on one occasion, the largest George had ever seen.

But George was very tired, so he kept things quick and vague. It was almost like he was reciting a dream, all hazy details and no connection. There was one thing that stuck in Armue's mind, though: the sighting of two massive footprints. He said they must have been from a bird, as they were the only prints left on the ground. They were quite fresh and deep, filled with murky water, and no animals were around at the time. When he listened carefully, George said he could hear a thunderous boom far away on the wind.

~

Armue lay in bed, flicking his eyelashes back and forth with his index finger. He wanted to sleep, but kept drifting awake and blinking for no reason. He was thinking of his dad's journey south, picturing the forests and animals in his mind; back and forth the images materialised. As he was being taken into the arms of sleep, he could hear the thunderous boom of wings above the forest; he could see the beast circling their farm, a large beak, but not quite a bird. His heart pounded. Lightning flashed above, and the creature circled lower and lower towards the fields. He felt as if he was riding on its back, looking down on the farm from above, with no control over direction. He gripped tight to the creature as it swooped down fast, crashing into their home and clawing the roof apart.

Lightning struck close by, jolting him awake, returning him to his dark and quiet room. Under his blankets, a cold sweat soaked through his shirt and a puddle lay in the small of his back. He struggled to take in a full breath, worried by the strong irregular pulsating of his heart. He calmed himself down by watching Tilly sleeping across the room.

Armue looked out of the window, just to make sure nothing was flying above. He listened intently for thunderous beats, but there was nothing. And he could finally breathe. He thought about where Boy was sleeping that night; he hoped that he was safe and no beasts lurked looking for dinner.

Beyond the farm's vegetable patch, moonlight shone through the tall trunks of the surrounding pine forest. Behind the dull light, Armue caught movement – an unnatural thing waited in the gloom of night. Two eyes shimmered in the shadows, moving between tree trunks, appearing then disappearing. Armue watched for a long moment, then decided that it would be better to show this to his father.

He stepped quietly on the creaky floorboards, not wanting to wake Tilly, then he looked back outside. The eyes, now red, pierced his window. He knew it had seen him move. He didn't know whether to yell for his dad or to hide or stay still.

The red eyes moved closer to the farmhouse, but the dark helped the creature to be undetermined. It moved behind a tree and, as the light from the moon vanished, so did the eyes. *Whatever it is, it's no longer watching me.*

~

Armue woke in the morning and remembered his terrible, vivid dream. He was happy it was daytime and that his father was home. During breakfast, he thought about the large red eyes passing behind the trees outside his window. *Nothing has red eyes that lives around here.* The more he thought about it, the more he was convinced it was a dream. He decided not to burden his mother and father with talk of gross creatures, especially since Boy was out there all alone.

3

Boy held his steering pole high in the air and inspected the dangling cloth; it only held on by a few strands and would be better replaced now than later. He ripped the tattered remains from his makeshift steering and retrieved a piece of cloth that had been left behind at the last camp by Gruldarht. He had kept it for this very reason, and he attached it to his light polished stick. It was long brown material with added weight that cut through the oncoming wind. He decided to call it his shepherd-stick from now on, and made a mental note to add a nice grip handle, soft for his hands, and binding to give it an almost regal appearance.

He smiled to himself and wanted to show his work off to others: his very own shepherd-stick that worked as a fantastic steering signal for his cumbersome friend. Boy would like to think that Beetie was mesmerised, that it was a magic of his own compilation. In truth, that was not the reason.

A long day of picking through the forests on winding deer trails followed. They regularly passed granite outcrops and bracken-laden floors before they finally reached the forest's edge. Ahead, a flat opening of grass surrounded a small spring that was the start of a stream running downhill. Rocks were half-exposed to the air and pools were created for animals to drink from. They watered their mounts patiently, a few at a time, and then began the orderly procedure of setting up a level camp for the evening.

Glohring seemed deep in thought all day, much deeper than usual. Boy had watched him silently all afternoon from the high perch of Beetie's shell.

Boy tethered his mount and began collecting their own firewood. Even though the warriors were happy to lend them plenty, he had been taught to warm himself when in need. He laid out a square rock barrier and crisscrossed the wood. That was the easy part; the tricky part was finding Glohring and getting him to light the fire, ensuring none of the soldiers were nosing around. Boy placed himself next to the fire, while Glohring hid behind him and placed his hands on the kindling. They heard the wood catch alight and the low rumble of the flames climbing off the wood. Glohring stood up from the fire and called Tendai over.

'Tendai, go and fetch your captain. I want to speak with him.'

Gruldarht soon appeared from the forest edge and walked through the camp. Boy shuffled away from the large fire and leaned against his bedroll. The captain approached and ignored Boy.

'You wanted a word with me?'

'More than a word.'

'Then, let's walk, Master Glohring.'

'I wanted to thank you personally for guarding Boy and I while we ride through unseen lands. Although, in some parts, it does look a lot like home.'

'Where is your home anyway? To the north? You look like you travel a lot. But your real home?'

'It's near your home, but a lot deeper into the mountain region.'

'I thought it may have been a stranger place. No offence.'

Glohring didn't respond.

'My young companion and I will be leaving on the morrow. We don't want to get too close to a large population. There is no need for us to go there. We have supplies and will be moving on.'

'What is your relationship with the boy? He isn't your son

or family? If you don't mind me asking.'

'I am travelling to the seaports, and he is trying to get home. As long as we are heading in the same direction, we might as well travel together.'

'The seaports? On the coast?'

'Of course.'

'Well, good luck on your journey. I will pry no longer, my good man. But one last thing, and I will not take no for answer. You will keep the extra horse we lent you, plus food, grain and blankets. It needn't be wasted on a pack of dogs like us.'

'Thank you. But you keep the horse. The other items will come in useful for Boy, I'm sure. And good luck for your journey home. Stay safe,' said Glohring.

~

That night Tendai once again joined Boy by the fire. They ate cheese together, and Tendai taught him an old dice game he had learnt from his mother. They were beginning to become friends: Tendai, a young man with a happy smile, but not yet welcome to the troop; and Boy, mature, smart and always happy to learn.

'Tendai, what is your troop going to do now because Glohring and I are leaving tomorrow morning to head south-east?'

'Well, I know we are heading to this castle for some meeting, but I'm not too sure what it's all about. Being the newest, I'm not privileged to any information. It's just *come on, you're coming with us; get your pack ready.* Then, I set off and do my role. Do they think it would help me do my job better if I knew more? The answer is no. So, they keep quiet. I'd be better off in charge.'

'Well, I hope the castle is nice. Do you think your captain will be able to give me the map he bought, seeing he doesn't need it and all?'

Boy was hoping Tendai would go and ask the captain for him. He didn't really want to ask himself since he'd been given extra supplies already.

'You will need to go and ask him. He's a closed man, but still, he may grant you the request. I would give it to you if I were him,' said Tendai, but doubted very much the captain would grant Boy any special boon, no matter how noble the cause.

'Well, if I don't see you again, it was nice knowing you. Thanks for teaching me this game. It's very interesting, and I just hope I remember the rules.'

'Oh, there aren't any that important to remember. The core of the game is there, but if you feel you have better rules to brighten the game up a bit, then by all means, go for it. It's not like it's a tradition. Your story has been very interesting. Good luck, Boy ... you will need it.'

Tendai shook Boy's hand and left the fire to find sleep in his lonely bedroll on the edge of the forest. Boy thought of what Tendai had said about the game not being a tradition. In his life, there had been tradition in a lot of things: it was passed down through the family, it was a habit through the years that made you feel good, you expected it, waited for it. The very idea of changing something to make it better was eye-opening. The freedom! Maybe one day, he would have enough power to even start a tradition, an annual or regular act that would enhance everyone's lives around him, people he loved. Boy sat and stared into the fire, considering endless options for an act that he would like to fulfil before he was too old and the idea became forgotten. Ideas dropped into his mind, but they always came back to one thing: something happy that involved his family.

Boy woke to an annoying stick poking his side. *Glohring.*

'Get up! Time to pack up the beetle and move.'

It was still dark, close to sunrise, and no light appeared from the east. By the light of the dying embers, Boy tied his bedroll and new bag to the leather straps on Beetie. It still took him several attempts to climb onto his smooth shell. He would have to take a long run up, leap, grab a rein and pull himself up into position. Beetie always wriggled and squeaked as if it were a game he found funny.

They began the day's journey at the first light of sunrise, giving one last signal to the two guards on post. They waved back and bowed low in a sign of respect. Boy was hoping Tendai was on guard to say farewell one more time, but he wasn't.

The sun rose over the pine-stunted hills. The birds woke up and became lively in the morning, singing their crazy songs: a thousand it seemed at once, yet only a few in sight. A small spring ran across their path and they stopped to water the mule, and the beetle, of course. Glohring finally felt awake enough to talk in private with Boy.

'I managed to get the captain's map for you. Now, Boy, this is important. That red-eyed wolf creature you saw. If you see any more on your journey home, then ...' He stopped mid-sentence, breathing heavily. 'Just know that things in these lands may be getting very bad. Stay as far away from them as possible. Don't get close to them at all.'

'Well, what happens if one talks to me again?'

'I don't know. I wouldn't even lie to them, but you could try that. I really don't know what's going on with them. I haven't seen them in years. Maybe they have just procreated and been forced to gain new territory. We all know that the more you breed your stock, the more stupidity is spread. They may not be powerful at all, but nonetheless, I would not test their wanting connection to you. Some creatures in this world have an agenda, have secret information on the future, and through their morbid powers, they are coercing with the oily layer of the afterlife. I wish I could journey home with you to make sure you get there safely. I would like to learn more about these beasts that have now travelled so far from home.

It is a very interesting and scary thing.'

He rummaged through his pack and brought out the map, holding it high to catch the morning light of its new ownership glory. It was written on thick flexible paper, without many creases. Glohring wiped down the map, and the coarse sound of the paper was unfamiliar to Boy's ears.

'I'm guessing your farm is somewhere down there, off the edge of the map, maybe further. Now, I think this is where you saw the first wolf, before this other fatter one.' Glohring pointed at the two locations, surmising the distance between them. He sat very still, considering this information.

'So, here is the fortress of Manne. I'll be travelling to the town by the lake, not far from the castle. In fact, the castle and this town may even link up to be a small city. We'll have to wait and see. I'll have to find an inn. You may want to come into town and buy more weapons.'

'I don't know how to use weapons anyway. I should have taken that spear from Gruldarht. Or taken the extra horse and sold it. I could have used the extra money for supplies along the way.'

'I don't think selling an extra horse would have been a good idea, especially when the map shows there is only wilderness heading south. You have enough food, and the beetle appears to be fine with the extra packs. Stay smart and you'll stay safe. I'll be making my way into the town by this afternoon. Come with me, then when we leave the inn, we'll both begin our new roads.'

'Okay … but I do worry about Beetie going into a city. There are too many people in these places, and I don't like them. I've already seen how these weird folks get offended and try to kill him. Stupid idiots who hate anything unfamiliar. If there's any sort of trouble, I'm just going to leave.'

'Fair enough. I'll keep an eye out if I have the chance. It would also mean the chance to find a larger map. A larger town means more chance of getting you the directions you need for further south. At least that's something.'

~

Boy and Glohring stopped for a quick lunch – sliced apple, nuts and dates – mainly thanks to Gruldarht and his team. Boy hadn't had dates since he was young. The image of Armue spitting them on to the ground as a young child was so clear. The taste brought back the smells and the sounds of home. He wondered if his family was also eating right now, sitting down at the dining table, with their elbows raised up high on the edge of the wooden table, each waiting their turn to hold the lone knife to spread cool butter over steaming bread. Boy sighed and concentrated back on the road as the beetle veered off onto the grass. He began to think Beetie did this deliberately; maybe the grass tickled his underbelly.

The land opened up to rolling farms with rammed earth dams, green paddocks and busy workers. The road became busy with wagons and traders, farmers and travellers. Boy monitored everyone with a suspicious scowl, but most of the people only half-looked. They were busy with their own lives, and he forced his mood to settle down.

Coloured flags hung low in the soft wind, their long poles coming from high walls of the fortress in the distance. The grey stone towers stood safe within double stone walls. Hundreds of rooftops lay ahead of them. As they drew closer, they noticed the town was built around a small river that ran out of the castle walls. Instead of the typical city design – surrounding a circle with a circle – the town lay in a long line along the banks of the river. Depending on what angle you approached it from, it either looked extremely large or extremely small. In fact, it was long and narrow, with no outer wall to defend the lesser people. If the castle was ever held to siege by an army, the town would be utterly defenceless.

From the crude design of the town, Glohring knew it was every man for himself. The ruler of this fortress cared little for the protection of his townsfolk, if at all. They kept to a hard clay path that ran behind the outer buildings, more of a service road. It was quieter than the last town, and it was harder to look for a decent inn. Glohring needed privacy and wanted this stay to be somewhere nice and secure, somewhere out of the way. A young girl, of about Boy's age, ran out onto the road to sell inks and paints. Glohring politely waved her out of the way.

'Sorry, we do not need any. Have a lovely day, lass.'

She moved off the road, watching the beetle with the biggest smile on her face, then turned and ran inside the building she had come from. Boy lowered his head to look into the open back door. A cat hissed and ran away, but he could see the little girl hiding behind a sack of grain, looking back at him. Boy waved at her to come out again, but she did not come.

Ahead, a sign with an arrow pointing down a dirt laneway hung high from a thick tree branch: THE BEARDED BARREL INN.

'Well, we'll enquire here, I think.'

As they turned down the skinny laneway, Beetie just squeezing between the buildings, the noise of music and laughter reverberated between the walls. The door ahead flew open and the hooting of men rang out. A skinny patron was launched through the air and out into the dirt lane. Four men followed, ranting and hooting with gravelled slurs directed at the grounded man. He stood up and calmly dusted himself off, standing erect and facing the men. A wrestle ensued between him and another before the others pulled him off, picked him up and dumped him into a horse trough. Laughter and jeers rang out, then the small mob walked back inside … most likely for another tankard of ale. Boy didn't like this, and he was glad they hadn't noticed him and Beetie.

'Glohring, I don't want to go in there. It's the same as the other horrible village.'

'We have to at least enquire. They'll be able to tell us of the other inns in town at least.'

'I don't want to go in.'

'I will only be a short moment.'

'Okay, but let's get out of here quickly. Don't take too long. I'm going to wait closer to the road, away from this door.'

Boy didn't like the town already. It was loud, with signs of a lazy culture: discarded items, broken and unused along the edges of the buildings. They would be useful to a farming or creative mind, but were just left, and noticed by no one. A weird smell hung in the air, and small spot fires were everywhere, even though it wasn't cold.

Glohring dismounted, tied his mule up to a pole and walked inside the noisy venue. Boy waited, fearful of anyone walking down the alley. His muscles vibrated, and his arms and fists were clenched, nervous and tense. A strange sound ran through his head and he realised he was grinding his teeth. He breathed in deeply through his nose. *Calm down, nothing has happened yet, and I have no basis to be worried. Just be cool and calm. I'm the master of a beetle, I carry a dagger. I am the one to be feared.* Another man was thrown out of the inn into the alley. Boy yelped in fear and tightened the reins. Glohring walked calmly out of the inn as another man rushed out and lobbed an empty tankard at him. He ducked, turned and held his ground.

'I got ya now, weirdo,' yelled a stained drunk.

Glohring pointed to the dirt below the man, and yellow flames began to flare up at the drunk's feet. He started yelping, jumping and hopping, like a foreign dance. The flares moved with him, following him as he yelped a high-pitched scream. Glohring waved his hand and the flames died, smiling to himself as he mounted his horse. The man ran down to the far end of the alley and around the corner.

'We follow the town to the very south-eastern end. A well-off inn stands in acreage of its own. Let's find it and sit down for a good stew.' They headed out to the road again and travelled at a slightly quicker pace, with Boy keeping regular checks on the road behind them.

'Some unsettling characters in the tavern there, but they sure know how to make a beef stew, judging by the smell. Mmmm, those herbs and the meat falling off the bone, I'll bet.' Glohring lifted his nose, hoping to sniff out any lingering stew in the air.

'So, what did they say?'

'They said we could sleep in the hayloft, but there were no more rooms. I don't think he trusted the look of me. Another patron at the bar told me about this inn for merchants and well-off travellers … an old out-of-town stone building … some kind of estate, I assume.'

'I meant, what did the drunk man say before he attacked you?'

'Oh, he just wanted me to stand him a tankard of ale before I left their company. When I said no, he told me to go outside, but I said *you first* and threw him out the door. That was fun though, seeing him dance with imaginary fire.'

'Chika chiko,' Beetie laughed, picking up on the mood.

'So, these things you do with fire are only imaginary? Aren't you worried he will tell someone at the bar of evil magic and they'll come looking for you?'

'No one's going to believe a man stinking of ale. Did you see the filth on his clothes?' He laughed out loud. 'I can manipulate fire, but what I did then was only a perception of fire. I could never harm anyone in a circumstance like that. Only for protection and defence, never to attack. Remember that lesson.'

'But I don't control fire.'

'Well, remember that lesson anyway.'

'I'd never want to be in a situation where I have to make that kind of decision. Do you think it's possible to avoid it in a lifetime?'

'Sometimes you are in a position with no choice, and you must act according to what you believe in. Decide whether to be a scummy pig-dog or a decent, loving human. Usually people make the decision their parents would have made. They go on their first instincts.'

Boy nodded in agreement and turned Beetie wide to go around an empty barrel that had rolled down onto the street. He was glad they were leaving the town. An acreage inn sounded nice and safe to him, away from these scum-bucket street drunks.

The further they moved through the town, the more savoury and familiar the environment became. The road meandered between buildings and shop fronts, all neat and tidy with fresh, colourful flowers exploding from their pots. The sites and sounds brightened Boy's mood. Smells from the bakery wafted by as children roamed the streets eating sugared buns. A fabric master, who was drying freshly-coloured shirts for merchants, waved them over to his shop. Glohring waved off the invitation to purchase any garments but did smile politely at the hard work he could see the old man doing.

The high perimeter walls of the fortress loomed above the rooftops ahead. The town scenery changed extraordinarily. It became emptier: fewer people occupied the streets and more vacant lots appeared where buildings had once stood, the ashes of a wooden structure, never to be rebuilt, blew in the wind. The remaining buildings were reinforced and bore the scars of past battles. The history of long sieges outside the castle walls could be seen all around. As to how the other side of the castle wall fared during years of war, Boy did not know, but he would rather be inside the wall if anyone had plans to siege the castle.

Boy felt something touch his mind: a life long-forgotten maybe. He brushed the thought aside and looked at the spring flowers sprouting from the vacant lots of rubble. He didn't want to be negative now. Boy tried to steer Beetie down a laneway towards another main road; they had no intention of riding up to the castle gates. This road would take them to wider acreage away from the town, and to the inn. As they passed an old farmhouse, Beetie stopped in his tracks. A dog approached and began to bark ferociously at him.

'Go on! Get out of here!' yelled Boy as a man from the farm came running over.

'Sorry, young man. That bloody dog is not even ours. He just showed up out of the forest and made our farm his home. Who knows where he came from. I'll take him out of your way. That's a fine-looking steed you've got there. He looks like he'd be good in the fields for ploughing,' said the farmer.

Glohring thought he'd let Boy respond, as he knew he would be protective of the beetle. *If he's going to be alone in a day or two, he'll be coming across this situation more and more.* He waited for Boy to respond, as did the farmer. Boy just stared at the dog, then leaned forward and patted Beetie as close to his head as he could reach. The farmer awkwardly grabbed the dog, nodded, and headed back to the farm.

'I want to find this inn. Why do I have to keep talking to strangers? I'm so tired of strangers and their questions and looks. It's annoying.'

Glohring raised an eyebrow at Boy's obvious lack of resilience. *He will have to adapt*, he thought, but let the matter drop.

'Follow me then. It's got to be around these hills somewhere.'

After a short while, the gravel road came to an end at an old wooden fence. Standing high above the decrepit fencepost hung a regal sign, all hand-crafted metal work, with a large arrow: WILLIAM'S INN. The road ran up the sloping hillside and into the afternoon shadows. Perched at the top stood a large stone building, built along a rock retaining wall at the edge of a towering forest of oak, tuart and tingle trees. The delicately crafted ironwork gates stood open to the public. They were magnificent: shiny and polished, just like Beetie's shell. Even he was impressed.

'Chikachika,' he sounded and twirled his tentacles.

A large stone hall stood high. Attached to it were several outhouses and stables, and at its rear was an impressive estate. Boy slowed Beetie to a crawl and let Glohring ride in front. They passed the entrance to a large fountain garden surrounded by rows of curved hedges in need of a trim, where a man kicked angrily at the stony path, unaware of the new guests.

'Whoa! What's this? Giant bugs?' The man held up his hands, crossing his fingers to ward off evil.

'It appears you haven't travelled much then, have you, my old man?' said Glohring.

'Well, no, not really. Lived here for sixty-eight years, going on sixty-nine,' the wrinkled man laughed.

'Well, you can drop those hands. He is merely a mount for us. You must know that around the world there are many types of transportation and farming help, and this is one of the most common. Now, we are here for a room. Do you have anything available?'

'Not sure, not sure. Master Donnelly runs the business these days. How about I go fetch him?'

'Good, thank you.'

Boy and Glohring waited patiently in the afternoon wind, both admiring the inn's grand stone hall. A man looked down at them from a window. When he made eye contact with Boy, he smiled and closed the curtain.

'Did you see the man in the window?' Boy blurted out.

'I did, but Boy, you need to stop being paranoid. It's good that you are training yourself to be on guard before you set off alone, but you will drive yourself crazy if you distrust everyone. It's a fine balance: sometimes it is the safest thing to assume all strangers are dangerous, but it will make you tired with stress and anxiety.

'We are now in what looks like upper-class living quarters. People here will be stranger than the country folk we've come across. Power does that to people, maybe because of their upbringing based on coin and status. Just remember: if you need help, always look and listen for intelligence. And don't be fooled by your own brain. Deciphering head from heart can be fraught with peril.'

'I understand. I'll be careful on the way home. But if I have to run, I'm not leaving Beetie behind. We are going to get to my homeland and start him a new life.'

A tall, burly man burst out of the inn door. Imposing as he was, Glohring strode straight up to greet him.

'Good afternoon. I am Glohring, and this is my friend, Boy. We are looking for shelter for two nights. Do you have anything available?'

The man scrutinised the beetle. 'What's this thing?' he grumbled.

'He is Boy's friend, transport and farmhand. We are journeying through and need a comfortable place to sleep while we stock provisions for our next leg through the wilderness.'

'We don't have any rooms available in the inn, but we do have an old cottage out on the edge of the forest. It used to be the old gardener's quarters before he passed away. We're still looking for his replacement, actually. We really should have hired an apprentice years ago, but who knew the old man would die from hard work. Anyway, the cottage has a small stable so you can store your strange steed away from here without disturbing our guests.'

'Perfect, thank you so much.'

'Without disturbing my guests,' the man emphasised, raising an eyebrow.

They followed the innkeeper who led them across the sloping hillside on a gravel path towards the tree line. The gardener's cottage revealed splintered timbers clinging to their final years, and unfinished repairs showed that the ongoing maintenance had stopped a while ago. A wall of thick warm air hit them upon entering, and the smell of damp curtains collecting dust filled their nostrils. But it was fully furnished and had a small well out the back. After the innkeeper said his farewells and wished them a pleasant evening, they immediately darted through the cottage opening the windows.

Boy left the cottage and set off to gather firewood from the edge of the forest, letting Beetie graze in the grass like an old colt. While he scoured the area for old dry wood, he climbed higher up the hill where he could see the castle towers, the red sunset colouring the flapping flags of the Lord's clan. He wondered what kind of man would rule such a magnificent place and hoped he was a good one.

Boy clomped down the hill, stomped through the long bracken and across the crunching forest floor, carrying an armload of wood for the night. Insects crawled out from their wooden crevices and down his arm; Boy shook them off casually and dropped their fuel at the back door. After stocking up the fireplace, he sought out Glohring to light the fire, softly knocking on his door.

'Come in, Boy.'

The room was small, with no hearth and only one chair in the corner. Glohring sat on the bed, looking over Boy's new map.

'I only got a few armloads of firewood, you know … because it's only for a few nights. Do you want to go over the map now?'

'After we have some food, we'll sit down and discuss my next move and our departure. There are some things I'd like to show you that may be of assistance.'

Boy smiled. He loved learning new things.

'But go and start that fire. I'll be out in a little while.'

'I thought you could just snap your fingers and light it for me.'

'Did your memory dissolve the knowledge that I will not be accompanying you home? There will be many a cold night if you don't find your way before autumn.'

'Okay. I'll have to get used to doing everything myself then.' Boy freely accepted the lesson.

'I don't like laziness.'

'I haven't used a flint in a while. I'm not all that good at it.'

'Remember, skill is the mother of repetition.'

Boy nodded and left the room. He succeeded in starting the fire then cleaned Beetie and ensured he was safe in the stables. He fetched buckets of water from the well, filled up their water pouches, boiled water for tea and walked outside in the cool air to watch the inn and listen to the noise from their tavern. Quite a few riders came and went, some galloping down the main road towards town, others returning in the dark, lit by small torches.

The door creaked open behind him, but no one was there. Boy turned and peered inside the dark cottage.

'Glohring? I'll start boiling vegetables if you're hungry?'

The candles had gone out, and the black silhouette of a hunched man stood in the room' centre. He held out his hand.

'Come inside, Boy,' a strange gravelly voice said.

Fire leapt from his hand, lighting a wrinkled old face. Boy quickly stepped back.

'It's okay. It's a pretty neat trick, isn't it? I even fooled you.'

'What the hell is going on?' Boy grabbed a nearby stick and held it up.

'Sorry to frighten you. It's me, Glohring. You didn't think I could meet with the warrior troop as me, did you? I need a disguise. I am, for the first and last time in my life, going to be a thief, so I may as well dress up as one.'

Boy hesitated. 'Okay, if you are Glohring, what's the name of the city I am from?'

'You're not from a city. You are lost, far away from your family and your farm. Sit down; it really is me. That's what I've been doing for the last few hours. It's a difficult process and I couldn't have any distractions. Now, Boy, let's get fed and we'll discuss our plans ahead.'

Boy threw the stick away and walked inside. Glohring relit the cottage candles and Boy prepared their meal, serving up slices of cheese, peaches, boiled vegetables and two slices of meat each.

'We are all out of the cured meat. Only this end chunk left.'

'That's fine. Now, please sit down. I took the liberty of transferring some detail from your map to mine. I'll be needing to leave tomorrow afternoon. I have an arranged appointment at the castle. I will make my trade and then head home. Quickly, I might add.

'I'm not sure what you want to do, but if you need additional supplies, I'll go with you into town tomorrow. I also need a few things. What were you thinking?'

'Well, I wanted to study the map with you tonight and work out the direction I need to head in. I was also thinking a large piece of canvas or leather would be good for shelter from the summer rains … not that we have too much, rain I mean. So, I guess I don't need to go to the markets. I should save the little money I have.'

Glohring agreed, nodding with approval while he gnawed on the piece of cured meat.

Boy and Glohring spent a long night discussing supplies and how to survive in the forest. They studied the map and talked about possible weather patterns. Glohring talked about certain fruits and herbs with healing powers that Boy should collect just in case he got hurt. Boy asked many questions, his mind beginning to lose focus from the amount of information he had absorbed. His eyelids grew heavy and, when his neck fell forward and he dozed off for a second, Glohring knew it was enough. He stood, put the fire out with a snap of his fingers, and clapped his hands to wake Boy.

Boy woke suddenly in the dark, not knowing how long he'd been asleep.

'It's time to go to bed.'

'I'm sorry I fell asleep. I was listening.'

Glohring snapped his fingers to relight the candles.

'I almost forgot. I have one last thing I want to give you, but you must be very careful with these.'

Glohring opened a cloth sack brought out four small pouches with strings attached to them: two brown and two red.

'What are they? More herbs?'

'I'll get to them. Now, do you have a flint? I've never needed one to start a flame.'

'Yeah, I do. I picked one up at the last town.'

'Good. Now, these are only to be used if you are in danger. They are for self-defence only. If you light the end of the string, you have four to five seconds before it catches alight. You want to have an accurate throw. They shouldn't kill anything … well, I hope they won't … but they will scare whatever you throw it at – bears, enemies, wolves. Now, you must throw it. You don't want it in your hands when it goes off. Very dangerous. Be very careful and use them wisely.'

'Let's hope I don't have to use them at all.' He thought of the wolves.

'Precisely.'

'Are the colours a different type? Or are they all the same?'

'They're all the same.'

Boy packed them into his bag with his revised map.

'Are you going to be okay, stealing the stone and exchanging with the troop?'

'I think so. We travelled with them, and they have honour, so I don't expect them to sabotage the trade. You knew one of them well, didn't you? The young one. He was a trustworthy lad, I thought.'

'Tendai was his name. He was new to the troop and they hadn't really welcomed him. He was an honourable warrior, I thought, but he just didn't seem to fit in. Tell me, if they come from the north and you do, why didn't you steal the book from them in the north? Why travel so far?'

'I thought you'd never ask. It's all a game of percentages, you see. A trade where each party gets something they desire, without any stealing, will not end in revenge or being hunted down and slaughtered. In short, being far away from the north, it is easier to hide from a Lord and his soldiers who are not familiar with the area and do not usually travel far. I would rather escape them than stealing from a forest filled with armed soldiers. I am familiar with fire-gems. I am aware of the power of these stones, but they are merely jewels for them. The book is of great power and needs to be in the property of a smart man … me. Do you get it now?'

'I understand.' Boy nodded. It still sounded dangerous to him, but what did he know about the far north or these strange lands?

'And how do you feel about heading into the unknown alone? Remember: be confident and trust yourself, and you'll stay safe and get home.'

'I don't feel anything yet. Once Beetie and I are out there and alone I think I'll decide then whether it's scary or not. I don't want to come across any of those wolves again.' His heart began to race at the thought of being alone and hunted.

Glohring suddenly looked fearful. He knew a lot about these beasts, but he wasn't going to speak further about them.

'Well, we have a long day ahead of us tomorrow. I'm feeling quite weary, the aging man that I am. This fire inside will only burn for so long. Goodnight, Boy.'

'I just have one more question about the book. You said it would be dangerous in the wrong hands, but a romancing book sounds kind of girlish, with lots of lovely flowers and kissing.'

'I'll give you an example – it's probably the easiest way to explain. Across the world, there are many types of Lords, royalty of different ranks and provinces. They all value power. If they did not, they would be crushed in battle and their clans become extinct, meaning their bloodlines would be wiped out by death. So, it is in their interest to align with more powerful bloodlines to ensure their clan's survival. If you have a young Lord, firstborn, of course, whose father is getting on in years and whose war-ravaged farms are bringing in no taxes, wouldn't you do anything in your power to have him marry into a powerful clan?'

'Or even the daughter of an emperor, if there is one where you come from,' Boy suggested.

'Yes, indeed. So, the dying art of romancing can fetch a hefty penny these days if there is a master willing to teach.'

'So, it's a job for money? I still don't get why it's dangerous.'

'If you engineer the arrangement of clans and power through bloodlines, I foresee warmongering taking the place of peace, and possibly a very long civil war.'

'That wouldn't be good at all.'

'It might not happen. But war exists and soaks through the lives of the living.'

After Glohring left the room, Boy locked and bolted the front and back doors, blew out the candles, climbed into a real bed, lay down on the soft mattress and slept.

He awoke in the middle of the night, confused for a moment. He rubbed his eyes, thinking he was at home again. But Tilly and Armue were not sleeping quietly across the room. He missed his brother and sister so much, and his eyes began to blink and water. Before he let the emotion out, he shook his head and focused on his gentle breathing. Feeling the air fill and expel from his lungs, and his sore muscles relaxing in the deep mattress, he drifted back off to sleep.

~

The cottage was not a place where one could sleep long into the early light. The surrounding trees were filled with the morning song of what sounded like a hundred birds: the high-pitched tweets of hopping wrens and robins, and the squawks of summer parrots and lorikeets. Boy splashed his face with a bucket of last night's water, still cool from the night, and went to say good morning to Beetie. He found him foraging in the forest behind the stables, shuffling his legs and face into the loose leaves.

'Good morning, Beetie. How did you get out? I'll give you a clean again this afternoon, but first I want you to stay in the stable because I'll be in town for a while. You can stay out in the morning sun for now, but when I leave, you'll have to go back in the stable. This time the door will have to be bolted, just in case someone from the inn comes snooping around while I'm away.'

Boy leant against Beetie's shell, reached up and patted him on the head. Beetie's small tentacles flung around.

'I'll leave you to your breakfast. Have fun!'

'Chika-chika.'

Boy stepped inside the cottage to the smell of milk and honey.

'Wow, I didn't know you had honey.'

'I purchased a small amount in the last town, and I was saving it for our last meal together.'

'Thank you so much. It's just like my birthday.'

Glohring served up a steaming bowl of oats, added cool fresh milk around the edge, and drizzled lengths of honey across the top.

'I always have honey for my birthday breakfast. Those memories are so clear. Dad is the only one who can go near the beehive. So, at my morning breakfast, he would always serve the honey and show me all his stings, swollen on his hands and arms. He would make up stories about how the bees were larger and angrier than he'd ever seen. He never complained, but I always remember him serving the breakfast as if to say *now see what I do for you kids?*'

'When is your birthday? Will you get home for it?'

'Oh, it's not for a little while yet, in the autumn. Do you have the same calendar as us?'

'Yes, I think we do. Four seasons. Just that we have colder winters in the mountains, further to the north.'

Boy scrunched up his face.

'I'm not fond of the freezing winters myself either.'

After they'd finished their morning oats and the dishes were cleaned and put away in the dusty cupboard, Boy retrieved Beetie from the edge of the forest and led him back into his cramped stable. This time he bolted the door.

Boy and Glohring set off down the grassy hill on foot, towards the main road that led back to the edge of town and eventually to the gates of the fortress walls. Boy would have preferred to ride Beetie, but wasn't in the mood to be gawked at today. He had too much on his mind without suffering the insensitive behaviour of the townsfolk.

The sun shone warm on their shoulders, and the sounds of people grew louder as they approached the town. The marketplace was bustling with villagers in good spirits. The stall owners and traders greeted them, cheerily offering their products and services without force. Boy slowly started to change his perception of the townsfolk. Without Beetie there, Boy could relax and enjoy the smells, sights and sounds: cooked meat on charcoal braziers, spices on the air, music from afar, and young golden-haired girls waving to him as they worked at their parents' stalls. Despite Boy's protesting, Glohring went ahead and purchased several items on his behalf. The stock would come in useful: rope, spare water skins, steel blades, and tightly woven string for cooking and hunting. He didn't know what he would have done without Glohring happily paying for it all, and he thanked him dearly. Boy wandered freely around the vibrant marketplace without Glohring. He stopped to look at some canvas sheets, thick and stretched for waterproof covers. A pretty young girl with large green eyes, maybe a few summers older than he, watched him in silence as he viewed her product. He rubbed it between his fingers and admired the strength of the material.

'It's a very strong sheet. I like it, but I have spent all my money. I am sorry. You must like working here very much. There are so many things going on.'

She smiled and nodded politely in silent understanding. Then she pointed to her mouth and ears and spread her hand out as if she was miming a vomiting action.

'You're feeling sick? Are you going to throw up? Do you have a bucket?'

She sighed and shook her head, knowing that he did not understand. She pointed at her heart, tapping her chest and then at her canvas product. She waved her hand in an arch pointing to the wooden structure of the stall. Boy looked confused.

'You've got chest problems? You're going to vomit on the canvas and all around the stall?' He took a few steps backwards. 'Is there anything I can do?'

She placed her hand on her forehead and pointed again at her mouth. *What a strange girl ... pretty but odd.* He slowly recoiled. She'd had enough of him not understanding and opened her mouth wide, showing a mutilated slab of flesh that was the remains of her tongue. Boy yelped and stepped backed. He looked around for Glohring, but forgot at first to look for the new disguised version.

When he located Glohring in disguise, they made their way back to the inn. With the warm sun out and the breeze cooling their skin, Boy began whistling an old song his mother always sang.

'What is this song you sing? Is it just a melody, or is it a story?'

'My mother used to sing it, but I think she just liked the melody. It's about an old miser whose silver and pennies turned to chocolate from a curse. Word got out and all the children came from all around town to eat it. When they got there, the miser had hidden the coins too close to his hearth and they'd all melted.'

'A lesson about greed. No one ever wins.'

'I don't know. It could be.'

Boy thought about what Glohring had said: no one ever wins. He had thought there was always a winner and a loser … in all the games and stories he knew anyway. *Why would you want to play if there was no winner and no loser?* He shook the thought away, not interested in exploring what didn't interest him.

~

Upon arrival at the cottage, Boy walked up to the stable and let Beetie back out to play in the dirt and the sunshine. Glohring spent the day packing his belongings and sitting in the sun talking to himself, going over the perfect plan and the obstacles that could present themselves. Boy heard some of it as he went through his own bags, sorting out his belongings. Glohring opened the cottage door and nodded at Boy, who knew to follow him to the stables. The horse waited, packed and eager to get out on the road again, and Beetie ambled over feeling the importance of the moment.

'Now, I'm not going down to speak to the innkeeper. As far as he's concerned, we're leaving tomorrow. When you leave, stay to the back roads if you are worried about the beetle. But, if you feel safe, then stick to the main roads because you may pass someone who knows more about where your home is than me. Stay safe and be smart.'

'Thank you so much for travelling with me. Everything you've done has been a gift I can never repay. I would never have been in a position like this without you. I may not agree with you stealing this gem, but I hope the trade goes safely and you get back home in one piece.'

'So do I. And thank *you*. You have made my journey a happy one. Good luck, Boy, and I hope you get home to your family. If I ever travel down that way, I'll seek you out, my friend.'

Glohring patted the beetle on the head.

'Farewell, Beetie. Travel well and take care of young Boy here.'

'Chaca chi chi!' he replied, accepting the responsibility.

'Before you leave, could you give me any tips on how to talk to a girl?'

'I'm afraid that's something you will have to find out yourself.'

Glohring smiled, mounted his horse and trotted down the path, stopping and turning for one last wave goodbye.

Boy watched him ride out to the main road until he could no longer see the dust rising from his path.

'Well, it's you and me once again, Beetie. Now we have food and a bedroll and lots of things to get packed, so let's get ready.'

'Chi chok!'

'Oh yes, I will clean you first. A good wipe down today and tomorrow I'll strap all the gear on, okay buddy? I'll probably use Glohring's pillowcase … the innkeeper can deal with it later. I'm not cleaning his linen.'

Beetie followed Boy around like a lost puppy all afternoon. He collected another load of firewood, cleaned the leather reins and his steering pole, and saw to the stretchy task of rubbing down Beetie's shell to a shiny, smooth surface. When he was finished, he threw the dirty pillowcase behind an empty horse trough in the corner.

An old tub sat at the rear of the cottage. He filled it with water from the well. *A cold bath is better than none,* he thought, before diving in butt-first, curling his shoulders inwards against the sides of the tub. He held his breath under the cold water for as long as he could. After submerging several times in the chilling water, he felt clean and refreshed and ran inside naked to dry off. By the time he'd changed into clean clothes, his body was still icy cold so he lit a fire in the hearth for warmth and company. Only when the fire was ablaze and the night sky fell dark outside did he really feel alone.

An old bookcase held a few dusty volumes on the shelf. He picked up two books and placed them on the ground in front of the fire – anything to distract himself until he felt tired enough to sleep. He opened up the middle of the first book and began to read. *The running peg was only designed to spiral left to right in accordance with pitch and tone for one's desired note.* Boy was already bored and closed the book.

The candles flickered as a rush of cold air pushed through the room. Behind him, he heard the sound of metal slowly scraping. He turned quickly to look at the door. *Did the handle just move? I can't be this paranoid … I've only been alone a few hours. What am I going to be like in a forest rumoured to be haunted?* He shook his head, annoyed, then blew out the candles, scurried to his room and closed the door. *The sooner I close my eyes, the sooner it will be morning.*

~

That same afternoon, Glohring walked through the busiest streets of town. They had not seen this area on their arrival, and it looked quite poor. Even though it had a large population, the houses and buildings all looked the same: cheaply and quickly built, or half-destroyed and crudely patched. Closer to the castle, a few buildings reflected the contrast of the classes in the small city, notably the cathedral, a stunning structure carved from something not of this world – carved by men but delivered by gods. It must have taken them a hundred years to add all the external detail. The priests' quarters were covered in gold-encrusted sculptures and designs. The overlord appeared to be very generous to the church, but Glohring knew it was most likely rotten with corruption inside. He left the holy square and headed towards the castle walls along winding streets of compacted clay in search of the main gate.

A thick-chested guard stepped onto the road to block Glohring's path. He wore old leather armour, chipped and scratched, with a crude iron helmet, but his halberd was as shiny as if it had just left the smith's forge that morning.

'Halt. What business do you have here?'

'I have a meeting.'

'With whom? I cannot let you get closer to the gate without more information.' He stamped the end of his halberd hard on the ground.

They are paranoid around here, which doesn't bode well for me, Glohring thought.

'Please let me explain for a moment. I'm here to meet Chamberlain Jorgan. I am the castle's temporary scribe.'

'Temporary?' the heavily-built guard snorted.

'I am here to teach, and I hear they are fast learners.'

The guard looked him up and down. 'I haven't heard anything about a scribe. Wait here.'

'Happily,' the old man grinned.

He stepped away from Glohring to consult another guard who was on horseback. The mounted rider took one look at the old scribe and trotted down the street to the portcullis watchmen. The burly guard stayed close, and Glohring thought it a fair idea to lighten the mood, so he began to whistle a sweet melody. He gazed up at the high walls he would soon be escaping from. One end of the castle wall met directly with the forest, which meant a constant source of firewood and rams for any besieging army. *Very dangerous if you live inside the walls,* he thought.

A wagon full of fresh fruit and vegetables passed him and

drew up slowly to the large guard. He gave the young rider a nod, waved him through, then turned back to Glohring, who was staring at him questioningly.

'We know him. He delivers fresh food for his Lordship.'

Glohring said nothing, and the guard turned away to escape his gaze. Eventually, the mounted soldier returned.

'Send him through,' he yelled from horseback.

'Good day,' said Glohring, tipping his hat.

~

Glohring was guided through the side door at the portcullis and entered a large area hidden behind the castle walls, an area most of the townsfolk would never see. As he passed through into the realm of the privileged, Glohring examined the gates and all their working details.

The paths were dusty with gravel stones; the castle did not yet have the grandiose cobblestone roads he had expected on the inside. *Very different from the wealth and splendour of the lords of the north.* Servants, pages and guards went about their business, with no royalty to be seen. Most people carried food or washing, focused on their immediate errands and not a new visitor to the castle. The guards did not have a uniform appearance; although each had at least one part of their armour stamped with the crest of the eagle. Their weapons were of any kind: old, used and poorly maintained. The majority of guards clustered near the portcullis while groups of two walked the top of the walls. Their spears and halberds gave their positions away above the high stone battlements. A small band of soldiers cantered through the main gates and passed him without paying any attention. Again, he noticed their armour was very shabby with cuts and patches, and their horses looked malnourished, frothing at the mouth and fly-bitten. Either the lord was a tight miser, or they were cutting their tax spending, saving for a future war.

The chamberlain came running out to greet Glohring. One page took his belongings, and another led his horse to the stable.

'Hello there. We've been wondering when you were going to arrive since we heard Master Eaman could not make it. I am Chamberlain Jorgan … and you are …?'

'Scribe Cobb. Here at your Lordship's service.'

'Actually, you are here at Lord Denham's service. He is the heir to my Lord, and has asked to learn how to read and write. Quite a strange request, I think, as a Lord has people to do those kinds of things for him. No offence to yourself.'

'Can you read, Jorgan?'

'No, sir. I don't need to,' he replied, confused.

'So, in the future, when the young Lord hands you a written list of instructions to complete immediately, what will you do?'

'Well, I guess I will get my scribe to tell me.'

'That's one hell of an answer, Jorgan.'

The chamberlain looked puzzled.

'I'll show you to your chambers. They are situated in the northwest tower.'

Glohring liked toying with Jorgan. The arrogance of royal chamberlains and staff usually irked him, but you could have a special type of fun with them.

They walked together across the grassy ward, staying off the unmaintained gravel paths that were littered with horse droppings, and headed in the direction of the tower, past the main hall. High and grand, the outside wall of the hall featured tall windows stained in yellow and red shaded glass: an expensive feature that would have been designed in more affluent times.

'You can come down to the great hall for food any time. Cook will always have something for you.' Jorgan pointed to the various kitchen entrances and service doors.

'If you don't mind, I have a lot of work to do. So, if someone can bring something up to my chamber, I'd appreciate that.' His tone insisted more than asked.

'Yes, sir. We can do that.'

They walked across the grass, then between old, round houses and past storage sheds, until they came close to the rear outer wall where an old tower stood detached from the main portion of the castle. Its stone walls were faded like no other, and all its windows faced the forest hills. As they climbed the steep stairs, there was not a single sound, and Glohring began to think he was the only one staying in the tower. This would be good for him, considering what he had planned.

'It is the quietest tower, so you won't have any trouble working up here. I'll let you get settled in, and then tomorrow we'll send for his Lord to start lessons.'

'Thank you, Jorgan, for all your help.'

'The page should be up soon with the rest of your gear.'

Glohring entered the dusty room, which was semi-circular in shape. An open hearth was at the far wall, clean and dry from the recent makeup of the room. There was a small writing table and chair set up by the window. He lit a fire with the wave of his hand and looked out the window. The view was over the outer walls to the rising hill, surfaced with pines. There was a soft knock at the door.

'Come in. It's unlocked.'

A young page pushed open the large door and unceremoniously dumped Glohring's bags at the foot of the bed.

'Your meal will be up soon, sir.'

'My thanks, young one.'

~

After his meal was delivered, Glohring barred the door and sat by the window pondering his options for escape. Without knowing the intimate details of the castle and the guards' routines, he would only have a few choices. He would have liked to stay there for weeks in preparation, but it was near the summer solstice and the evening would have a full moon.

It would have to be that night, and besides, the warriors were already waiting with his prized possession for trade. There was little time to keep them waiting. Now that he knew the rough layout of the castle grounds, he could plan further. *There is always the possibility of just walking out the front gates,* he thought, but that would mean stealing from the chamber during the light of day. That would be too difficult.

From his quiet tower, he could see over the outer wall, which stood about twenty yards away. It was possible to get a rope to the wall and, if it snagged, he could climb across. However, if something went wrong, the fall would certainly break his legs.

~

Boy could not sleep. His thoughts raced back and forth, barring any stillness of mind. The night winds had picked up through the trees, whining and whistling on bending branches. It reminded him of home, lying down in his own bed.

A thud sounded from the front door.

Boy opened his eyes, rolled onto his side, and held his hand up to cup his ear. *Knock, knock, knock* came clearly on the timber door. He peeled back the blankets, carefully placed his feet on the creaky floorboards, and tiptoed quietly to the bedroom window. The knocking stopped. He inched the curtain open and looked into the dark. An old man stood there, still, staring back at him. With a yelp, Boy flung himself back and fell to the floor.

'Hello, in there! I didn't mean to startle you. May I have a word?'

Boy's breathing quickened. 'Wait there.'

He scurried around the room, searching for his dagger to no avail. He put on his shirt, fumbling with the buttons, and stomped on the floorboards loudly into the next room. He picked up a cup there and dropped it; he hoped it sounded like there were several people inside the cottage. He held onto the door handle, took a deep breath and quickly opened it, just enough to pop his head out.

'Oh, hello. I was wondering if your master was available for a quick word?'

'I am the master,' said Boy viciously, vexed at this rude intrusion.

'Oh really?'

'The master of everyone here. And who are you?'

'Oh, um, I'm Nikkotto, a master merchant. I was merely hoping for a quick chat. May I please come inside? My old bones don't take too well to the damp of the night.'

'Hold on a moment. I just have to light the place up.'

Boy closed the door and ran around, lighting as many candles as he could find while still looking for his dagger. It did occur to him that it was not a damp night whatsoever, and the man must be lying, but he decided to give Nikkotto the benefit of the doubt.

Unarmed, Boy opened the front door, further this time, wide enough for the stranger to glide through the doorway and into the cottage. In the light of the candles, Boy could see him clearly. He was smiling with little, blackened teeth that dug into his bottom lip. He was an ugly man, with rippled wart-like bumps across the side of his nose. Boy drew himself up to full height, and the hairs on the back of his neck stood up. Only the merchant's eyes moved around the room. Then he licked his lips and stepped forward. Boy stepped back.

'It's okay, little master.' He held his palm open to calm the child.

'What did you want to talk about? Take a seat. It's rude to discuss things standing up where I'm from.'

Nikkotto bit his lower lip again, pulling out a seat from the dining table and sitting down. His mouth and eyes were black and slimy. Boy remained standing.

'And where are you from, young man?'

'I'm from this town. What did you expect?'

'And why would someone from this town, who dresses like a traveller, be staying at an inn for merchants and traders?'

'Okay … I lied. I'm from a far distance to the south. And you don't look like anyone in town. You must also be from far away.'

The merchant smiled, showing his black slimy teeth again. This time when he bit his bottom lip, it bled.

'Tell me your name, young man, before we start.'

'We have started. What is your business? I'm busy, so out with it.'

The merchant tilted his head like a dog to observe him, and Boy felt his ugly eyes all over him like a bad itch. Nikkotto licked his bleeding lips. Outside the window, in the darkness, a torch moved toward the cottage. Then another passed by the window. Nikkotto could see the fear on Boy's face. A few of the candles blew out.

'Are you also from the south?' Boy finally asked.

'We are from the south,' hissed a voice behind Boy.

Out of the shadows, a man who looked like Glohring appeared. Nikkotto viciously grabbed Boy's shoulders, but he twisted and shrugged him off, making for the back door. He grabbed a vase and flung it backwards, hearing it shatter near the men. He kicked the backdoor open and ran towards the barn. Four men were pulling on ropes, trying to hold Beetie down.

'No!' Boy screamed. A lasso fell over his shoulders. He tried to wriggle out, but it tightened so hard the rope cut into his skin and crushed his chest. Nikkotto picked up the middle of the rope and viciously tugged, pulling Boy forwards. Boy stumbled in the dark and careered into the ground. His head hit something hard and sharp, and blood flowed warmly down the side of his face. He could see stars flickering and heard an agonising sound from Beetie that he'd never heard before – close to a squeal, close to a growl if a giant bug could sound as such.

~

High in the lonesome tower, a heavy oak door creaked open across the dark landing beside a spiralling stone stairway. A man stopped in the doorway and snapped his fingers to set the hearth ablaze. The dancing light joined the present chorus of candle flames, settling a warm glow across the room. The soon-to-be-thief had a flabby sallow face, with bad skin and a large head filled with white hair. You would not have known this was Glohring; his disguise was set and the night awaited. He had spent the evening adding to his masked make-up and considering his best options to escape the walls. He left the relit fire in the hearth to burn brightly high in the tower, so it could be seen glowing through the window.

He flung his gear over his shoulder, started to close the chamber door, but walked back to the window for one last view of the rooftops and sheds. The layout needed to be stored in his memory. Standing at the window, a warm breeze blew; it was a hot night and the stars hid behind thick clouds which trapped the heat and darkened the night. The large moon had only been seen momentarily earlier in the night, and there was a glow from a campfire at the edge of the forest. The troop would not have been allowed to come close to the fortress gates, and neither did they need to. But they had camped a questionable distance from the outer walls. Glohring shut the window and left the chamber. Luckily no one else was staying in his tower, so he crept down the stairs without a guard.

He left the tower and shuffled his way across the moonlight, keeping to the shadows alongside the sheds and stables – far from the main gate with limited surveillance. He reached the kitchen's backdoor unseen, and paused to listen: pots clanged and splashed against water as the midnight servants progressed through their sloppy chores after the night's feasting. Glohring left the busy kitchen area before someone noticed him and continued along the stone wall towards a doorway closer to his needs. The Lord's law chamber lay in a small tower off the grand hall. It wasn't the hardest to get close to, but guards were coming off duty and relaxing with a trencher of ale by the fire. Even late in the evening, the great hall was seldom empty. Glohring casually entered the cook's door, grabbed an apple and kept walking as if he did this every night. At the far end of the kitchen, he stopped, waited, and peered into the grand hall. Limited candles burnt long and dim, and two men sat in front of a fireless hearth at the far table, talking quietly over an ale.

There were two main entrances to the grand hall: large double doors for the many men and servants that serviced the ward, and a third smaller door that led to the royal chambers in the Lord's tower. A fourth led to the women's quarters, and a fifth that Glohring instinctively knew led to the chamber of justice. This was the door he needed, but it was closer to the guards than he. Glohring decided to take the casual approach. With a snap of his fingers, the hearth burst into flames. The men jumped to their feet with a shout.

The fire vanished without a trace of smoke, then burst alight again in a show of lengthy flames. The men left their ale unfinished and scurried out in a panic – no doubt running to the soldiers' barracks to hide in their blankets. Glohring tiptoed across the room and pulled open the wooden door, which opened to a wide hallway.

The floor was laid with smooth broad stones, the entrance to the chambers representing wisdom and power. There weren't any stairs, but the stones rose with the incline of the hill they were laid upon. All the chambers, except for residence, came off this hall, and no one should really be there in the dead of night. Each door had a symbol, attaining to the chamber's use.

At the far end of the hall, barely visible in the dark light, were double doors – the entrance to a much bigger room. Marked on the door was the symbol of two carved scales – one black obsidian and the other smooth bone – hanging from a sequence of polished silver rings, and aloft a pair of crossed battle-chipped swords, self-honoured by the evidence of battle glory. It could be none other than the chamber of justice.

The room was long, with an impressive wooden table in an elevated position. An intricately decorated throne stood tall and imposing, giving ultimate power to whoever sat within it. It was beautiful and superior-looking, with golden banding and gems encrusted in its decorative oak carvings. Above the throne, large tapestries featuring the Lord's bloodline hung high. Below them was a giant hammer, woven gold wrapped around it, with diamonds and rubies working their way through the handle, much like the workmanship of the throne. This was obviously not used as the actual hammer of justice, as the impressive piece of metalwork was too valuable and would clearly crush the oak table. Glohring was impressed, but then he remembered the poor unfinished buildings in the ratty town.

He stalked across the chamber but could not see any other metalwork that would hold something as valuable as a fire-gem. It had to be part of the throne or the hammer of justice. This Lord, whoever he was, stunk of pomp and righteousness. Glohring held up his hand and invoked the fire; a red glow emanated from the rear of the throne. Carefully treading up the large step, he moved closer to the glowing light.

The stone was displayed, red and fierce, on the back of the throne. He dragged the throne around to face him, the smooth material on the base of the legs making it easy to slide. The rear of the giant chair was more of a sight than anything else in the room, again decorated by a master craftsman. He had once read that, long ago, Lords began their legal hearings with their backs to the people, who may or may not have disobeyed the rules of their realm. So, he supposed it would be quite normal to have this grandiose display on the rear of the throne.

Usually, at least two master jewellers and a smith with a great big furnace would be required to remove the giant fire-gem. However, as Glohring could not exactly drag the throne through the gates to the local smith, his only option was to damage the fine piece of craftsmanship. As much as it irked him, he commanded the fire gem to glow white-hot, until it melted the claws and burnt the surrounding metalwork. It revealed its full size, as large as a plum, and dropped into his hand. Within a moment, it was ice cold, as Glohring transferred its heat to within himself. He safely placed the cool treasure in a white pouch he had bought specifically for the fancy stone. The smell of burnt metal lingered in the air; the grey smoke held its shape for a moment before shifting and dancing across the room, moving faster towards the door. The smoke was vacuumed beneath the door's gaps and into the hallway, and there was nothing Glohring could do about it.

A voice called from beyond the door, echoing in the long hallway.

'Who's down here? I saw someone enter. No one is supposed to be allowed in this wing at night. If it's you, my young Lord, playing around, your mother will be most displeased. Come on out! You should be in bed anyway.'

Glohring quickly dragged the throne back into position. He stepped backwards and clumsily knocked over a candelabra behind him. The metal bounced and clanged, sending an echo bounding across the night chamber. Then silence. Hearing his heart thumping in his chest and the whistle from his nostrils as he breathed, Glohring picked the scabby mucus from his nose to clear the cavity and switched to breathing through his mouth. He listened. Footsteps on stone, the jingle of metal buckles, the iron door handle screeching as it turned. The wind had picked up from the east and rattled at the window.

Glohring sat still, leaning back on his heels and low to the ground. The door was slowly pushed open, and the guard stepped inside the chamber.

'Who goes there? Is anyone here? You are not allowed in this wing.' The guard cautiously took another step, peering around the dark room. A beam of pale moonlight broke through the passing clouds and shone through the window. It caught the guard's attention and then it was gone, taken by the cloud cover.

'Oh hell, a full moon, masked by the clouds.' He crossed his fingers to ward off any haunts awoken by the moon and slowly stepped backwards. Then stopped. He had seen a hooded figure sitting on his Lordship's throne. The guard began to shake and reach for the hilt of his sword.

'Who are you? How did you get here?'

The robed figure did not move, and a black hood covered his face.

'Are you okay, sir? Are you lost? Speak up, or you'll be arrested for trespassing.'

It looked more like a corpse on the throne than anything living. A crow squawked at the window and the wind howled through its cracks. The guard moved towards the window and peered outside, catching a glimpse of several campfires burning in the forest. When he turned around, the robed figure stood in the middle of the room. Where its eyes should have been, only a cauldron's flame burned brightly in each socket. The guard drew his sword.

'Step back, foul creature!'

Glohring flicked his wrist and sent a small flame careering to the guard's feet. The guard let out a girlish scream and stepped rapidly from side to side in panic, before tripping and landing on the floor on his side. He shuffled along the stone floor to the edge of the wall, dragging the sword with him.

Glohring held his glowing hands above his head, in an attack position, all the time keeping his watch on the soldier. He moved across the chamber until he reached the door that had been left ajar. Hooking his foot against the door, he pulled it open, moved into the darkness of the grand hallway, and shut the door behind him. The guard sat on the floor, shaking with fear and crossing his fingers to ward off the evil magic.

Now Glohring sprinted down the hallway. He hadn't run that fast since he was a child. He stopped to open the other chamber doors, regretting he did not do this earlier, but they were locked. He did not want to head back through the grand hall, so he gathered a sphere of flame in his hands and launched it at the bottom of a wooden door of an unmarked chamber. It burnt white hot for a moment, then the flames went out. He stepped back and put a heavy kick into the door. His boot punched through the crumbling ash, causing his leg to get stuck momentarily. When he got his leg out of the hole, he reached his arm through, up and around, and unbolted the lock.

It was the scribe's writing room. *Very regal*, he thought, but there was no time to ponder his fake tutoring position.

He closed the door and ran to the window. Below it was a twenty-foot drop. *Enough to easily break your body.* He pulled out a small rope from his bag and tied it to the leg of the writing desk, then climbed up to the window. *It's a long way down, you fool.* Nevertheless, he grasped the rope tightly, lowered himself off the window ledge and started his descent. The guard peered through the burnt hole in the door and watched the evil creature drift out of the window and disappear.

A sense of relief washed through Glohring as he set his feet on the ground. He lit the rope on fire, ensuring the guard would not follow, and ran towards the outer stables. The guard appeared at the window, waved and shouted to the perimeter walls, attempting to raise the alarm, but none of the night watchmen were present. It was too late. Glohring disappeared into the shadows of the ward.

The gate to the city was barred at night and covered by two guards; another four manned the upper walls. News had not yet reached them of an intruder in the castle, and as shouting was quite common in the late-night barracks and stables as drunk soldiers returned to their beds, it was disregarded. Two guards sat with their backs against the portcullis facing the dark castle grounds.

'Warm night tonight. Don't know why there are so many campfires lit in the forest.'

'Well, a warm fire is never too far from a man's heart, especially out on the long road.'

'Strange things always appear with the full moon.'

'You mean normal things are perceived stranger during a full moon. It's just a few people with campfires in the forest.'

'Maybe. Wait ... look! What the hell is that?'

Two glowing eyes moved in the dark. A figure came from the shadows of the stables and its footsteps approached quickly.

'Halt! Who goes there?'

Suddenly, a ball of fire launched the soldiers' way. They screamed and dived clear of the flaming orb. Before they could draw their swords, another fireball exploded at their feet.

'Get out!' screamed the running, glowing-eyed figure.

The guards deserted their post as another ball exploded behind them. The noise attracted attention from the upper walls, and arrows were released at Glohring. He dodged left and right, then dived to the base of the gate, pulling the lever and rolling under the opening portcullis. The archer on the tower peered out from the battlements, arrow notched and ready. He only saw the glow of light briefly before a fireball exploded on the stone before him. Diving to the side, he landed on his bow, then waved the accompanying guard, who was crouched low with sword in hand, over to him.

'On the count of three, we will both stand and attack,' ordered the archer.

'But, I only have my sword,' the guard responded.

'Why aren't you on the ground then?'

The guard did not answer him.

Peering over the wall, the archer watched helplessly as the intruder dissolved into the shadows of the town, a cloaked man with eyes of flame, wielding fire on a full moon, then disappearing into the night. *The swordsman had better back my story, otherwise no one will believe me*, he thought.

~

The troop of warriors gathered close in the dim light of the fire. They had set up a quick camp in the pine forest overlooking the town, far enough away not to disrespect the laws of the castle. Gruldarht arranged all his men in a small circle around him. Usually, councils of war would only be a select few, but he wanted to speak to each and every one of his men and didn't like wasting his time on repeated breath. He walked around and looked all of them straight in the eyes, ensuring they were all paying attention. Tendai made sure he looked strong and stood tall.

'Tonight is a full moon, and this man should arrive before first light. Now, I know a lot of you are not going to like this, but I have explicit orders from my Lord to keep the book if we can. I know what you are thinking. It will have to be an ambush of sorts. I've been thinking about it, and we have no idea if this person will have people with him. He shouldn't. I was informed that he may be a travelling scholar. If any one of you doesn't want to be a thief in the night, well, you'll just have to erase this night from your memory. I want you all packed and ready to go before first light. I don't want you to leave any scrap of our gear from home. I don't want anyone knowing where we are going.'

'Captain? Where are our extras sitting for the ambush?'

'Do not interrupt me. I'm getting to that. Maybe I'm trying

not to echo across the hills, you fool.'

The soldier looked at his feet.

'Darkin! Tendai! Where are you? You'll be the scouts. I want to know when he is arriving and how many he has with him.'

Darkin, another young soldier, grumbled that he had to be singled out to work with Tendai. They exchanged a sour look, and Tendai's shoulders dropped.

After the meeting, the soldiers dispersed to pack their gear and get into position. Nobody, except the few left as a decoy around the fire, would be getting any sleep that night. Tendai couldn't find Darkin anywhere, and they were meant to scout as a team. Not wanting to be seen hanging around the camp and not following his orders, he made his way into the forest to scout the area and hopefully find Darkin, who he thought was probably doing the same. Slowly, Tendai made his way through the pine trees, the soft pine needles underfoot quiet enough for sneaking around the area. He came upon the night shadow of a large fallen pine tree and moved hidden along the trunk towards the large unearthed root system. A bird-like whistle sounded in the darkness. *That must be Darkin*, he assumed. He crept forward and low along the edge of the trunk until he reached its end. Someone was in the shadow of the root system. He waited for them to speak first.

'Tendai? Come here,' said Darkin. He was a young, strong and handsome soldier, extremely skilled, and one of the finest swordsmen they had. He could be a captain of a Warband in the future, but not for many a year.

Tendai stepped into the shadows and crouched beside Darkin. He kept one eye on the forest, looking for any movement. Darkin didn't bother looking at the forest; he concentrated on Tendai.

'You want to stay in the troop, don't you?' asked Darkin. Tendai was taken aback by the question.

'Yeah, I do. It's my job.'

'And you've got a hunting bow with you?'

Tendai nodded.

'So, when this scholar, or whoever the hell he is, comes ... and if he's alone ... just fire an arrow into his chest. It's not a hard target.' Darkin didn't blink, wanting to read Tendai's face in the dim light, to watch him squirm.

'I'm just scouting. That was my order.'

'Just as the rest of us have always thought. No guts, no loyalty, all weakness and complete selfishness,' Darkin taunted.

'Now wait here ... I'm just following orders.'

'I can handle the scouting myself. Maybe you should just go back to camp and see if anyone even wants to sit next to you.'

Darkin unsheathed a small table dagger, slowly enough to grab Tendai's attention.

'What? If you want me to murder, then I don't belong here. There's no place for me here now? I know I'm better than you anyway. You can rot with men, while I succeed more than you ever will,' Tendai said, a little too loudly.

'I knew you would say that,' Darkin grinned and sheathed his table dagger.

A stick snapped behind them. They both turned to see Gruldarht calmly walking towards them. He crouched at a tree, looked Tendai straight in the face, then glanced at Darkin.

'I heard talking and wondered why in the hell my scouting team are only twenty yards from me. My eyesight surely isn't that horrendous.' He waited for an answer, but they gave him nothing.

'So, Tendai, you just said that you don't belong here. I'm not sad to hear that,' he grinned. 'But you were given a job and I don't see one inch of effort so far. I don't think you would have made it much longer anyway. No doubt it will be another dangerous road going home. You probably wouldn't have made it.'

'Of course, I would have made it back,' Tendai said through gritted teeth.

'Yes, maybe as a loner, but not as one of my men. We work as a team. Get back to the fire and, on the morrow, I'll pay half your wage. That's as much as you have done … and poorly, might I add.'

'We'll be better off, Captain, without a weak link amongst us.' Darkin started to laugh under his breath.

Tendai locked eyes on him, with a look of restrained fury. Darkin placed his hand on the cold hilt of his sword.

'No swords,' said Gruldarht. The captain stood up, wanting to see them duke it out.

'Hello!' said Glohring, still in disguise, suddenly appearing on top of the fallen tree. They all stepped back in surprise at the old man standing on the log.

'I happened to hear your amusing conversation, and I just had to meet the captain who is casting this young soldier aside.' Darkin and Gruldarht drew their swords.

'And who are you? I want a name before we speak further,' said the captain.

'That information is of no use to you. All you need to know is that I have the gem. Do you have the book?'

'The book is safely back at the camp. We will take you there.'

'Surely you jest, for that bulge in your chest pocket appears to be kind of book-shaped. And I hate liars.' His eyes began to glow red, and he jumped down from the log to face them.

Tendai slowly stepped back and behind a tree drew his bow and arrow.

'Don't point that arrow at me. It'll get you nowhere.'

Darkin and the captain held their ground, their faces stern and without emotion. They watched Glohring carefully as he reached into his jacket and retrieved a white pouch which he held in an outstretched hand, showing without a word that he was ready to trade peacefully.

'Slowly open it. I have to see it,' said Gruldarht.

'Of course.' Glohring pulled the magnificent gem out of the pouch, held it for a moment, and then placed it back. 'Now you have seen it. Can I please see the book?'

Gruldarht didn't move, but held his sword armed and ready. He glanced at Darkin, who held his sword tight, then to Tendai who had an arrow notched but pointed at the ground. There was a long pause.

Glohring felt the tension in the air. He reminded himself that he looked to them like a frail old man, and that the guards in the castle would soon be rallying to hunt for the thief. He threw the pouch into his left hand and created a fireball in his right. The men stepped back in shock. Finally, the captain stepped forward.

'Let's make this trade and get it over and done with, you disgusting creature.'

'I'm not disgusting. I wasn't the one thinking of stealing from an innocent stranger. Put your sword away please,' he smiled, showing a mouth full of jagged teeth.

The captain slowly sheathed his sword, and kept watch on the foul man's glowing hand. He hoped Tendai would loose his arrow, but knew he never would. The coward can disappear into the wilderness for all he cared.

'Now, arrow boy, you can be the witness to a fair trade.'

Tendai, frightened, just nodded, still with his bow in hand.

'Open the book. Show me,' whispered Glohring.

The captain pulled the book out from his inside pocket, exactly where Glohring noticed it had been, and began to turn the old pages. In the dim glow emanating from his eyes, Glohring could see that it appeared to be the correct book. He let his eyes fade. Tendai was unnerved and didn't want to see more displays of glowing magic, so decided to intervene.

'Okay, so on the count of three, you swap.'

The captain and Glohring glanced at the nervous Tendai.

'One, Two, Three!'

The exchange was complete. Glohring stood next to the fallen tree, holding the book as the captain pocketed the fire-gem.

The captain grabbed Darkin by the shoulder, and they slowly backed away into the forest, then disappeared. Glohring watched them retreat into the pines, then turned back to Tendai.

'I'm sorry, young man. I forgot you were there.'

Tendai stood silent, with his arrow aimed directly at Glohring. He began to shake – he just couldn't help it. For the first time since leaving his home town and joining the Warband, he was alone. Before him was a man whose eyes glowed red, and he knew he didn't dare challenge him. Glohring leaned casually against the side of the tree trunk.

'You can put the arrow down. Don't be rude. I imagine you are no longer part of their Warband. It looked like the captain was going to let the other man murder you before I showed up. And this is the thanks I get! … An arrow pointing at me.'

Tendai dropped his aim, acknowledging that this strange man was correct.

'I'm not one of them. I never was and never will be anything like them. Some were good men, but I don't belong with people like that. I'm better than them.'

'Do you know where you belong?'

'Well, I …'

Suddenly, a dagger spun from the darkness and lodged in Tendai's quiver, breaking an arrow or two.

'This way. Keep low and head towards those rocks.'

Tendai obeyed hesitantly. There was nowhere else for him

to go, and his old troop were now trying to kill him. Running, he and Glohring made it to a cluster of tall jagged rocks. An arrow whistled by their heads. They stayed low and made their way around the far side of the rocks.

'Let's slow 'em down. Fire a few arrows into those closer bushes. We have the wind on our side.'

'They're much further away. They're not in those bushes.'

'Just trust me and do it.'

Tendai began loosing arrows into the bush in front of them in a wide arc. As each one sailed through the air, Glohring set it on fire. A spectacular lightshow for the forest dwellers, until they had to begin running from the fire.

'Come on, let's go. That'll slow them down and blind them for a while.'

~

The remainder of the night dragged on as they bashed their way upwards through thick bush. Dawn broke as they reached the top of the hill. It looked back to where they'd come from: a view of the town that stretched south along the banks of the river. Looking down, the other side of the hill was quite open and devoid of trees, with no farms or fences. *An unused or unclaimed farm from the past,* Glohring thought.

They kept to the edge of the clearing, jogged along a fire break that divided the forest and what would have been a farmer's paddock. Tendai ran with more vigour and energy than Glohring, and maintained a distance in front. He stopped and examined something peculiar on the ground.

'These tracks are very fresh.'

'Good eyes. I didn't see them myself.'

'I've never seen tracks like this. It's most interesting, but let's go. We have to make speed.' Tendai thought he was saying the right thing to his strange companion.

'No, change of plans. We follow these tracks. Take a closer look, Tendai. You've seen them before. These tracks were made by a large beetle. There are also a number of horses and a wagon. Then these small footprints walking behind the beetle … dragging his feet. He looks tired.'

'How did you know my name?'

'Give me a moment and you'll see. Keep watch.' Glohring emptied his water skin over his head, turning his makeup to a sludgy mess. The liquid loosened the adhesive of his wig, and he pulled the clumps of hair away from his scalp. He dumped the remains of his disguise on the ground and washed his face. 'Ah, that's better. Now you see. I am Glohring, and we have met.'

Tendai stared, open-mouthed in shock.

'But, why the disguise? We camped with you before.'

'Questions can wait. These are slave tracks: the curl of the toes and the dragging of chains. And they are beetle tracks for sure. We follow them. There is only one reason they would have avoided the village road, the sneaky dogs.'

They both jogged tiredly, following the tracks as the sun rose above the treetops. The morning was hot already, and they would soon need water.

4

A large wooden door slammed shut, and the sound echoed through the open stables. In a decrepit stall, Boy lay asleep in a pile of straw. His arms and feet were bound by rope connected to a brace and chained across the middle. The smell of excretion was in the air. Approaching footsteps stomped louder; Boy heard them clearly reverberate through his throbbing head. He sat up and wiped the straw from his hair. Nikkotto stood on a wooden box and peered over the stable door, his mouth clapping together coated with thick stringy saliva. He held a raw-looking turkey bone.

'I told the men you'd be able to jump over this door. I guess I was wrong. Did they bind you tight?' Nikkotto's scabby lips bled dark.

Just watching his festering mouth smack up and down was torture for Boy. He was repulsed by this vile man, his captor. He sat up straight as best as he could, not wanting to appear weak, but his tired body ached. He hoped he was stronger-minded than this fat worm of a man.

'Where is my beetle?'

'Well, he's right over there at the end of the stable.'

'Where are you taking us? And what do you want with him?'

'I'm taking you to the harbour with me. I hope you like boats and the sea. And your beetle friend is going to find himself a fine new home, if we can get him there. That's enough questions for today I will answer no more.'

Nikkotto smiled, dribbling salivary blood. He took another bite, tearing the turkey skin away from the bone. It flapped on his bottom lip for a while, then he sucked it and left.

'I have no more questions. But I can tell you that if you want Beetie to go with no hassles, there is an easy way.'

Nikkotto returned to the wooden box and looked over the stable door again. He appeared interested, but feebly tried to hide it.

'You know, I am not his master. I have only known him for a few days, and I was sick of walking. Do you think he comes with me out of the goodness of his heart? Well, I'll tell you that's a no. He comes with me for one reason, and I'm willing to part with that information if you are ready to parley?' Boy was quite surprised at his own burst of confidence, trying to negotiate with the slime of humanity.

Nikkotto thought for a while, staring at the far wall, then turned to look around the stables to see if they could be overheard.

This is too easy, Boy thought, reminding himself to stay on guard. He didn't know if this was just an act, or if he really was plain stupid. *I guess if he is doing illegal things and he is not in jail, then he can't be that dumb.*

'What is your request? And how do we know if what you say is valid information?'

'If I give you the information to control and be the master of the beetle, I want to be released with all my belongings *and* a horse complete with saddle and tack.'

'And why would we want to grant this? We already have two extremely valuable items. There is nothing in that deal for me.'

'A few of your men will probably be killed by him once I depart his presence, if you try to take control of him. Men will die by his fury. You need to trade for the information to control the creature, and you know it.'

Nikkotto smiled and walked away.

'We will just have to torture you until you tell us. Goodbye.'

Boy listened to the footstep of the slimy slug. Thirty-eight steps and then the slam of the door. He lay on his back in the itchy straw, his stomach cramping in pain. He hadn't eaten in a long time, and the forced march in chains had exhausted every ounce of energy in him. There was a bucket of water near the stable door to quench his thirst but it was too tiring for him to stand up, so he fell back down into the straw, rolled himself across the floor and drank half the bucket. Then he dunked his sore head into the cool remains. It woke him up and gave him a clearer head. Sitting back up, Boy leant against the door, and looked around the stable. Either side had wooden partitions, too high to climb, and the stable door was also too high to climb. He attempted to finish the remaining water, even though it cramped his stomach. He tipped the remains out, placed the bucket upside down and used it to gain extra height.

It was hard, but he managed to climb on top of the bucket and jump towards the top of the door.

As he landed, he hit the side of the door, grazing his knees on cracked timber. If his hands and feet weren't bound, he believed he could make the distance – it wasn't that far. He didn't want to give up, but on the second attempt, he bounced back off the door, landed on the bucket and hit the ground hard. He lay in pain for a moment, then, rubbing the stable dirt out of his eyes, he noticed the gap under the door was only sand, with no wooden flooring. Boy quickly grabbed the bucket and started to dig. Thankfully, the ground didn't hit hard clay straight away and, by laying his cheek in the sand, he could slide his head halfway under the door. He could see all the way to the left and to the right. To the left, where he thought Nikkotto had walked, was a larger door, possibly a double-sized stable – *enough room for Beetie.*

'Beetie!' he called out. 'Chika chika chika!' he yelled, imitating his friend as best he could.

There was no response. The dusty blackened dirt hung in the air, drew into his lungs, and settled in his eyes. He pushed his head into the dirt and under the door. Further around the corner he could see long ropes tied down and anchored to something.

'Chika chika chika!' Boy called out.

The ropes began to tug and move. Boy dug as fast as he could with his limited movement. He pushed the bucket back and forth through the hole and, lying on his back, he shuffled against the dirt and under the door.

Distant voices began shouting. Boy pulled his chains tightly apart to prevent a rattle, and ambled along on his hands and knees like a clumsy bear. An empty stable's door was open, so he removed the bucket from inside and dragged it in one hand, heading towards the moving ropes.

'Hang on, buddy. I'm here.'

Hanging on a wall was a selection of old rusted rabbit and bear traps. Boy unhooked the rabbit trap and placed it on the ground. He set the clamping vice into position and placed his feet either side with the chain across the middle. The steel claws slammed shut with a rusty clang that broke the chain. He reset the vice and placed his arms either side of it, his face pulled away from any possible recoil. Above him, the ropes tugged hard, creaking from the roof beams.

'It's okay, settle. I'll cut the ropes down. Chika chika chika … say that with me, Beetie.'

There was no response.

Once free of his chains, Boy tried to help Beetie. Sawing the rope on the rusted claws of the trap, Boy slipped and sliced his wrist open. But he also managed to snare the rope. He let his wrist bleed; there was nothing he could do to mend it now. Beetie pulled hard on the ropes, making the roof beams creak louder. The friction finally ate through the fibres and snapped some of the ropes.

Boy placed the bucket upside down and reached the rusty

steel latch unlocking the door to the next stall. It burst open, swinging outward and sending him falling onto his back. There was another giant beetle next door, lashing around and pulling at its remaining ropes. It was rippled in black hardness, with sharp horns surrounded by red spikes pointing out from his shell. Boy lay sore on his back in the straw, watching the black-horned beetle. Two men stepped inside cautiously to see what the noise was about.

'What the hell!' one shouted.

'What have you done? You let him out!' said the other. They scrambled out the door in a hurry.

Boy dived into an open stall and pulled the door closed. He peered through the crack and watched the horned, black beetle charge out of his pen. The men dragged in a large net, but they were too late. The black beetle charged past them, shredding the net and trampling the men as it crashed through the door. Boy ran to the men. They were alive but in severe agony. They wheezed out crushing sounds of pain from their internal injuries. The cracking of trees and branches echoed in the distance as the horned, black creature smashed its way through the bushes.

Boy found his bags sitting outside the shed door. It seemed like they were on some kind of farm, surrounded by a dry-looking banksia forest on the slopes of a steep hill. A perfect place for illegal dealings: an old run-down farmhouse, a few sheds, and two large stables. He jogged stiffly to the other stable, but no one else appeared to be on the farm grounds at the time. He opened the stable door quietly and peered inside. It was the same layout as the other and, at the far end, ropes were tied from the rafters holding something down, something large.

Boy rummaged through his bag and found his table dagger, then walked towards the roped stall, his chains rattling. He could hear sniffing, an intense, almost competitive sniffing, followed by a foul smell. Boy walked closer to the noise and the smell, not realising it was him who was being sniffed out.

'Come here, young man,' a gravelly female voice said from behind the cell door.

Boy found an old chair, dragged it into position, climbed up, and peered over the wooden door. An old woman was tied up with a rusty chain, just like he'd been. She looked like the witches in his father's books, with a large nose, thick bulging scars down her face, and rich violet eyes. Her skin looked like charcoal in places, not bruises but something else, giving the impression that she'd been recently burnt, her skin crisp and flaky like ashen paper. Her clothing was hundreds of torn shreds of cloth.

'It's okay. I'm not as creepy as I look. Can you please help me?'

'I'm here for my friend, the beetle. I'm sorry, but I have to go.' Boy jumped down off the chair and ran to Beetie. The beetle looked exhausted, and not even a wink of his tentacle responded. Nikkotto and his men had left the leather harness on, undoubtedly wary about getting too close.

'There you go, Beetie. I hope you aren't injured. We have to go now, back into the cover of the forest.'

'Chik,' Beetie answered tiredly.

The witch started to cough incessantly.

'Please, what is your name? Come and help me. I have also lost my beetle. He is the last of his kind. Have you seen him in the other stable? I can sense it. Oh, please. I need to get out of here to finish my journey.'

Boy gave Beetie a bucket of water and ran back to the old crone.

'What type of journey are you on? I have learnt not to trust anyone in these parts. Why should I help you?'

'I am a mother, a grandmother and a carer of forgotten animals. I am on my way back from finding a secret herb, thought to be extinct. It will cure my beloved granddaughter.

She has gone mad and is doing terrible things.'

'I don't believe you for a second. If I release you, you will try to get rid of me and take my beetle since yours ran off into the forest.'

'Did he? Which way did he go? I must find him.'

'I have always been kind and gentle to old ladies, but the more I see of the world, the more lies and selfishness I see.'

'You are right, but you do not know of their agendas. Maybe people are doing noble deeds but, when they cross your path, they need to do one selfish thing to keep going. Then that's all you have experienced of their story. If you leave me here, that is exactly what you will be doing. I can see you have an injured wrist.'

Boy grabbed his hurting wrist, blood dripping from his arm.

'Here. Take one of my strips of clothing. It will heal your arm to better than it used to be.'

Boy hesitated.

'Why has your granddaughter gone mad?'

'She was born with a strange power. Most people don't believe it. In some ways, it's a curse and others a blessing. She has a connection to animals … only the weak-minded ones, and her beloved pets. She has been having terrible nightmares, seeing things, not knowing what is a dream and what is reality. She talks of visiting another girl out there who controls the wind in the forest. I think that's all nonsense. The air isn't a living thing with a brain.'

'Neither is water,' Boy blurted out, thinking of Tree Deep Trundle. The old lady ripped a piece of her ragged cloth with her teeth.

'Take it and heal your arm. Don't go mad like my granddaughter.'

Boy grabbed a long stick, and reached over and hooked the rag. The old lady lay down in the dirt and closed her eyes. Boy blew the dirt off the rag and wrapped it around his bleeding wrist. It suddenly tightened like a tourniquet, and he squirmed in surprise.

'What have you done, you old crone?'

'No need to call me names. Just take a deep breath and relax.'

Boy did that and felt instant relief. The rag turned to polished steel, and he tapped his dagger on it with a clink.

'It feels just like my normal arm, but the wound is now steel.'

'I hope that is okay. If you really wish, you can take it off and let the arm heal by itself.'

A sense of comfort wrapped around Boy. He felt as if he saw the world with new eyes; something was in this steel, something warm. The daggers of mistrust were replaced by faith in the choice of kindness.

'Your beetle ran west through the forest. I'm sure you can follow his tracks. Do you think you can catch him? He looked very fast.'

Boy opened the door and walked up to the old lady.

'You think he is fast? Well, you're in for a shock when your beetle grows up. They live long and have a few surprises that come with age. I'll find him. I know his true name, and I have tracked animals my whole life.'

Boy cut the ropes from the woman's hands and legs and helped her to her feet.

'Thank you for helping me.'

'You're most welcome. Thank you for the magic cloth. My arm feels great.'

'Oh, that isn't magic. Now, where did they put my things?'

Boy shrugged, whispering a few reassuring words to Beetie. The old hag searched for her things and eventually appeared from the last stall carrying a burnt-looking wicker basket and a walking stick. She helped Boy up onto the saddle as he lacked the strength to get there himself.

As they were about to set off into the woods, a rider on a black horse cantered towards the shed. It was Nikkotto. He carried many a small pack on the rear of his poor horse, appearing to have returned from the morning markets. He stopped by his men who lay still on the ground, passed out from the pain of their internal damage. He kicked his horse in the direction of Boy and the old lady.

'Stop there! We can parley!' he shouted.

'This is what you get!' yelled the old crone. She threw a spear at Nikkotto. He attempted to duck, but it caught him flush on the shoulder, snapping his collarbone and sending him off the back of his horse. His flabby body landed with a resounding thud, and the witch approached him and grabbed the reins of the black gelding.

'That's my revenge, you bastard. Next time I'll kill you if you try to harm us.'

She unceremoniously ripped the spear from his shoulder, swung up onto the horse with surprising agility and kicked it into a canter.

'Goodbye, Boy, and good luck.'

She followed the broken path of trampled flora created by the stampeding beetle, and disappeared into the forest. The ragged strands of cloth in the wind looked more like a flurry of leaves than a person.

Behind Boy, Nikkotto writhed in pain. Boy was tempted to inspect the fallen man – as much as he was a slimy worm, he was still a human. He didn't think about it for long before turning and leaving the farm without a backward glance.

He entered the forest and started working his way through the path of crushed trees and broken branches trampled by the witch's creature. As the damaged vegetation gradually subsided, he lost the tracks of her horse and her beetle, as if they had disappeared or became one with the forest. The path soon vanished and only dry low-lying trees stood in the hot gravel and hard clay earth beneath him. He drained the water skin onto his rough tongue; like a sponge, the warm water dissolved instantly, with near to nothing soothing the back of his throat. He dragged the reins of his bulking beetle, and head down, focused on undue hazards. When the earth became treeless, he raised his head and viewed the flat clay road that ran roughly north to south in front of him: a view that inevitably would require a decision.

Gravel compacted in the clay verified that a fair amount of traffic moved back and forth along the road, possibly straight to town and the castle. Without wanting to go back into town, he decided to head south until any crossroad branched off to the west. If not, he would cut straight across the lands and forget the roads. At least then he wouldn't be annoyed by strangers.

The sun was now high in the sky: not a comforting warmth, but a very hot burn to his dehydrated skin – he and the beetle needed to find water, and soon. The land had some old clearings, which appeared to be long-forgotten paddocks of once-worked land. An old stone structure lay crumbling in a disused paddock, with what seemed to be a well standing hunched behind it. Boy berated himself for the decision to stay on the road. He knew it was a vulnerable position so close to Nikkotto's farm, and knew he had to seek shelter in the shadowed woods as he was most likely being hunted.

A stone path wended from the road to the well, which had a decrepit rope and a cracked bucket in place. Boy collected water until he and Beetie had drunk a bucket's worth and his water skin was full. He sat down on a dusty sand mound, his stomach bloated, and leaned against the well. His body ached, and he was in pain from the chains tied at his wrists and ankles. His lower legs burned with fire from his shackled march. He realised he had forgotten to thoroughly inspect Beetie for injury. Reprimanding himself for being so selfish, he circled Beetie looking for injuries or bruises left by the ropes and chains. Luckily, Beetie appeared to be in good order. He also liked the inspection and chattered the whole time, 'chika chika' this and 'choka choka' that. Boy was pleased that he wasn't hurt and smiled. Then his smile turned into a giggle that he could not stop until the sudden call of nature interrupted him.

'Beetie, sorry, but I'm absolutely dying to go to the privy. You'll have to follow me over to those trees. I don't want you staying out in the open alone where anyone can get to you.'

Beetie probably didn't understand, but when Boy stumbled away clumsily, he rose his shell off the ground and followed. He meandered at his regular pace in Boy's direction. Every now and then, he stopped to bury his face in the dirt and scuffle around, attending to his favourite pastime.

Boy finished completing his business behind a tree and turned back to see Beetie far away grazing in the field, happy to be free of the stables.

'Beetie, you're mine now. You should come to me when I call you.' Boy called, but the Beetle turned away.

'Hey, if you don't listen to me, you'll get caught and butchered by strangers out here. Do you want to be caught and tied up again? Or made into bug soup? Big bug soup!'

The beetle looked at the ground, tentacles slowing twirling.

'I know you understand what I'm saying. I want you to come home with me, and I'll look after you. You'll have a good life. I've never had to look after someone in my life, but I can do it. I know I haven't even discussed this with you, but I thought I should.'

Boy stood, looking into Beetie's eyes. He held out his hand, full of blueberries.

'Look what I found.'

Beetie's tentacles swirled around his head in response to the berries.

'Chick chokachoka.'

'I found them over in the trees. I am going to look after

you now, so you must do what I say. Because I love you.'

His giant shell began to flutter as if in a mysterious breeze. Four shelled sections separated and vibrated together dramatically, echoing the flutter of a flock taking flight. Minute blue bolts of lightning struck out from under the overlaps. The beetle stretched his legs and squeezed out a sound of pleasure, like an elongated sneeze. The colourful episode was soon over, and Beetie lowered his head back down to inspect the dirt below. Boy smiled, accepting another interesting event, and patted Beetie on the head.

'Okay, well, that was a surprise. Maybe next time give a little notice, so I can make sure no one else is around. Let's go.' Boy picked up the reins to spare him his weight and led him south towards some wide peppermint trees.

~

Glohring and Tendai continued tracking Boy and the beetle's movements. They had led all the way to a farm, where the crowded footprints and the distinctive prints of interesting events were written in the ground in feet and blood. It was the blood that worried Glohring the most. He didn't have the heart to head straight home without ensuring Boy's welfare.

At the rear of the stables, a crudely made fence sectioned off a patch of dry grass where grazed two bay geldings.

'I thought I'd retired from thieving, but here I am. Tendai, saddle those horses. The stables should have what you need.'

A few minutes later, they trotted onto the broken path, following the tracks.

'What if these horses have a brand on them? I don't want to be hunted as a horse thief,' Tendai said.

'So, look for a brand then. I can't imagine those kidnappers to be the very heart and soul of the law. The horses are probably twice stolen already. When we find Boy and make sure he's safe, we'll take the horses back if you really want to. If there is any chance they want to sell them, then we'll buy them. Or you can at least buy yours. I'm fine with taking this one.'

'I don't have any money to pay for a horse anyway.'

'You mean you never got paid for being one of their soldiers?'

'Not much. The supplies were provided for me, so I didn't have to have money. We were to be paid on arrival back home.' Tendai looked like he'd bitten into a lemon. He kept a keen eye on the gravel, reading the tracks and continuing in silence.

'Look over there, in that field. A beetle!' Tendai pointed.

'What the hell!' Glohring shielded his eyes from the sun, and from a flickering of overlapping colours as the giant beetle entertained a spectacular show across his shell. The beetle then began to move away from them, heading for the distant trees.

Glohring nudged his horse into a trot and followed their tracks into the field. Far above them, against the developing summer storm clouds, two large birds circled the meadow. Even though the fields were their normal hunting ground, something didn't feel right to Glohring.

'They move in the fashion of a trained hunting bird, one that signals the owner. We must leave. Hurry, this meadow bodes ill.'

'I think you're right. I can feel it too,' agreed Tendai.

They kicked their horses into a canter along the flat meadow grass. They could see Boy struggling to mount Beetie, attempting to pull himself up into the saddle before sliding back down the shell. Feeling the deep rumble vibrating through the ground, Boy turned to the noise of the horses.

'Boy!' shouted Glohring, waving his arms over his head.

Boy dropped his head in sudden relief; the incoming hooves were not carrying evil with them. He sat and smiled, allowing himself a second of peaceful rest as he waited for Glohring and, to his surprise, the soldier Tendai to arrive.

'We came across Beetie's tracks, and tracks of small feet tied by rope. I'm glad we found you. Are you okay?' Glohring asked.

'We're okay. Just a few cuts and bruises. But I am so tired now, Glohring.' Boy leant against his steed, hugging Beetie's shell. The relief and joy of doing nothing ran through him, even if it may have been rude to his friends.

'I don't want to alarm you, but we can't rest out here. We should get under the forest canopy. Did you notice two large birds circling above you?'

'I did not. I only heard your horses coming.' Boy looked up. The two birds had climbed higher and were now only small specks in the sky.

'Follow me. Tonight we can talk, and you can tell me of your remarkable escape.' Glohring smiled proudly.

'Boy the Brave, that's what you are. It's a very dangerous place for people like you,' said Tendai.

'Thank you,' said Boy.

Boy thought about what might happen if they ran into hostile townsfolk again. He could have lowered his guard and saved mental energy with Glohring there; however, the opposite happened. His thoughts zoned in, calculating everything that came into his mind. The three of them rode their steeds at a slow pace, south-west across the field, leading them to the canopy of a forest which descended into a small valley. In the distance, a hill rose high, thick with forest. A blackening storm cell grew higher against the rising heat of the land.

5

When Armue and Tilly were sent to gather water from Tree Deep Trundle, the river was not its usual self. Gathering water was a chore that they'd had to learn after Boy's disappearance, and they knew that the river would become angry if you lingered by its banks. At their parents' request for water, Armue and Tilly would stop what they were doing and head north-east along a narrow dirt trail that twisted through sharp boulders. At this section of the river, the rock formations filtered a small stream where they could fill their buckets in peace. It was not always that easy though; on the days that Tree Deep's moods were unmanageable, they would have to retreat to the slow collection of the farm's spring, or even the drying well.

This morning was the same as any other when they would sneak quietly down to the shallows, carefully scooping up the fresh water until all four buckets were full. Armue was scooping the final bucket, standing in the shallows and being careful not to pick up any sand from the bottom when he heard the river reverberate a loud boom. He dropped the bucket and stepped back from the water. Again, the sound thundered, and Armue's attention was drawn to the sky.

A large beast flew over the southern shore of the river, its straw-coloured wings stretched wide and flat to glide on the wind. Like that, it whistled through the air. It carried something in its talons – *a basket,* Armue thought. The beast soared gracefully up the river, releasing the item from its talons. Then it landed on the rocky cliff-top, upstream on the far shore. Armue squatted in the water, shading behind one of the sharp tooth rocks.

'Armue?' Tilly whispered, trying to locate her brother from her hiding place in a small crevice.

'Just wait. I want to look at this thing.'

The bird-like creature began stomping around in circles on the clifftop, rubbing its head amongst the shrubs and salt bushes, attacking an itch.

'Tilly, the beast dropped something. Maybe it was a deer carcass?'

'Armue, I don't want to be here any more. Let's go.'

'No, we can't go. The thing will see us. If it's swooping down, eating deer and ripping their guts out, then we are going to look like a nice treat. Dessert, sweets, human toothpicks.'

'Hide then, Armue. Hide quickly.' Tilly ducked and scurried up against a flat rock to hide in the shadow. Her lips began to quiver.

'Just don't move and it won't see us.' Armue crawled over towards Tilly and the flat rock.

'But *you're* moving. Stop it. He'll eat us. I want to go home. Let's go home. I want Mum.'

'Shhhhhh … it's probably got good hearing.'

Tilly began to cry quietly, sniffling the snot back into her nostrils. Armue placed a comforting hand on her shoulder.

'Okay, okay. We'll sneak back through the shadows of the rocks and go through the underbush … are you listening, Tilly?' He grabbed her by both arms, demanding her attention.

Tilly stopped crying and sat up straight, trying her hardest to listen to her brother.

'Follow me, and we'll head to the big trees. Then, when we get into the cover of the forest, we'll run back home as fast as we can.'

'Wait! What are we going to do about the water?'

'We'll tell Mama and Papa that a beast was going to eat us, so we had to run home.' Tilly burst out crying again and clung to her knees. Her brother put his arm around her and pointed to their regular path to the rocks.

'I'm sorry. Look, it's just a big bird which is probably going to fly away, and we'll never see it again. It's nothing. But, when I tell you to, go quickly, stick close to me, and stay low. It won't even see us and probably won't even be interested in us. It'll be fine,' he gulped.

Armue looked up to the cliff face; the beast was staring directly at him. It could see him move, and he knew it. He froze for a second, then grabbed Tilly's hand.

'Run! Come on! As fast as you can.'

He ignored any plan he'd had, and took the straightest and quickest route home. Behind them, a distant screech of the beast rang from the clifftop. It sounded like an angry sow. He ignored the temptation to turn around and sight the beast, focusing on his next foot placement, one fast footstep in front of the other. He never let go of Tilly's hand. The sound of the air beating like a drum against the cliffs had stopped, replaced by deflected wind approaching fast from behind. Armue began to turn. He would later regret it, remembering the sharp claws whistling through the air before him, and the sticky, thick putrid smell that he would forever hate.

6

For some days, Boy and the beetle waited for Glohring's decision to part ways with them. On the first day, Boy decided again to pick his brain as much as he could about what to expect in these parts of the world: the geography mainly, as a giant beetle is not the most agile of rides if things turned sour.

The last attack on him and Beetie had shattered any confidence he'd had after the previous question-time with Glohring. But, he did not want to exhaust the man's patience: Glohring was ready to go home. He had completed his task, and Boy knew he should mentally prepare himself for the lone journey ahead. At this time, Tendai decided to speak up; it was most unlike him, but he felt more welcome amongst this group and wanted to share his thoughts.

'We've had a good run, without any danger. I say we let the horses and the beetle have a break … renew their energy just in case we need some fresh legs,' said Tendai with purpose. There was a long pause.

'You are quite right. I need to make a fire,' said Glohring.

It was the middle of a hot summer's day with a fair breeze blowing from the east: not ideal conditions for a flame, but Boy thought better than to question Glohring about fire and the possibility of it losing control. *So long as Glohring doesn't leave when the wind picks up*, he thought. Glohring assembled a few dry twigs, sat down, crossed his legs, closed his eyes, and fire sprang forth without any psychical action from himself.

Without wanting to disturb him, Boy sat quietly, watching for detail he had not yet seen from Glohring during his powerful arts. He was itching to ask a barrage of questions.

He did not want Glohring to leave now but knew it was inevitable. He would be alone again with the beetle, susceptible to dangers of the wild and civil. He asked himself how he should use this time instead of worrying about the future, and concluded that he should focus on happy times from the past. He imagined picking blueberries near the shore of the river. He remembered the smell of fresh bread. He thought about how his dad would act surprised when he found food stuck in his beard – chunks of bread he would show off before eating.

~

Boy lay asleep, eyes closed and motionless, in a comfortable position amongst soft grass in the shaded roots of a tree. Tendai stood guard, scanning the skies for changes in the weather. Glohring sat in front of the small fire, snapping his fingers with loud clacks of old bones. The fire feathered out, then relit, then disappeared, then appeared again.

'Well, I can let you know that we are not being followed from the north. I sense no impeding hunt.'

Boy opened his eyes and sat up to speak.

'Do you know that for sure? Or is it just a feeling?'

Glohring laughed at this.

'Your sharp wit will see you far one day. But, no, it is just a feeling. I could never be adamant. But, it's better than guessing, eh?' Tendai and Boy exchanged questioning glances. 'Well, okay then, don't believe me. But before I leave, we have more pressing information to go over again. This is based on memories of travelling out this way to the west. The land heading south and towards the river at this time of year is probably dry and fuel-loaded. You will be able to travel quicker if you find a recently burnt area, but you will have limited cover from danger. South east and the river will be harder terrain, hillier, filled with forests and rocky gullies.'

Glohring paused to let them speak, but Boy had drifted

back off to sleep.

'Well, I have no care which direction I go, as long as it is further away from my troop. I would say my experience would be advantageous closer to a river and forests. But I've never travelled with a giant beetle. I will head south-east towards the great River Hew you speak of,' Tendai said, trying to sound confident. He was devoid of his own surety, and Glohring sensed this. Glohring needed him to be the best he could be, for Boy's sake. *The young child needs to get home, and this young man can help him, if only he doesn't run away back to where he came from.*

'That is probably your best choice, to go south-east to the river Boy knows of. Stay away from the north. Good luck. I will wait for Boy to wake up, and then I'll be on my way. Farewells are not always more important than sleep. I'll wait here for him to wake up, but I'm sure you have other things to do?'

Tendai took the hint and set off into the forest to collect firewood and herbs.

It wasn't much longer before Boy stirred. He yawned, stretching his arms above his head, and sat up, blinking slowly.

'Sorry I fell asleep. I didn't realise how tired I'd become.'

'When you are ready, come and sit by the fire. I'll put it out. I don't need it any more.' He snapped his fingers and this time only smoke rose from the ashes. The flame dropped so quickly, it was as if the oxygen was strangled around the hungry flame. Boy stood up, moved towards Glohring and sat down next to him.

'Boy, what are you thinking?'

'Ummmm … well, I guess I'm just wondering if we are heading in the right direction and how far we are away from the river.'

'Good. Make sure you don't let your thoughts get sidetracked. If you know the river will lead you home, keep moving.' Boy was confused at the simplicity of what Glohring was saying and waited for him to elaborate.

'I am leaving now, Boy. I have my own agenda, as you know, and I have to be on my way. I'm glad you were able to escape from those men. You may need to escape more than once.'

'I understand. What of Tendai? Is he going back north with you?'

'No, he cannot come with me. Not at all. He doesn't have a choice any more. Do you want him to go with you?'

'Well, he is a warrior. And I'm just … it'll be easier and safer.'

'It will be a damn-sight easier travelling with a man. Hunting, tracking, cooking, defence. If you are happy for him to go with you, I will not persuade him otherwise.'

'Of course not. That would be rude. Thinking about the advantages, I'd be silly not to have a warrior of my own. Well, not of my own … I don't own him … but a travel companion. Someone always there at least.'

The words hung in the air as Tendai came out of the forest with a handful of berries. He placed the berries down with his belongings, eyes averted, not wanting to be accused of eavesdropping. Glohring stood up and packed the last of his bags onto his horse.

'Boy, stay safe. Get to where you want to go. Goodbye.'

Glohring walked off, leading the horse down an old deer track into the forest to the north.

'Thank you again for all your help. Thank you, Glohring,' Boy's voice trailed off.

~

Boy stayed seated on the ground, watching the old ash as it settled after the burn. The sun beamed down onto Boy's face, and he picked himself up to rest in the shade. He didn't want to walk in the heat of the day; once the air cooled later they would be able to make further ground and find a place to camp for the night. Boy fell asleep again until a butterfly landed on his nose. He felt it tickle his face as it crawled onto his upper lip. Boy sniffed once, then twice, and violently sneezed the butterfly onto the ground beside him. He watched it try to take off in flight, but a thick length of snot clung to each wing. Boy apologised, and removed the snotty string, so the insect could fly away safely.

'I hope you're not getting sick. We don't have any healers with us. Drink plenty of water, have plenty of rest, and we shouldn't have any trouble,' said Tendai.

'I know a few herbs that can be made into a brew for certain ailments, but that's about it,' Boy replied.

'Good. Have a snack while we ride. I have some berries. We really should have left by midday.'

Boy still believed it was better to travel when it became cooler, later in the day.

'So, you are coming with me then?' asked Boy.

'Of course. I would be a dishonourable man if I let a poor innocent child wander into the forest alone with nothing. The honour of men and good deeds make the world a better place.'

'I understand that. Glohring did not need to help me, but he did. I hope he gets home safe and your old friends don't find him. After everything he helped me with, I wish him the best.' As he said it aloud, and even with Tendai there, Boy felt lonely again.

'I think he knew how thankful you were for his help.'

Tendai picked up their bags and slung them onto the beetle. He had not seen his mother (or anyone else close to him) for a long time, and he didn't tend to make bonds as quickly as Boy did. However, Tendai assumed that Boy had developed respect for him and was at ease in his presence, and the feeling was mutual. It was grateful knowledge to him after so many years of rejection and isolation.

They wound their way down a jagged crevice alongside a

small stream. There they found remnants of a recent camp: ash from an old fire, a broken arrow, turned earth, and the skeletal remains of a rabbit.

'Boy, this looks to be from a camp of about three or four people. I'd say close to mid-spring, twenty days ago maybe. Hard to tell but it looks like they left here heading northwest. Nothing of use here though. Remember to tell me if you see anything familiar or anything your dad may have told you about. Two sets of eyes can join the dots better in unfamiliar territory.'

'I will. I haven't seen anything yet, but I know in my heart that we are still a long way away. We need to head further west and find the river that will lead us straight home.'

~

Boy's mind began to daydream – heat combined with exhaustion. Beetie's calming pace also didn't help keep sleep away. He began to dream about getting home and arriving with his family. He imagined Tendai standing around the farm awkwardly when he hugged his mother and father. *I guess he'll travel further and find a town for work.*

'Why did you leave your job?'

'It's rude to ask a soldier such a question. But, if you must know, I would not have been a man of honour if I had stayed. I'm better than those men.'

Boy left it at that. *I guess he has nowhere to go. I need to get home, so he may as well come with me.* Something deep in his gut throbbed in the dry heat; it took his mind off wondering about Tendai, but his stomach hurt nonetheless.

'One day, Boy, you will grow up to be a great man,' Tendai said, without any eye contact.

'Thank you. I hope so,' he replied awkwardly. The silence clung in the air between them again.

'Tendai, do you still have that game with the dice that you taught me? At least at night we can play a few games to pass the time.'

'Unfortunately not. It was left in my other bag.'

'Damn.' Boy wanted to play it again.

The day ran long and hot. The afternoon wind stopped, and the heat could not be escaped. The giant beetle soldiered forward through the rough underbush of the forest. Only a few birds could be seen flying around in this heat; every other animal would wait for the cooler night to forage for food. At least the trees gave some relief in the shade.

'Tendai, have you been south of here before? Do you know the general area where we are?'

'No, I have not been to these lands before. I have spent most of my life to the far northwest of here, where the mountains fall before the sea.'

'I've never known of such a place.'

'It's very far from here. The mountains to the north are very high, always white, and always watching. For a little while, I grew up as a barge hand. My mother was working in the town and we would send the farmers' stock down the river to the sea to trade. It was a hard upbringing but fun sometimes. There were many towns and people to meet, but I left and never looked back.'

'Why did you leave if it was fun? It sounds nice. I love rivers.'

'Sometimes you have nothing to go back to. Now my bow and my sword are my family and my destiny.'

'What's destiny? I've never heard that word before.'

'Destiny is just a word for the tools you have to get you to your place of death.'

'Sounds like a morbid word.'

'It is. The tools should not be analysed in that way. They just speed you to where you should be going. Even just moving forward is destiny – which is the opposite of what we should do now. Let's have a break at the bottom of this hill.

Hopefully, there is a stream.'

'Okay. Um, Tendai, did you have a wife or a betrothed back in your home?'

'Why do you ask?'

'Just because you are a man, and men usually have wives. Well, they do in all the stories I've been told, and the men with farms close to ours do.'

'Did you have a woman in mind for me where you live?' Tendai chose not to answer the original question. His response left Boy slightly confused.

'Umm, no. I don't know of any woman free for you. It's not a city or even a town. I think I told you that.'

'No, you didn't tell me that. Be clearer next time.'

'Well, it's just remote farmland anyway.' Tendai didn't respond, and Boy chose to return to the previous subject.

'Are there many girls my age in your village or town? I might need to travel to find a wife when I am older. I won't be finding any lost in the forest.' Boy laughed. Tendai ignored the joke and remained silent for a long time before responding.

'You'll be fine, Boy. When you grow up, the girls will come to you. You're a handsome young man, and smart too. There will be plenty chasing you.'

Boy blushed.

At the bottom of the hill was a clearing where the trees thinned out and an animal trail wound through fallen trees and boulders. A small stream could be heard beyond the clearing.

'Wait here in the covers,' Tendai instructed. 'Trails and water mean strangers, people or traffic.'

Boy stayed seated on the giant beetle and watched the trees upwind for any movement. The trail was small but looked to be used, with old footprints and recently crushed grass. Tendai returned, scanning the ground for tracks as he approached.

'The trail looks used, maybe every few days. It doesn't appear to be a scouting backroad. That would be on the other side of the stream. Let's have a break, and water the mounts.'

'I'll keep an eye on the road for travellers and an ear on the wind for trouble,' Boy said.

'Good. Do that. You have great hearing.'

Boy smiled at the compliment. He took Beetie's reins and led him through the trees to drink from the stream. *I do have good hearing*, he thought. *I always have.*

It wasn't until Boy had a drink himself that he realised just how hot and exhausted he was, even after his midday sleep. He lay down on the bank and dunked his head into a small pool of water. It was so refreshing that he decided to roll his whole body straight into the stream. He lay in the shallow water looking at the sky, rocks digging into his back. He listened to the water and looked at the leaves above him, which drifted back and forth in the welcome breeze. The sound of water trickling through the rocks made him smile, and he thanked the forest for its current beauty. Eventually, his core temperature dropped to a normal state.

He didn't realise how long he had left Beetie alone and scolded himself for being selfish and not keeping an eye on him. He found Beetie not too far away, as if he were keeping a watch on Boy, and quickly walked him back to the path. He pretended to scan the surroundings for humans and beasts alike when Tendai appeared from the forest.

'All clear. No sign of anyone,' said Boy.

'Good work. Your eyes and ears are built for the forest. You can do that every time we stop from now on.' Boy didn't know whether he liked the compliment of responsibility. *I'm always on the lookout anyway*, he thought.

The path wound downhill along the valley floor, easing its way around rocks and trees close to the water. The stream chattered peacefully to the right of them. Across the valley, a clanging of pots came to them, and a man singing to himself *hum-ho the blind man and the bowl, as it were to the top, not knowing when to stop, hurried moods of your wife, will send a man out to sea, forever on the breeze.*

The man rode a small horse and had a pack pony trailing behind him. He looked to have all the possessions one would need for a life on the road. He waved as he approached Tendai.

'Hello, young man,' the old man said. His beard was cropped short and grey, and his voice sounded gnarled like the stump of a burnt tree.

'Good day, fellow traveller. My name is Tendai, and I was hoping to know where this path might lead. And possibly beyond that.'

'Well, that's an interesting question. You must be far from home then.'

'I have no home.'

'The road is mine, so I know a great many things about the paths and tracks through these forests. And beyond if that's where you are headed.'

'Well, we are looking for a large river which leads to this young boy's home. We are unaware of what direction it may be from here, except possibly south.'

'There are several large rivers that run south and out to the coast in the west. The larger ones run off the mountains and into the plains. Young man, please tell me more. I may have passed through the area in my long life on the roads.'

'We call it the River Hew. It winds through rocky outcrops, not extremely wide but very deep in some pools. There is a small cliff on the far eastern side, just near my house. The western side turns to low hills and forests between farming paddocks. We don't live near a town, but a road, where we can meet merchants, lays half a day's ride to the west. We have cold winters but never snow. We have sun through most of the year, but it can get very windy.'

'Thank you, young man. My name is Joe, but I have never set these eyes on such a place. Since I am travelling in the opposite direction, I doubt I ever will see it. Good luck to you, and good day. One last question: did you have any trouble with bandits on the path you just came from?'

'No, not bandits. We had no trouble in the forest whatsoever.'

'That's good to hear. You're lucky you weren't alone, young man,' Joe said to Boy. With a tip of his hat, he set off up the gravel path.

~

The late afternoon was still very hot in the valley, and regular water stops were necessary for all. Walking back from the stream after filling his water skin, Boy had a sour look on his face.

'How can that man not even know what I described? He sounded like he had travelled everywhere, but he didn't even know Tree Deep Trundle. He said there were other rivers. I have never seen any other like Tree Deep. He really got my hopes up. Come on, I wasn't brought up completely in the middle of nowhere. There are some other farms nearby.'

'We'll be fine, Boy. You are a smart kid, and you'll be able to spot the lay of the land. You are also a very good travel companion.'

Tendai kicked his horse to a trot. Boy was taken aback hearing another compliment; he thought he had some brains and made good decisions but didn't realise it could be seen so easily by others. *It's nice getting to talk to Tendai some more*, Boy thought.

The path became overgrown with extremely tall trees that shielded any distant view, but they soon found out the valley they were in was atop a small range. The path rose slowly to a sudden drop: not so much a cliff, but steep enough to have only one way down. The path down veered back and forth, cutting in and around vertical rock faces and tall timbers. As the steep hill petered out and the forest became clearer, a crossroad appeared in front of them. Now, this was even more confusing. What if they chose the wrong way? It would lead them even further away from Boy's home.

The sign read that they were heading towards WOOD-TOWN and they were coming from STAINBIRD. Neither of them recognised either of the names. To the left was GRASSHILL, and to the right it just said THE SEA.

'I think we should just keep going on this track,' said Tendai.

'To Wood-Town?'

'The one that's straight ahead.' Tendai trotted forward and let Boy follow in his kicked-up dust.

'I'm just going to consult Beetie!' he shouted. Tendai didn't appear to hear him, and kept moving forward.

'You know what, Beetie? I don't think he can read.'

'Chika chika,' he agreed.

Boy laid his head down on the beetle and whispered to him, attempting to gain some kind of psychic power from the giant bug. Nothing really came to him.

'Oh well. That was relaxing, but a waste of time. Let's just keep going straight.'

They camped that night not far from the crossroads, off the track and hidden without fire. Boy slept all night, without dream or interruption, waking to the chatter of birds in the morning light. Tendai was brushing his horse with an old rag he kept tied to the reins; it wasn't much, but he did it out of routine more than anything.

'What food do you have, Boy? We need to ration it out correctly. I'm used to doing this, from being on the road.'

Boy opened his bag, pulled out all the cured meat, cheese, stale bread and dried fruit, and lay it out in front of him. He knew that rationing meant life and death, and wanted to organise and discuss this as a team. Tendai silently counted the rations of cured meat, then picked up one large portion.

'What type of meat is it?' He took a large bite. 'Tastes like pork.' He placed the gnarled piece back with the others and did the same testing with the other dried fruits. He sorted it all into two piles, one clearly larger than the other. The smaller pile included the half-bitten meat.

'That's your food for the day, and this is mine.'

'Well, that's not fair. You have the larger pieces.'

'You're a smart kid, so you should know … I am obviously bigger than you, taller with more muscle, so I have to have more. I'm the soldier.'

Boy let it go, and mounted Beetie. He wanted to get to this town. They set off early with an abundance of energy and walked all morning and into the afternoon, only stopping briefly to water everyone and refill their skins.

Tendai was chatty, talking to Boy and listening intently to his answers. It was a sign that Tendai was comfortable and opening himself up; they were good friends at this point, and enjoying each other's company, without danger.

Beyond the tops of the trees, the colourful thatched roofs of the town appeared. The town sat peacefully in a valley with a good-sized river winding its way through the streets and buildings. The road became wider now they were approaching civilisation again. Farms lay on each side of the road: one stone-fruit-laden fields; the other side citrus of all descriptions in long rows. A group of chickens scattered on the road, clucking and driving their feathered party below the paddock's wooden fence. A little girl picking fruit waved to the strange travellers, and a dog barked from a newly-built barn.

The road became compact clay, hardened from traffic. As they came around a large bend, the view of the town became clearer. Above the colourful rooftops, the smoke of the town's industry hung high, dampening the natural light even with the drifting breeze. There was a large spire, probably rising from a town square, or a performance and market area. Villagers passed by without any real shock at seeing the beetle. A few young girls smiled towards Tendai with a giggle.

Boy desperately wanted to know if there was a library, or a scholar who could tell them more about the area and where they should go. He was beginning to think like Glohring, keeping a keen eye on people who may have the information he required. Before they could reach the main wall of the town, a young guard stepped out onto the road. He wore quality leather armour and held a spear that appeared more for ceremonies than battle.

'Halt in the name of the Lord Byron.'

Boy immediately disliked the arrogance in this young guard's stance and expression. He stopped Beetie quickly and didn't say a word. Tendai did the same.

'And where are you travelling from?'

'From that road. We came from the forest,' said Tendai.

'From the forest!' the guard said, huffing incredulously. 'It would do you a world of good to just lower your voice and tell me the truth.'

'We have travelled for weeks from the dangerous lands of the north. This young man is seeking his family. They have a farm which we believe to be south of here. I am his guard, and we are only passing through the town to pick up food rations and general supplies.'

'General supplies? More like poison traders. No one walks around with a beast like that. It's clear you've had dealings with a witch.'

Boy had had enough of the guard's attitude.

'Yes, you're right. This was a warrior horse from the north, but a powerful witch turned him into an insect. We took her head for her actions. We are not to be trifled with. If you have an issue, let us speak to your captain.'

The guard and Tendai both stared wide-eyed in surprise.

Boy suddenly regretted his little outburst; it had stirred the melting pot of the guard's hurt pride.

'You cheeky little vermin! Don't you make demands of me. If we weren't at the town gates, I'd give you a …'

'It was not a demand, but a mere option. You seem to be unwilling to communicate with us, after stopping us here on the free road,' Tendai cut him off mid-sentence.

The guard laid his hand on the hilt of his dagger. A tall man with a thick bushy moustache and a lion crest on his tunic marched up behind the guard and forcefully grabbed his arm.

'Garvian, what the hell do you think you are doing? Don't be a fool. We obviously have travellers to the town, and you've started a confrontation with the threat of your weapon. Your father will hear of this.'

At the sound of his father, Garvian turned pale. He took off in a hurry, yelling at another guard to replace him on duty. The man with the moustache looked Tendai and Boy up and down.

'Where have you travelled from?'

'We were asked that by the other guard. Is there a war or a dispute down this way that we are unaware of?'

'Answer the question, and I'll elaborate.'

'We have travelled from the far north, looking for young Boy's family farm. We believe it to be south of here, but these lands are unfamiliar to us.'

'Young man, how did you get so far away from your family without knowing the way back?'

'I was taken by this large flying beast. I was dropped somewhere far from my home.'

'Kidnapped then, eh? You must be from the southwest of here. It's a dangerous place along the coast, where thieves and pirates go into hiding. Sounds like your family knew some bad people.'

'Excuse me, but my family does not deal with any

criminals. And no, my farm is nowhere near the coast, as far as I can tell. We come from a peaceful area, in between a large river and a vast forest. I need to find a map in your town.' Boy was red with rage.

'I understand, young man, and please forgive my ignorance of your situation. We live in growing fear of the next attack from the pirates I have spoken of, around Port Joranup. The last we heard, the regent of the town was preparing for a siege. Other rumours say that they will be deserting the city. But where to? That's the question we have been asking ourselves. We all pray it's not in our direction, for only bad things will follow them.'

'The last thing you want is criminals taking over a port. They'll only grow richer, and you will be left with trade scraps.' Tendai shook his head.

'That is precisely right, young warrior. Now, after my assessment, I don't believe you to be spies or a threat to our Lord. You may enter the town for the next two days to gather supplies and ask about maps. Unfortunately, we are not a learned town with lore-masters and libraries. I have no use for them. But, I hope you can find something you were hoping for. And we could always do with a strong swordsman here after you have found this young boy's home. Good luck and good day.' The soldier strode away, yelling at the guards to let them pass for two days and two nights.

A sense of fear came over Boy. He did not like the sound of heading south into possible danger in unfamiliar territory.

'Tendai, I think we need to camp outside the town walls. We don't have any money for an inn.'

'There's a farm that we rode past with a sizeable shed out the back. I'm sure that, for the little money we have, the hayloft should serve us just fine. You need to start looking out for things like that, Boy.'

Boy whipped his head around to look at Tendai but stayed silent. *I did notice it.* They headed back to the farm they spoke of, where fruit trees engulfed the front paddocks, corn grew in the field, and cabbages, carrots and broccoli grew closer to the farmhouse. Tendai had a sour look on his face.

'Great,' he said sarcastically. 'With all this ripe corn, there are bound to be rats. Large ones that come out at night. I think they are the most disgusting things ever. There'd better not be any near me!'

Boy wasn't really listening; he was keen to see what type of people lived at this farm. An old woman with a straw hat and a wonderfully coloured parrot on her shoulder strolled over.

'Hello. What may I do for you and your magnificent beetle? Wow. He's a big boy, isn't he? Haven't see one like him since I was young.'

'Big boy, big boy,' said the bird.

'Oh, shut-up, Mervyn,' the old woman said to the bird.

An old man – the husband, possibly – stepped out of the house to see who the strangers were. He waited in the doorway with a grizzled scowl on his face as if it was etched in stone. *His poor wife*, Boy thought.

'My name is Tendai, and this is Boy. We are travelling through the town and were hoping for a night's sleep in the hayloft out the back. We have little money but strong backs for compensation if required.'

'No, no, that's fine. A copper each should do it. Stay a few nights if you wish. Old grumpy inside has a fine pot of rabbit stew on the fire. At sundown, I'll bring some out for you. If you could kindly return the bowls to the chest on the back porch, that would be much appreciated.'

Boy could smell the stew, the meaty scent, and the soft earthy smells of potato, carrots and rosemary. It transported him home like nothing but the sound of his parents' voices could do. He stopped his daydreaming as the woman strolled away, because he wanted something answered.

'Excuse me … um … sorry, but you said he looked like a

boy. I mean, the … errr … my beetle. How do you know it's a boy?'

'Oh, an unlearned owner of a beetle … this is a surprise. Where did you get him from?'

'I saved his life. He wasn't owned before. He was in the wild.'

The old woman looked shocked.

'Well, this just gets more interesting. I would have you know that, where I come from and when I was young, these creatures were only owned by people who were rumoured to be sorcerers, or had some unique magic of their own. You couldn't just tame a wild one.' The old woman looked at Boy closely. 'But you could have one of these rare gifts. No one really knows if it's the beetle who chooses, or the owners. You are a lucky young man. Enjoy your stay, and I'll be around if you require anything.'

'Thank you,' said Boy and Tendai in unison. Tendai scowled: he didn't like it when Boy spoke over him.

They found the large barn, which was very neat and organised. Tools and hoes hung across the left-hand side near a long repair bench. There were numerous jars filled with old blades and farming tools, all labelled and left within reach. Although the barn was large, the hayloft mezzanine was quite small.

'I'll have the hayloft. You ride the beetle all day, but I'll need a comfortable bed for all the walking I do. The beetle can't get up here anyhow,' Tendai said, climbing the ladder to the loft.

The more hours Boy and Tendai spent together, the more Boy noticed Tendai's sly intentions; it was how he decided to go about things that made him a curious subject.

~

Boy wanted to put this new behaviour down to lack of sleep, and just tried to ignore Tendai. He rolled his bed out across the hard clay beneath. He could smell the mix of old grain bags and rat droppings. *If a rat so much as runs near me in the night, I'm going to sleep on the back porch of the farmhouse,* he thought.

The sun set in a cool clear sky. Boy could feel the rats' stench clinging to his face as he sat down in his bedroll. He wanted to rip it away like cobwebs at a window. The skin across his arms began to itch in various places; each time he scratched an itch, another one would start somewhere else on his body. There was a noise at the barn door, a shuffling of dirt.

'Hello? I have a nice meal to warm up your tired bellies.'

The door opened. Boy could see the steam pouring out of the wooden bowls, but all he could smell was rat droppings. He leapt up and ran to the old farmer.

'Hungry, are we?'

'Oh, yes. I have longed for a home-cooked stew for many days. This really is a treat. Do you mind if I eat quietly on the back porch?'

'Of course I don't mind. Just don't peer into our home. I'd thank you if you didn't.'

'As you wish, good lady. Thank you.'

Boy grabbed the spoon and bowl, then quickly shuffled towards the farmhouse, trying carefully not to spill the precious stew.

By the time he reached the long timber bench on the porch, his mouth was watering in exuberant anticipation. The smell of the earthy flavours steamed into his face.

The old woman disappeared around the other side of the house, and Boy put his head down and greedily shovelled the stew into his gullet. He lifted his head for a breath of air and noticed Tendai walking towards him with his bowl of stew.

'Why are you sitting here?' he asked.

'I didn't want the smell of the barn ruining my food. It's

nice out here.'

'Well, you could have invited me to come and sit over here with you. Anyway, it's not even smelly in there. And what if it rains out here? Then what are you going to do?'

Without being too obvious, Boy looked up at the first stars of the night: *no chance of rain*. Boy was again surprised at Tendai's change of character but stayed silent. Tendai stepped past him to the patio and sat on an old chest to eat his meal. *I just want to eat alone now*, Boy thought.

That night, Boy lay down on the cold ground and could not sleep. He tried to make a soft base out of the loose straw, but it only made it lumpy. He could hear Tendai make an annoying grunting noise as Boy shuffled around; it would be a long night. His eyes burned, the stench felt coarse on the back of his throat, and his head was heavy and cloudy at once. He gave up on sleep.

~

The morning air was clear and crisp, but Boy felt dirty and ragged. He considered asking the nice farmer for a warm bath, but thought he might be pushing his luck. He decided to walk to the stream at the back of the farm, out of view of the farmhouse. After a quick cold dip in the water and a clean shirt, he felt refreshed to begin the new day. He returned to find Tendai looking through his bag and knowingly waiting for him.

'Where did you go? Found a stream, I see. You could have told me that.'

'I needed to wash the scent of grain and rat off me. I didn't have a good sleep at all.' Before Tendai could interject, he kept going. 'What are you doing going through my things?'

'You didn't tell me you had food in here. Why are you being selfish?'

'I did tell you I had some rations?'

'Why are you lying? There's food right here.'

'That's what I mean, I do have food.'

'And not to share? What are these things?' Tendai pulled out the colours balls Glohring had given Boy with a warning.

'Glohring gave them to me – they are special,' he said.

'Good, we can sell them in town for more food. That's more important.'

'We need to find someone in the town who knows the lands south of here. A scholar of some kind, or a cartographer.'

'I highly doubt a cartographer would be lodging in a small merchants' town. There are no libraries or places to study.'

'We don't know that for sure, so let's go into town and ask around. They could be fleeing the siege at the harbour town … Port Joranup, or whatever it was called.'

'Fleeing the siege? I think that defeats the purpose of a siege.'

'I mean, someone in the area, or someone who left before trouble started.'

'I highly doubt it.'

Boy realised that Tendai always needed to have the last word, no matter how contemptuous it sounded. Tendai left the barn and headed in the direction of the stream.

'Well, we'll head into town when you get back,' yelled Boy.

'We'll go when I'm ready,' said Tendai, again proving that he would have the last say on everything these days.

Close to midday, Tendai returned from the forest stream. Boy had let Beetie roam in a small paddock behind the barn where he foraged contentedly in the moist shadowed ground rich in seed, worms and grubs.

'Tendai, do you want your horse set loose in the paddock too? The fences and gate appear in good order.' Boy only really offered to make the mood more peaceful, but Tendai didn't respond. Boy closed the gate, said bye to Beetie, and headed back to the barn to grab his coin pouch. As he rummaged through his belongings, he heard a shout from Tendai.

'Boy! Come on. What are you doing? I'm waiting to go into town.'

Boy jogged out the door and found Tendai mounting his horse.

'Wait! I'm coming. Hold up.' Boy ran after him panting. Tendai turned in the saddle to watch him catch up.

At the town gates, the older soldier with the moustache was there once again. Much to Boy's delight, there was no sign of the young, arrogant guard.

'I have been waiting for your company. Did you manage to find a warm place to shelter for the night? It's very rare to have a cold night like that at this time of year. Winter is too far off.'

'We managed to stay at a farm up the road, thank you. Is there something you needed?' asked Tendai.

The guard ignored Tendai and turned to Boy.

'Well, as matter of fact, I have come into some information that may please you very much, young man. Garvian! Where are you? Get here this instant.'

The arrogant guard from the day before came strutting out from behind the town walls.

'Tell them what you told me.'

'Everything, captain?'

'Yes, of course, everything. Get on with it.'

He spoke directly to Tendai, and did not acknowledge Boy's existence.

'I have some news that may please you. A young merchant and his relative, who are lodging at the Protecto's Inn, are personal collectors and sellers of maps and cartography, amongst other things. I immediately remembered our encounter yesterday, and I told the captain. We are not just soldiers of our town, but we like to help wherever we can.'

Garvian bowed low. Boy could feel the stench of rat in his throat at the site of this man.

'Thank you for producing this information. It brings us vision of finding young Boy's family home. With any hope, we'll be leaving your wonderful town on the morrow,' said Tendai courteously.

'Stay as long as you need now.'

Boy was shocked back to reality. *I might actually be able to put a number of days on how long it will take me to get home, if this merchant has the information I require.*

'Thank you. Thank you so much,' Boy said, close to tears.

Tendai bowed to the soldiers. They turned and headed back through the town gate, disappearing down a street.

'Enough blubbering, Boy. Let's go and find this inn, and see what we can trade for these maps.'

Boy gritted his teeth and wiped away the tears.

'We are not bargaining for anything. This is my life, and I have to get home. It's not a trade deal of jewels that may or may not happen. I am getting the information my way. You aren't trading anything of mine.'

'What did you say? You disrespectful little cub! If it wasn't for me, you would have been dead out in the forest. You heard that old man's talk of bandits. You will never make it to your farm without my skills. Now, I'll do the talking and we'll get the information.' Tendai grabbed Boy tightly by the arm. 'You are coming with me.'

Boy tried to wriggle his arm free.

'No! I don't want to go anywhere with you now. Getting to my family is my mission, not yours. I don't need you.'

Tendai tightened the grip on Boy's arm. His nails began to break the skin. 'You won't bloody survive without my help. You're staying with me. Now, come! Let's find this inn and get the maps. Then we can get on the road. People are watching. Stop it now.'

In fact, no one was in the vicinity or paying obvious attention to this rabble as Boy ripped his arm from Tendai's reach and strode through the newly-built town gates. He could hear Tendai's feet right behind him, and felt the intense stare burning through his back. The townsfolk all glanced in their direction: new visitors who were not merchants … maybe refugees from the rumoured war on the coast. Boy couldn't take the intense pressure any more. He turned to Tendai.

'I'm going to be sick.'

Tendai stepped back.

'Well, don't do it on me. Filthy.'

Boy shuffled quickly to the base of a tree in between two stone buildings with freshly thatched roofs. Down on his knees, he felt like he could empty his stomach. Not out of physical illness, but disgust. Disgust at Tendai's actions, at the young guard, at people who had hunted him and Beetie. He hated them all. He hated this moment. He hated Tendai. He hated the thought of having to buy information just to get to his family. He hated the rat barn. He hated not having the choice to be alone. He hated not having control. He felt as if everything was flowing against him, and it made his stomach cramp in pain. *At least I can pretend to be ill, and maybe I'll be given some space.*

Boy looked up. Tendai was standing on the road, looking at a market stall and waiting for him. He didn't vomit, but instead brought up the acidic taste of the liquid, then swallowed it back down; the burning aftertaste of last night's stew clung to his breath for the rest of the day.

Boy accepted that he had to keep moving forward. He would ignore the annoyances around him, and find the information he needed. He stood up.

'Let's find this inn,' he said and, for once, Tendai didn't answer back. He kept an extra few strides behind for fear of himself becoming ill on the roads.

They walked through the town's twisting streets and stopped at several carts selling fruit and cured meats. Boy spent the remainder of his coin: it could well be the last place to get rations for the days ahead.

Amongst buildings and markets, they finally found the inn. It had a thatched roof with four chimneys, sending out high plumes of grey smoke. The smell of the kitchen hung over the rooftops like a lucid crown of crispy pork and burnt oak. Music and laughter filled the streets here, rather than horseshoes impacting on the cobblestones. It was surely the busiest area of town. People came and went from the large inn's busy tavern.

'Don't get lost in here,' Tendai said.

'I won't,' said Boy confidently.

Boy followed Tendai inside, where women rushed around serving ale and roast pork, and men shouted for more ale. A large barrel was rolled in through the rear door and cracked open. Tendai and Boy squeezed uncomfortably through the crowd, looking for anyone who appeared to be a merchant. Tendai found a small table with two vacant chairs in the corner, and pointed them out to Boy.

'You sit down, and don't go anywhere. I won't have you lost again. I'm going to have a look around for this merchant.'

Tendai left the table, and Boy almost felt like crying. He looked up to see strangers staring at him. People passed by with tankards of ale, and looked at Boy like he was a strange beast. He wanted to stick his leg out and trip someone up. He had reached the point where he needed to run away from being lost. *Why am I sitting here doing nothing? I am the one needing to find my way home, not Tendai. For all I know, he is going to try to sell Beetie or me. What's in it for him? I don't want him anywhere near my family anyway. I could run away, find Beetie and leave. I can reach the forests further down the hill … or I can just wait to see if this merchant has any information.*

The more Boy pondered his situation, the more he knew

running away wouldn't work. Tendai would follow them. He had some idea of tracking, especially a slow beetle. And Boy would still be as lost as they were before. A heavy-chested waitress strolled by and caught his attention. She reminded him of a younger version of his mother.

'Are you supposed to be in here? Who are you with?' she asked with a cheeky grin.

'I'm here with my bodyguard, and I'm fine. He has gone to look for a merchant.'

'Oh yes, I saw them over in the far corner. You must be important to have your own bodyguard at your age.'

'I'm not important. I'm nothing.'

She winked before moving along with her work. 'Have a good day.'

'Thank you,' Boy said, smiling. *It's amazing how the polite smile of a stranger can suddenly warm your heart.* He snapped out of his gloomy mood, sat up straight, and looked around for Tendai. He was strolling across the room with a smile on his face. *Here is a man trying to help me get back to my family. He's trying to find a map, and I feel like an ungrateful fool.*

'Boy, come with me. I have some great news.'

He jumped up, tucked his chair under the table, and followed Tendai around the corner to the far side of a room. Two middle-aged men in colourful clothes and hats occupied a table by the fire. The hearth was wide and a day's worth of morning coals glowed under a dry log. The men were clearly merchants, wearing jewellery and fancy shirts embroidered with their family emblem. On the emblem, two griffins – one gold, the other green – passed a scroll between their talons. Boy liked this. It told him of a story, a family, a history, of always being connected to your blood kin. His family didn't have an emblem, as far as he knew. He would have to ask his dad when he returned home. If they didn't, he would begin one, and perhaps Beetie could be in it.

Tendai introduced them. 'Esteemed merchants Harondi

and Peat, this is my travelling companion, Boy.'

Harondi, the elder of the two, nodded while Peat said, 'A pleasure to meet you, Master Boy. Tendai here has explained your situation to us. Quite a precarious predicament.'

'I'm going to the latrine.' Tendai stood up.

Boy watched him leave and turned to face the merchants.

'Thank you. It's a pleasure to meet you both. I come from an area of forest and farm that I cannot find. I was hoping to see if you had maps or some information about a large river with steep rocks on the eastern side. To the west is a vast forest over rolling hills. I believe it's probably to the south-east of here.'

'A notable description. Thank you, Boy,' said Peat. 'We are traders, merchants. We care not for lore or meaning but only for value. You are interested in a map. We may have that map. What do you have?' Peat's greedy eyes pierced into Boy's soul.

'May I see the map … to make sure it's the right one?'

'No, you may not. Not until a deal is done. The compensation must meet our requirements.'

'So, I won't know what I'm trading for until the deal is done?'

Harondi's eyebrows dropped, and his face looked tight.

'We will speak no more of maps. Who is this Tendai man? Is he your guard or your slave?' asked Harondi.

Boy began to breathe deeply through his nose. He looked towards the back door of the inn and saw a cloaked man leaning in the doorway.

'I would never hold a slave. No, I don't own him.'

'We won't be trading for him then. That would be terribly unfair and not part of the deal. You seem terribly keen to get home.'

Boy disliked the tone.

'I will get home, one way or another. A map would just be

quicker.'

'It's terribly dangerous out there on the roads, in the forests, dealing in strange towns. Believe me, I know. My life has been trading on these roads. I understand you want to get home to your family as quickly as possible. As a family man myself, I think it would be in your best interest to facilitate a trade of the largest map I have. It ranges to the south of here, in great detail. It's a very old map.'

'Then you must already know what you want from me. If you are willing to let go of something so old. You look desperate, Mr Harondi. I can just walk away.'

Boy leaned in close to the pair and whispered, 'You are not getting my beetle.'

Peat slammed his fist on the table.

'The map is ancient and precious. It is worth a lot more than you know. We will throw in coin, silks, and silver. Lots of silver.'

Boy didn't realise that Tendai had already negotiated the deal with Peat. Tendai was supposed to get a side deal of money, enough for a small farm, for bringing the trade to the merchants.

Unlike common folk, the merchants knew of Beetie's worth in the distant land across the sea, where only Kings and lucrative Lords could afford such coveted creatures. Tendai justified his actions to himself by thinking he was helping Boy get home, and Boy had found the beetle anyway. He thought that it was fair and everyone would win; he'd just seized the opportunity when it arose.

Boy sat in silence for as long as he could. He wanted the upper hand, and he wanted them to speak themselves into a different offer. He wasn't in control of the situation, a feeling he hated, but he thought the merchants were more eager to trade than himself. Finally, Peat needed an answer.

'So, what is your answer?'

'What was the exact question again? Worded exactly.'

'Look, kid, stop messing around! I have the scrolls you want, and we are busy.' He pulled out a handful of rolled-up paper maps and then some older deteriorated folded cloth maps. 'You can go through them and pick which maps you desire.'

'I cannot make a deal without the guarantee that they will lead me home by the shortest route.'

'You stupid kid. These maps have so much information. If you can read, you will know where you are based on your surroundings. It's easy. '

'I'm leaving. Thanks for your time.'

'Sure, you can leave. But one more thing. What about this Tendai character? When you are both lost in the remote wilderness, will he be a warrior and protect you? Why would he do it? Out of the goodness of his heart? You are a kid with a very rare creature. Tendai will now know you are taking him blindly into the wilderness, the dangerous countryside, taking him directly to danger, possibly taking him to his death, all because you didn't want to sell something you found.'

Peat knew he was making Boy think, so continued. 'What is your goal? To get home? I hold something that can get you home. But, as a trader, I cannot sell it under its worth. You should know this. I'll have my man bring Tendai in to have a chat with you.'

It became too much for Boy, who started shaking. It was clear to him that Tendai had given them all the information about Boy's story. Peat smirked.

'Leave me alone!' Boy yelled and bolted for the entrance door. He turned and ran up the stairs, entering a large upstairs theatre room. He ran to the balcony to look down onto the street. The hot wind had picked up, with dark storm clouds moving in from the west. He climbed over the balcony and reached for a tree branch. Tendai and the merchants appeared at the front of the inn. Boy launched himself off the balcony and grabbed the branch, which creaked and snapped. He fell hard on the ground, and Tendai ran up to him.

'Are you okay? I'll help you up. What's going on?' Boy shook his head at this fake display of concern.

'You are asking me what's going on?' Boy dusted himself off.

'Yes, Boy. I am asking you that.'

Boy froze as he contemplated the situation. *I'm in a corner. If I don't go along with this charade, they'll take Beetie by force. I'm outnumbered, and I don't think Tendai would try to stop them.* There was nothing else he could do; Boy put on the best acting performance of his life.

'I'd like to go inside, have a meal, and discuss the maps after all. I'm hungry.'

'Then we can get you a meal,' said Harondi.

~

After Boy had ordered his food, he spiralled into a silent pit of shame and disgust. The table now welcomed his silence. Tendai sat and spoke politely to the merchants about the trading docks off the coast, and the general demand for supplies from the harbour ships to inland markets. They did learn that the seaports were not under direct threat; it seemed that most of the fear had been fuelled by rumours. The port was their home city – they knew it well and were both confident of it staying at peace.

At least I'll get a free meal out of this mess, Boy thought. The stew and fresh bread melted in his mouth, and reminded him of home. He mopped up the gravy with the last of the bread and thought about his predicament. I have no idea how I can get Beetie out of this. *Will Tendai kill me? I don't think he would. He doesn't have the guts. That greedy little miser can go to the hogs with his new wealth, for all I care. He'd better not have already told them where Beetie is. Surely he's not that stupid. They could have stolen him while we are here. This is the end. I must escape with Beetie … with or without the maps, I don't care. I can survive.*

'May I see one of the maps please?' Boy asked, looking down at his empty plate.

Harondi considered. They had already made a deal with Tendai. The child could not refuse a trade now.

'Okay, but I will hold it on this side of the table.'

Harondi carefully unravelled the parchment map and held it open for roughly two breaths. Boy scanned the map, saw what he was looking for, and froze. *Tree Deep.* He could see a valley with a winding river and a steep range on the northern side. *That's Tree Deep.* He didn't know where he was on the map, but he could find out. He thought of his family and seeing them again. Then of Beetie, who was his only family now. He couldn't desert him, especially considering the beetle's own family had died at the hands of greedy poachers. Boy shed a tear. It was all too much, the outside world.

'Well, the young man's getting emotional. Let's go and get this creature. You can have your maps and two pouches of silver. Tendai, you can also have a pouch of coin as the facilitator,' said Peat.

'Everyone agree?' asked Harondi. They all nodded, except Boy, who they ignored.

Suddenly, the door to the inn burst open with a strong gust of wind. Dust and leaves blew through the room violently, and a man struggled to shut the door against the wind. Thunder sounded in the distance, its crack echoing along the valley and bouncing off the hills. The splitting of wood in the trees could be heard. This was no normal storm. The group rose and left by the back door, struggling to walk in the wind.

'I can't travel in this storm,' screamed Harondi. 'Where is your farm stay? We will have to find you tomorrow.'

'Out the north town gate, and I will meet you on the road outside the farm. It's not far,' yelled Tendai. A flash of lightning opened up the sky, and the thunder cracked immediately. 'It's right on top of us. We'll see you tomorrow morning. You have my word.'

'Tomorrow morning,' yelled Peat, moving back inside.

Boy and Tendai ran back to the road and headed through town. The thunder was instant and very close, and the wind moved anything that was not tied down, picking up objects from the ground and flinging them into the air. A branch cracked and fell in the middle of the road in front of them. They climbed over it and ran towards the town gate.

'What about your horse? You forgot him!' Boy yelled, worried about the poor beast tethered at the front of the inn.

'I sold him earlier, along with those stupid coloured balls you had,' Tendai said. Boy couldn't believe what he'd heard but decided to think about it later.

The afternoon sun couldn't cut through the storm clouds. The grim darkness of the sky covered the roofs and alleys and sunk the fences. The town gates were still wide open, with the guard taking shelter from the wind and debris. It took them a long time to make it back to the farm as they stopped several times at points of shelter.

They found the giant beetle sitting on the ground, using the barn as a windbreak. Boy inspected him to see if he'd been injured by the storm. Some branches had become caught up underneath him, but nothing too severe. *Good thing I took the harness off him,* Boy thanked himself.

'Beetie! Come inside the barn with me. Follow me.' he shouted. Once they were both inside, Boy shut the large door. Tendai had already lit a lantern and sat relaxing on his bedroll, high up on the loft.

'Go and sit down, Beetie. Over there in the corner.'

'Chk ch chk ch,' Beetie responded.

Tendai sat up on his knees to watch.

'He'd better not take a steaming turd in here, or you are both going outside!'

'He isn't going to.'

'How do you know that? He's going to stink this place out,

and I'm not going to be able to sleep. You're a bloody idiot. And selfish. Why do you do these things to me? You're a moron … a useless kid. You'd be dead without me. You owe me now, you useless meat bag. You and your beetle …'

Boy didn't even hear the end of the rant. He was busy grinding his teeth. He didn't want to listen. There was no point. He just wanted to sleep, to be away from everything, to escape his mind for one solitary moment. The day would not be light again, even if the storm finished soon. He focused on his breathing to calm himself down. It was time to sleep, but the air smelt of rat, dust and hay, and the wind and thunder screeched and cracked. He lay still, staring at the inside of the thatched roof.

He did not want this: he was trapped. His face burned with rage. How did it come to this? He couldn't let Beetie get sold to someone. He was not a prize to be locked up on foreign shores for entertainment. He could feel the tension in the air warming his ears. He needed space, and he needed to relieve himself. Boy got up and went to the door.

'Where are you going?' yelled Tendai.

'I'm just going.'

'You're not going anywhere. You get back down in your bed and go to sleep.'

'I need to pee.'

'I don't want to hear it. You've woken me up now. What the hell is wrong with you?'

'You weren't even asleep.'

'Yes, I was!'

'I'm going outside to pee.' Boy started to open the door, and Tendai jumped down off the loft with eyes wide like stars of control.

'You're not going anywhere. You're not leaving!'

Tendai wrenched him back inside with such force that his feet came up off the ground. Boy flew across the room and stumbled, landing against the barn wall. A hot ooze ran down the side of his face. Red covered his hand in the dim light.

Boy would later think of that moment as a dream: when you fall and there is a moment of excruciating fear, then relief as you realise you are awake. But it was not a dream. His eyes were open.

He walked towards Tendai, who he once thought a good man. 'You know you hit like a child?' Boy said.

'What did you say to me?'

'You're not deaf. You hit like my little sister. Looks like you've failed at another thing. Maybe you should try to get one thing in your life right, and then move forward from there.'

'You shut up, you ungrateful little turd! After all I have done for you, you talk to me this way. You'd be lost, starved and slaughtered without me. Now lie down, shut up, and sleep.'

'I need to pee. I'll just be a short moment.' Boy stepped to the door, but Tendai moved quickly and grabbed his arm, almost pulling it out of the socket.

'You are not leaving.'

'You can't tell me what to do. I'm going outside.' Boy pushed him away. But Tendai grabbed him hard on the shoulders, shoved him against a bag of grain, then violently stuffed handfuls of hay into Boy's mouth.

'You don't ever tell me what to do! You shut up now, or I'm leaving with your precious beetle.'

He threw Boy into the back wall of the barn and watched him curl up into a ball on the floor. Tendai then climbed up to the loft, grabbed his bedroll, and dropped it down so he could sleep at the foot of the barn door. He pulled each corner of the bedroll out so the base was meticulously flat and massaged the cushions at the end. It seemed like any other night for him; he lay down, seemingly at peace, and shut his eyes.

At the other end of the barn, Boy, exhausted and panting, picked bits of dry straw off his tongue. He had bruises on his arms, and his head throbbed. The giant beetle cowered in the corner, his legs and head tucked up inside his shell. Boy lay down in the straw and curled up into a ball. He had seen a different side to Tendai; a sniff of the merchants' money drove him to his true self. *He hates himself. He's scared and weak with no friends, and all he cares about is control.*

Boy got up, hid behind two hay bales in the back corner, and relieved himself. *Do rats hate urine? I hope so.* He lay back down and, within a few minutes, the adrenaline wore off, the stench returned, and he was asleep.

~

Boy woke up in the dark of night with a throbbing headache and a dry mouth. The rain had clearly passed, but the wind continued to blow. He placed his hands on his head and felt flakes of old blood through his hair. He combed the dried blood through his fingers and felt a fresh scab come up with a clump of hair. It burned with pain. He rolled over and fell asleep again, allowing the wound to air itself out.

He woke again with a thrust, a stab, a crush of sharp pain. He jumped up. At first he thought Tendai was stabbing his skull, then he felt little claws scratching; a rat fell off his head and scurried towards a hole in the wall. Fresh blood oozed down his face, courtesy of the rat's generosity.

Neither Beetie nor Tendai were inside the barn. Beams of the morning's first light pierced through the cracks on the eastern wall. Panicked, he ran outside. He found Tendai on the edge of the forest, throwing grass and seeds down for the giant beetle.

'I need water. I need to clean my head,' said Boy.

'By all means, go to the stream. It's flowing magnificently after the rains,' Tendai smiled.

Tendai looked happy. Boy knew that he wasn't feeding

Beetie out of the goodness of his heart. He was merely guarding him in case the merchants and their men tried anything.

Boy strolled through the wet grass to the rocky stream, which was flowing cool and fast. He dunked his head under a small waterfall, and immediately the cold water exacerbated his headache. He flinched in pain as the water hit the wound. It felt like a trench was dug into his scalp. The shock at least helped bring the focus back to his mind. He was still physically sore, but his mind was back on high alert. He decided to have a full wash, not knowing when the next wash would be.

When he was clean and back into his spare shirt, everything came back to him in a flood of emotions: fear, anger, worry, excitement, loyalty, disgrace. His mind wouldn't stop. There was no plan, but he knew that he could not leave Beetie behind. He couldn't kill anyone, and he couldn't run away and disappear with such a lumbering friend. They were smarter, they were richer, they were stronger, and they were trained. *All I have are ragged clothes and a giant beetle that everyone wants.*

'I wish I knew magic and could just make them all disappear,' Boy said to the ground.

'But magic is not real. So, keep on wishing. It's only an illusion,' Tendai said, appearing from behind a tree casually nibbling on a slab of cheese.

Boy let out a sigh of defeat and watched the ants crawl past his feet. There was nothing more to do: no reason to walk, to pack, to smell the air. He was drained and dead inside. Tendai had crushed him. Tendai had taken control. He picked up his old shirt and started his way back to the barn.

'You'd better hurry up, pack and get Beetie ready. We need to get out of here before those merchants come to trade for him. We need to be quick, and we need to be invisible today,' said Tendai, leaning casually against a thick tree. Was Boy dreaming? Had Tendai changed his mind?

Boy ran back to the barn, where he found his bedroll

tossed in the corner, covered with hay. He collected his mess, stuffed his old shirt in his bag, and ran back to Beetie. Tendai was standing in front of the beetle.

'You do what I say. Otherwise, we won't get far into those woods. They have armed guards, remember? And they are not going to be happy with you.'

Boy wasn't dreaming, but he gave up guessing the reason for this change of plan. He wanted to shut everything out and get Beetie to safety.

Boy tied his gear to the giant shell and ran back to the stream to fill his water skins. He returned to find Tendai strapping his own bedroll to Beetie.

'I'll just go and thank the old farmers for their hospitality,' said Boy.

'No! I'll do that. Just get ready. We will head straight to the top of the hill through the forest. We need a fresh view.'

'Chka Cicka Chicka,' Beetie picked up on the sense of urgency. Boy pulled the leather-bound reins and hurled himself up to the top of his shell.

Tendai walked around to the far side of the farmhouse in search of the old woman.

'Hello? Anyone there?'

He peered inside the cracks at each window, and looked out to the fields. The old man creaked the door open, and the smell of herbal tea rushed out into the morning air.

'Good sir, I thank you for your generous hospitality. The barn was comfortable enough, and the stream provided us well.'

'It's no problem at all. I don't even use that barn. I think it's haunted anyway.'

'Well, thank you very much for letting us know that now and not before. Thank you for the shelter. We are leaving now through town to meet up with merchants. Thank you for your time. Have a wonderful day.'

'It's a good day to be free,' said the confused old farmer.

Tendai jogged around the side of the house with the old man's words echoing in his head.

Boy sat high on Beetie's shell, back straight, surveying his surroundings. He was waiting under the cool air of a stripped peach tree; its unripe fruit lay strewn across the ground from the recent storm, keeping Beetie entertained.

'Let's go now!' said Tendai, slinging his bag over his shoulder. They headed straight for the stream at the rear of the farm and deeper into the brown forest.

~

The old farmer headed back inside his house. He counted the bags of grain and flour in his kitchen storeroom while his wife cleaned out the farms chicken coop.

'One more of each should be enough for winter.'

He rotated the bags to get some movement through the stock. As he lifted a bag of grain, his lower back tweaked, a sharp stab long-familiar to him. He began to spasm and fell to the ground, his head hitting the side of the door and his elbow crashing into the floorboards. He rose to his feet with a grunt and heavy breath as a knock at the door sounded through the dusty house. He answered the door, clutching his bruised elbow.

Leaning on the doorframe to support his back, he felt a warm trickle of blood running down his forehead. The merchants were taken aback by the sight of the old injured man.

'Who are you?' asked the disgruntled farmer.

'Are you okay, good farmer?' asked Peat

'Of course, of course. Now, what do you want?'

'We are merchants from the great harbour. We have been staying in your town as we do every year, and we are here to make a trade with Tendai and young Boy for the giant beetle. This is the right farm, is it not?'

'Yes, yes. I know, I know. It is the right farm.' The farmer just stood there. The two merchants looked at each other.

'So, where can we find them?'

'I don't bloody know. They left. They said they were going to meet merchants. They were heading towards the town.'

Harondi and Peat turned to speak to each other.

'We would have seen them on the road. Do you think other traders may have outbid us?'

'There's no one else trading here with that kind of coin. I would know.' They both turned back to the farmer.

'Pardon me, good farmer, but did they say exactly who they were meeting and where?'

'Nuh,' he grunted, and slammed the door in their faces.

They looked at each other in bewilderment. Harondi walked back to untie his horse, and Peat trailed behind him. They were looking to the paddocks and the forest's edge, thinking the beetle would be long-gone. They mounted their horses, took one last look around, then made their way back to the road where their team of guards waited.

'Do you think that Tendai chap had a change of heart?' asked Peat

'Well, it is very rude. You don't back out of a deal just because your wife is in a mood,' said Harondi.

'But …'

'It's a figure of speech.'

'I haven't heard it.'

'Do you get the point?'

'Yes. Well, it would have been one hell of an exercise in manpower to get that beast to the dry world anyway.'

'Yes. You win some, you lose some. That's the nature of our business.' Harondi accepted their circumstance.

'I can't help thinking of Uncle Ben's trade when we were young. Dad never saw him again after that deal. He said it made him so rich in the far lands that he was elevated to Lord status. That's probably why he never returned. Who would want to leave their castle and coin?' Peat whistled to himself.

'Castle, coin, servants … it does sound like fun. But, things would never be the same again. I would miss the long road and the work we do,' Harondi reflected.

'Well, let's put this down to a wasted morning. It's not that bad when I think of seeing the harbour soon.'

'I agree. Let's get back to the inn and pack up. We should try to make it a good distance south by the afternoon. We've had a good run, and transporting that beast would have been one hell of a task.'

The merchants regrouped at the inn with their crew and caravan.

'So, I assume they didn't show up?' enquired a guard.

'No. It's disrespectful and rude, but it's probably for the best. We will head off home now.'

'I was just wondering why Tendai would take off. Did we give away too much information about the worth of the creature? Maybe he is going to sell it himself,' Peat said, raising an eyebrow.

'If he is, it'll need to pass through the shipping port, and it won't be unseen. It could just be that his loyalty to the young Boy was more important than money. I didn't see that in his eyes, though.'

'Let's be on our way. It's been a fine trading run, bar this last mishap. We all deserve to be with our families,' said Harondi, trotting down the road and signalling the end of the conversation and the beginning of the journey home.

~

Boy and Tendai walked in silence all morning, as alert as guard dogs. They reached the top of the hill and had a good view of the range as it continued south towards the sea. The view to the west was obscured by trees.

Tendai called out for them to halt, and they had a much-needed stop to refresh themselves. They drank from a grassy-edged stream, flowing cool and clean in the heat of summer; the source could only be a spring.

'Stay here. I need to go and drop a turd. If there's any danger, just call out,' said Tendai.

After a long while, Tendai came jogging out from the trees.

'I've found a rocky outcrop higher up and can see the country to the south-east. I think we should head south, and then east.'

'Why don't we head straight east from here? We may find Tree Deep Trundle, and then we can follow the river home.'

'No, that's not a good idea. Your way will take us through open farmland and towns. I could see the smoke. Remember, we don't know how these merchants feel. If their party comes hunting, I don't think they are going to trade peacefully again. They'd take your beetle by force as punishment for the disrespect you have shown. We stick to the cover of the bush and stay out of towns. A merchant's caravan cannot bush trail it like us, eh? Do what I say from now.'

'Keep an eye out for smoke on the horizon,' said Boy.

'I'm already doing that. Don't you alert anyone to our presence. It's already bad enough that these people are hunting us.'

Boy turned to find Tendai staring at him. He held his gaze but finally broke away.

That night, they camped high on the hill to get a better view of any campfires and to stay off the road running south. At some point, they would need to cross it, and the chance of a safe crossing would come down to luck. They would have no idea how busy the road was and who might be watching. They didn't camp with a fire that evening. The summer heat was lasting through the short nights and, unless they caught fresh meat, there was no real need to light one. Boy set up camp in silence and found a flat area of hard clay to stretch out his bedroll. Without the light of a fire, or friendly company, there was no point in staying up. He lay on his back and stared at the stars. His eyes closed.

'Aren't you even going to say *goodnight?*'

'Goodnight,' said Boy.

'That's better.' Tendai had to have the last word.

Boy thought of what he wanted to say in angry response to him. He wanted to put him down, and to make him feel the way he felt. *Why can't he just be normal like he was in the beginning? Why can't he just let me be? Why the hell is he even here? I don't need his help. He has no life, and nowhere to go. He thinks he is a great man for tagging along with me, but why would he wake up each day just to put me down?*

It took Boy a long time to fall asleep. He thought about escaping: how he could get away, where he would hide … but in these thoughts he never made it home. There were too many obstacles. What about Beetie? What if it rained? What if Tendai found him? He knew that if he were ever to get away from Tendai, it would need careful planning, and not a spur-of-the-moment decision. He was too tired to plan an escape now; it would just have to wait until the next day.

~

'Wake up. It's time to get going,' said Tendai. 'Here, have some bread and cheese. There's some pickles too.' He handed Boy a small wooden board with a generous amount of food.

'Yum … pickles … thanks,' said Boy, rubbing his eyes. He wasn't quite awake, but took the board of food happily.

Tendai ignored him and started tending to Beetie.

'Where did you get all this food from?' asked Boy with a mouthful of bread.

'Where do you think?' barked Tendai.

So, this is the tone of the day. I'll have to walk on eggshells from now until I sleep. If I speak too much, I'll be told to shut up. If I offer any ideas, they'll be immediately labelled as stupid. If I don't speak at all, an insolent comment will be made about my mood.

They packed up their bags in silence. Beetie seemed to pick up on these thorny moods that hung like mist in the air. He wasn't chika-chiking as usual, which made Boy secretly worry about him.

'Before we head downhill, we should talk. We are going to have to cross the main road running south. I believe it runs to the ocean and the merchants' harbour town. They will have their men patrolling the road looking for us, and a beetle's tracks would be easy to see. They know the area well and also know that the beast will travel slowly. It's going to be a dangerous day, so do everything I tell you or we both may die. Okay, let's go this way.'

Tendai led the way: the obvious way, downhill and forwards.

They picked their way along animal trails. Rocky streams carved their way down the hillside. It was a serene area to walk through, but Boy didn't feel peaceful. His thoughts and feelings were again being pulled in every direction: anger, shame, revenge, misunderstanding, power, bitterness, and helplessness.

They arrived at a rocky outcrop with a thick forest nurtured from several springs in the area. The leaves were green and the frogs were out in the midday shade; it was that lush. Tendai held up his hand to stop. Boy pulled the beetle's reins and quickly slid down his shell to dismount. Tendai kept low, crept on his hands and knees, and leaned against the beetle.

'I'm going to scout what's ahead of us. Stay low, keep quiet and don't go anywhere.'

'Tendai, do you really think these merchants and their men are out to hunt us down?'

'Yes, Boy. The world is cruel and people are evil. You'll learn that.'

'But we didn't do anything wrong. We didn't steal from them, and we haven't harmed them.'

'Boy, these are lifelong merchants. They said that the beetle would fetch a large amount of money across the sea, enough to buy yourself a castle and claim to be a Lord. These traders live for profit; they live for money. Greed is a disease. Remember, they have servants, guards and caravans. You are a weak child, who owns a beetle, wandering lost in the woods not too far from them. Of course, they are going to do anything to find you and steal their prize.

'All they need to do is pull you off him and throw you in the bushes. Then the beetle is theirs. They win, they profit. If they regularly trade in this area, though, they wouldn't want anyone speaking out against them. They would need to get rid of any witnesses, and that includes you. They could strangle you, or crush your head with a rock. You would slowly bleed to death, then the jackals of the night would drag you away. Meanwhile, they would live like kings.'

Boy looked down at the ground.

'That's why you're lucky I am here. Now, stay here,' Tendai said.

I wasn't meant for this world. I wasn't meant to connect with other humans. I only want to be with my family and some animals, by the river on our farm. Why would people want to leave? I now know why my dad chose the farm: the isolation, the cliffs, the river, the fertile soil, the security. The more I see what the world is like, the more I understand my parents' choices. I need to get back there. I don't care about anything else.

Boy knew it wouldn't be very long before Tendai returned, out of boredom most likely.

A twig snapped behind him, and Tendai fell to the ground in the clearing. He stood up, holding his knee, and hobbled over towards Boy. 'The crap I do for you.'

'Are you alright?'

'Of course I'm not alright. Now, there are no fresh hoofprints on the road. I couldn't see any sign of anyone. If we are going to keep you and the beetle alive, we should probably cross now. We can get some coverage through the trees for the rest of the day.'

Boy untied Beetie's tether and kissed him on the head.

'Stay low, my friend. I know that's hard for you.'

'Chk chikiki,' Beetie replied.

'Shhhhhhhhh!' Tendai scowled at them

'Oh yeah, and stay as quiet as you can,' Boy whispered.

They made their way to the edge of the forest, looking out at the road. Tendai would go first, and then Boy would walk Beetie across into the green forest on the eastern side. Boy hoped that this forest would lead to Tree Deep Trundle. Crouching beside the road, Boy looked around and tapped Tendai on the shoulder.

'What? I'm going first, and you come after. Wait until I signal you to come over.'

Boy tapped Tendai again and pointed up the road. A dust plume rose into the sky in the distance; it was definitely a few people on mounts.

'They must have scouted out the beetle's tracks,' Tendai shook his head at Boy as if it were all his fault.

Tendai climbed up a nearby tree, shielding his eyes with one hand as he clung to a branch with the other.

'A caravan alright, and a few extra men on horseback I think. It must be them. They are most probably armed.'

Tendai trembled, and his voice shook. It reminded Boy of a panicked child, and Tendai couldn't hide it.

'Let's get the hell out of here. I can't fight them all off.'

Tendai jumped down from the branch and rolled his ankle on the uneven ground.

'Arrgghhh!' he screamed, and Boy ran to him.

'Should we backtrack? Go back to where we came from and hide?'

'No, just move, and quickly. Get into the forest and undercover. Find something to hide him under.'

Boy grabbed Beetie's reins.

'Chucchchuchuchchik,' sounded the beetle as he was wrenched across the road.

With no time to find wider paths, his shell scraped against the bark and he bounced off trees. They were far enough into the forest to not be seen from the road, and Boy guided Beetie around the root system of a huge, recently fallen tree. He peered over the lower bushes, thinking Tendai was right behind him.

Where did he go? Boy began to shiver, and a thousand voices started again in his head. *Tendai has left you. He hates you. You cannot protect Beetie by yourself. He is setting up a trade with them on the road. He knows where to find you. Keep going, keep running away from him. You can use fear as an excuse if he catches up. You are finally free. Why wouldn't they just kill you and sell Beetie? Tendai will kill you. Nobody cares.*

A tear ran down Boy's face, and he shook more. *What if Tendai was on his side, but he'd been caught by the merchants' men?* He decided to wait longer and see what happened. He couldn't face another verbal attack if he ran away. *I don't think Tendai would kill me; he's too much of a coward. That's probably why he left his Warband contingent because no one likes a coward.*

~

Peat and Harondi led their caravan along the south road towards their home on the coast. The harbour city was a hard-working port, with many different cultures and a steady economic climate. The city based around the harbour, with its imports and exports, was an exciting, diverse and always entertaining town.

They rode their expensive steeds out to the front of the van, and left their bodyguards – Gerard, Dawin and Watiti – to breathe their dust in the warm afternoon. Their servant, Silvern, drove the van and was responsible for cleaning and food throughout the long tours of trade across the country. He was always paid well, and the term 'servant' did not sit comfortably with him. He was a long-time friend and worked with them as a team, but his duties labelled him a servant. He looked after them, like the mother of the group, although he would never say that aloud.

They were only a four-day ride from their city and, as they were crossing into their province, it was safe and familiar country. Rumours of their city becoming infiltrated with violence were laughable to them – anyone who lived there knew the overlord would stamp out unruly behaviour instantly. The guards had considered riding with no armour and no iron weaponry for the last few days.

Gerard rode up to Harondi. 'Sir Harondi, would you allow us to lighten by stripping to minimal weight for the last few days … for the horses and ourselves? We are within our borders and quite safe.'

'Gerard, you ask me this every time we are four days from home, so I knew it was coming. But no, not this time. We've been lucky in the past. However, if we did this every time whilst being watched by bandits, it would not turn out very pleasantly.'

Gerard nodded and stroked the coarse hair of his gelding.

'Oh, don't give me that sour look. You are a man of the sword and should know full-well the reasons for your work. I pay you well. Unless you want to take a pay cut for the lighter travelling, then don't ask again. I will let you know when you can strip down. Don't do it any sooner.'

Harondi stuck his stubborn chin up in the air, and Gerard retreated to his position without another word.

'You can be damn near mean sometimes, Haro,' said Peat.

'If you let your guard down for too long or too soon, something will happen. I can be fair and open-minded in trade, but not when it comes to safety.'

'I know. It's better to be cautious, even when we are nearly in our homelands.'

'To be sure that you are safe is better than being unsure if you are safe. I know we have done it in the past, but not this time. Our men have been brilliant. I couldn't have asked for a better job once again on this tour, and I will let them know when it's time.'

'I agree. All the men on this trip have done a marvellous job, and I consider them all my friends.'

'Don't let personal emotions get in the way of business, Peat. We were not brought up that way, and neither was Gerard. Hard work is number one. Focus on the job until it has been completed. I don't want to hear another word about this.'

'That's fine. I'm done with it anyway. I'm more thinking about a nice home-cooked meal.'

'You're thinking more about young Sarah and taking her home.'

Peat smirked.

'Can she cook? She must be able to cook. Otherwise, you shouldn't be marrying her.'

'Of course she can cook. She can cook very well,' Peat said confidently.

'Good, good. What has she cooked for you?'

'Well, for her family and myself a guest, she cooked us a spiced venison with stewed beetroot and cabbage.'

'No potatoes? No dumplings?'

'Well, ummm no, but it was still very tasty.'

'How are you meant to mop up the sauce? It's a stew.'

'We had some crusty bread, fired twice, and drowned in cows' butter. Sounds good now, doesn't it?'

'Oh yes,' Harondi rubbed his belly. 'And what are the plans for you two as a married couple, when we have to work away for weeks? Can she look after your land without a servant?'

'Oh yes, of course. Her family are very self-sufficient. No

big house with maids and cooks. She will clean the house, tend the vegetable gardens, see to the chickens and fish, as well as all the other chores.'

'May I ask why she needs to tend to the fish? They live in a dam. Just leave them be until you need them.'

'The dam isn't big enough to just let them be. If they spawn too many or the water turns green, it can cause problems and then we will have no fish.'

'You can always have her walk down to one of the jetties and buy some. Nothing like the fresh catch of the day.'

'I prefer fresh water and a bit of hard work. I don't need to waste my money. I would rather save it.'

'What are you saving for?'

Harondi had taught Peat from a young child all there is to know about being a merchant and the trading industry. He was like an uncle to him, although they were actually more like second cousins in their family tree. Harondi hadn't considered that there would be any change in how they worked the trading business together for decades. He was stubborn like that.

'Well, maybe someday, long into the future, we might want to move to more land. Sarah may want to start something of her own, like an arts and crafts hut.'

'Crafting! That's never going to make you any money. Better off raising bovine if you want land.'

Peat just nodded. He wasn't going to tell Harondi yet that he was saving for his own caravan. He wanted to have his own merchant trade route. He would never cross over or trade where Harondi had always gone, but he was sure that wouldn't be enough to appease him.

They continued in silence until the sun began to set.

'Peat, what have you done to me? All this talk about stew. I'm goddammed hungry now. I think we will stop early and send Gerard out to stick a deer. I think I'll even open one of those bottles of northern red we have in the back. I never really did toast your engagement.'

'Well, you've been very busy. That's very thoughtful of you and eagerly accepted. I'll tell the men to get a fire going and start making a coal pit.'

'Good. And you can give Gerard and the men the good news. They can strip down, and tonight we celebrate you and Sarah. We'll toast your healthy fish, your savings, and your crafts!'

Peat smiled. Turning in his saddle, he signalled the caravan to halt, and jumped down from his horse. Here was as good a place as any to stop.

~

The caravan came into view and was soon to approach the thin section of the road. Footprints could be seen embedded within the clay on this part of the road: two people and some kind of weird creature. The trouble with the path they had crossed was the dryness of the ground, and Tendai knew their tracks were a beacon screaming the way to find them. He did not know that the caravan would stop to make camp just before reaching the unique tracks stamped in the soft clay.

Tendai crouched low behind a thick area of lush reeds. He watched as the two horses on the distant road came closer. The caravan followed, then the guards choking on the dust. He breathed deep into his lungs, the dry dust that floated on the breeze reminding him of his usual riding position at the rear of the troop.

He watched nervously as they slowly approached, and began to shiver. He'd never been hunted; he'd never even been in a real battle. Mentally, he did not know how to cope. He felt like a sailor being swept overboard and remembered the tales he'd heard when he was young, of men falling into the ocean and the waves taking them – all they could do was wait and count down the seconds until they died. *Hurry up, you bastards. Let's get on with this.*

Tendai wondered if he could bargain with them but realised he'd had his one chance and lost it. *They are here to take revenge. Why else would they have tracked us all this way? They should be heading north in the summer. Traders always stick to their routes. That cursed beetle has brought about my death.*

Tendai would never know that they were on their usual route, and one day ahead of schedule, returning to their loving homes.

~

Boy had had enough of hiding. He secured his pack tightly to his back, reached for Beetie's reins, and slowly stood up, scared to look. He couldn't see any people, but he knew he couldn't flee if they were close. They would see or hear him straightaway.

A branch cracked in front of the giant log. Boy slowly placed the reins on the ground and looked underneath. A set of boots were on the other side, but he didn't know if they were Tendai's. He couldn't remember what boots he wore. Hands, silently placed on the ground, appeared, followed by knees. Tendai whispered to him.

'They're here. Don't run away. Untie my bow and quiver from Beetie's back.'

Boy crawled around the back of the hole, removed a few branches placed on top of Beetie, and began to untie Tendai's things. A poorly-packed ceramic mug fell out of his bag, shattering on a rock. Boy felt Tendai's hand on his shoulder, pushing him to the ground. He was wrenched around onto his back with Tendai looking down on him.

'That's your noise! And why would you break my things?'

'Sorry, it was an accident,' Boy whispered, lying vulnerable on his back. 'Are the guards armed and ready to get us?'

'It appears so.'

Tendai crawled on his hands and his knees back in the direction he'd come from. He shook visibly.

~

Gerard dumped his armour and flat steel blade on the ground and found a nice flat spot to roll out his bed for later that evening. Silvern helped the fire along by blowing a full chest of air to fuel the flame. Peat stood close, poking the beginnings of the coals. Gerard joined them at the fire, and patted Peat on the back.

'Thank you. Our backs are starting to feel the weight in our old age. Was it another quiet word to sway his mind?' asked Gerard.

'You know how he's always been stubborn but logical.'

'I understand, and I thank you again. But it's quite early in the afternoon to stop. Is it just to give us a rest? I don't want him thinking we are getting lazy or complaining. We all need this job, and we all like it. We can't go working on the docks to feed our families.'

'Hush hush, it's nothing like that. We started talking about my betrothed, Sarah, and her spiced venison.'

'She spices deer! What, in the forest?'

'What? No! When she's cooking. Anyway, Harondi and I both had thoughts of a lovely charcoal venison. We could taste it, we could smell it, and that's what changed his mind, I think. And more good news. He's going to open some of the wine we have from the northern hills. But first, we need this venison,' Peat winked.

'Yes, sir. Leave that to me. This is good hunting country. I shouldn't be too long.'

'Take this horn, and sound it when you've got the catch. I'll get the other men to come and help carry it back. Better to not blow out the old back, eh?'

'Well, I certainly don't want to injure it before I can see the wife,' he laughed.

Gerard grabbed his bow and large hunting knife. He used the knife not only to end a beast's life but also to throw. He was better with the steel than the bow. He wasn't too bad at hunting but didn't have anywhere near the skill of the people from the northern forests; everything they ate came from the ground and from the bow. Gerard's culture was more comfortable with nets and rods in the sea, but he enjoyed all forms of hunting and gathering.

The forest trees swayed in the light winds. He scanned the ground looking for deer droppings, tracks, or maybe a clump of fur caught on ragged bark. He pointed his nose skyward, and smelt the air. Something moved behind him.

'Gerard,' whispered a bush. It was Watiti. He was a young man, a rebellious type who was always quick with an objection. But, in his heart, a good man with moral tools from a good family. He was the newest to the merchant industry as a travelling guard.

'Which way are you going? After today's long ride, I need to lay down a huge steamer. I'm going to go that way, so just don't shoot me. This turd's been nagging at me all day.'

'Stay downwind. No one wants to smell your festering after-meals. I need to do exactly the same thing, and I'm heading in that direction.'

~

Tendai sat waiting in the reeds of a weak spring. The ground was damp and his bum was muddy. He watched the men and horses from a distance, unable to make out who was who, but he knew why they had stopped. He smelt the faintest of smoke on the air. *They are going to burn us alive. I don't want to smell myself burn … although they won't want to burn their prize beetle. They'll only burn the men. I can stay covered behind his shell, and maybe I won't be harmed.*

Tendai watched from afar as shapes began to move from their camp and into the forest. A man passed behind the tree trunks, then a second man appeared and they chatted. Tendai imagined there were more of them – many more – and they probably had him surrounded. He breathed heavily through his nose; it was too loud for his own patience and betrayed his focus. He watched and tracked the first man heading towards him, but the other man vanished. Tendai began scuttling sideways like a crab, with his sight fixed on the dark figure. The hunter was moving, shoulders bent, creeping slowly. He held a bow in his left hand and, in his right, an arrow notched and ready to pull. The birds above went silent and watched Tendai move in the direction of a large shell hidden by covered branches.

Boy lay in his dirt bunker, hidden by the giant fallen tree, with his head close to the ground. He couldn't see much, so had to trust his hearing. The giant beetle lay hidden under branches and foliage behind him. He seemed to be doing exactly as Boy had asked: staying very still and not chattering.

A footprint crunched through the bracken on the other side of the tree, and a man cleared his throat. From Boy's hiding place, all he could see was a pair of boots. A bow and arrow dropped next to the man's feet. A buckle sounded, and some horsehair-covered pants fell to the ground. The man's knees bent, and his white bum dropped into view.

The man groaned and sighed in relief. He cleaned himself with some dry leafy foliage while Boy held his breath and closed his eyes.

When Boy opened his eyes again, the boots were heading away from him. Suddenly, the man shrieked and fell to the ground, into the warm faeces. A liquid gurgling noise expelled from his body; an arrow had pierced through his neck, and a pool of blood was forming around him. His glassy eyes caught sight of Boy, and he reached out his hand in a last desperate attempt for help.

Boy crawled away towards Beetie. He could still hear the gurgling and twitching of the struggling man behind him.

When he stood up, he witnessed his worst nightmare right in front of him. Tendai stood over the man, holding a large rock above his head. He slammed it downward. Chunks of meat and bone were shattered, and the red pool spread. Boy would have to live with this sight for the rest of his life; he could never unsee that man on the forest floor. Out of all the things that Tendai had done, this was what Boy hated the most.

'Come on! We have to go,' Tendai said, grabbing Boy's arm. Warm blood ran from Tendai's hands onto his own. 'Stay quiet, and move fast. There's more of them. Grab the bug.'

In shock, Boy found it hard to breathe. He held Beetie's reins and ran panting through the forest. The wind picked up, and the smell of smoke blew their way.

'Hurry up, or we'll be burnt alive.'

'What?' yelled Boy.

'Get out! Get out! Just run! The forest … they are going to burn us alive!' Tendai screamed.

Tendai overtook the slower duo, and Boy never saw him look back. He wasn't surprised.

The forest became sparse and the ground rocky. Boy stumbled in exhaustion and his legs gave way. He held the reins tight to break his fall, almost pulling the beetle straight on top of him. The massive beast looked concerned at his fallen friend.

'Chika chiki.'

'I'm okay. I'm okay, Beetie. Come on. I can't see anyone in the trees, but that doesn't mean they aren't after us. Quickly now. We are warriors, Beetie.'

They gained height and turned back for a glimpse of the view. There was no large forest fire and no evident threat; Boy could just see the faint glow of a small campfire far, far away. As he reached the top of the hill, he found Tendai sitting on a log eating a handful of berries.

The sun was setting, and they had run all afternoon, but they decided to carry on through the night. There wasn't any cover to be seen – no rocks or large trees, no thick bush, no gullies or valleys – and the ground became flat. It would be close to a full moon that night, and Tendai wanted to sleep hidden in the shadows. Boy agreed with him.

They searched long in the darkness for a place to hide, to pass out in the dirt and hope to hell no one found them. They walked under the moonlight for close to an hour, but nothing was found on this flat sparse hill. Out of sheer need for sleep, they gave up locating their perfect shelter, dumped their gear at the base of a desiccated tree, flung open their bedrolls, closed their eyes, and collapsed.

~

Boy woke to the hot sun beaming down on his sore body. A puddle of sweat pooled in the small of his back. The giant beetle lay close to him, the shadow of his shell not far from where he lay but not offering him any shade. His tongue peeled away from the roof of his mouth like sandpaper. He reached into his bag and threw back his neck to find the water skin was all but empty; he hadn't realised how much he had drunk the previous night. It was all a blur after the sun had set. He rose slowly and packed up his camp, pushing through the stiff pain of his aching body.

Tendai woke and began doing the same. They could survey the land much better in broad daylight. It appeared the previous night that it was flat ground, but it was clear they were coming to the end of the tabletop. Boy pointed out the vast valley to Tendai.

'Look ahead. Another valley and a steep hill to the east. We should head there and attempt to scale that ridge. I know we have been heading slightly southeast, but that's not where my family are. It's further east. I'm trusting my gut on this one. I also need water badly, so we have to head downhill.'

Tendai pretended he wasn't listening. He packed his

bedroll and threw it towards the beetle.

'Sling that onto the beetle. I'm too sore to carry it today.'

Boy strapped it next to his damp, smelly blankets. Tendai drank from his plentiful water skin and placed it back in his bag.

'Well, we must have covered a good distance from those soldiers last night. But they're not going to give up now. Let's go. We shall head straight down this hill and into the valley. We can lose them in the forest,' proclaimed Tendai, marching forward.

Boy's joints ached more the more he moved. He slowly climbed up on to Beetie and rode him forward, following Tendai's tracks. The hill sloped downwards and larger trees began to appear again. Tendai obviously wanted them to follow his path quickly, but it was slow and difficult with Beetie. They cut through low bushes, in between large tree trunks, and annoyingly close to thorn bushes. Progress was slow.

Boy kept thinking of the man who'd died. The crack of the rock and the sound of his skull collapsing echoed through his mind, playing on a loop all day. He tried to ignore it but could not.

The day brought no wind, but many flies and thirst. Boy's eyes hurt from the sun, his neck was burnt, and his lips were blistered. There was no more water in his skin, and he didn't want to ask Tendai. He would prefer to die of thirst. Boy guessed Tendai was probably still shocked about yesterday or just scared that he would be hunted down.

They both noticed what looked like a small stone wall ahead of them. They approached it and saw it was an enclosed stone wall around a deep hole, about the width of the beetle. It was filled with water, but not from a natural spring. The stagnant liquid sat calmly in the heat, layered with a thin film across the surface.

'I don't think you should fill your skin up with that. Not

unless the pool is extremely deep.'

Tendai grabbed the longest stick he could find, snapped the twigs off the side, and leaned over the wall. Boy looked at his reflection and barely recognised his dirty dry face. He leaned in close to the water to inspect his red and tired skin. Tendai's stick hit something under the surface, which he forced further down.

'I just pushed a load of stuff down under the water. It's not fresh at all, or deep enough to be okay. It's pretty disgusting.'

Boy's reflection rippled. Suddenly, the rotting face of a dead deer surfaced from the water. He shrieked and fell backwards into the dirt. The swollen carcass bobbed semi-submerged in the water. Tendai prodded its mushiness, and the stab of the stick pierced the skin. The carcass let out a long squeal of festering air, and the smell of rotting flesh in the heat was unbearable.

'I told you it wasn't any good. Lucky you didn't drink from it. That deer must have fallen in and drowned. Let's get out of here.' Tendai laughed and threw the stick away.

The sound of a hunting horn echoed in the distance. It blew three times, each time longer and louder than before, sending a shiver down Boy's spine. Tendai turned and ran. Boy had no idea if Tendai saw someone, or knew exactly what that horn meant. He had never heard it in his life.

'Go, Beetie! Follow Tendai!'

Beetie picked up the pace a little but was still picking his way along the ground. Boy knocked the reins and kicked him on the side of his shell. 'Faster! Just a bit faster, or we'll lose Tendai.'

Beetie appeared to understand, and they picked a fast path down the sloping hill. Boy ducked under branches that raked the top of his head. They were trying their hardest to catch up with Tendai. Boy imagined arrows piercing his back each time they had to slow down. He couldn't see Tendai's tracks any more, and he felt Beetie slowing down. He hoped Tendai would wait for them but knew he would be angry. It was a proper forest now, lower in the hill, and the shade grew long and full. Without the wind, it was humid and hot under the canopy. Boy kicked Beetie back into a trot as they chased for safety and water. Tendai could no longer be seen, so they had to guess the path. Nothing was evident behind him, and the horn hadn't sounded again.

~

Tendai found a fresh spring at the base of a tree, and sat on the ground, panting for breath. Sweat beaded across his forehead, which he washed away with the cool earthy water before dunking his face deep into the spring. He had drunk a full skin of water and filled it up again by the time Boy caught up with him. Tendai filled his other spares with water and stored them away, while Boy sat silently, dying of thirst, waiting for his turn. Finally, Boy dropped his face into the water and sucked up as much fresh, cool, clear water as he could.

'We need to hunt today. We are out of rations. I only have half a carrot left,' said Tendai.

Boy knew they needed a good meal, but the sound of the horn returned to his mind.

'What was that horn? How far off do you think they were?'

'They were pretty far away, but I know they will be coming after us. They're going to want to steal the beetle and take revenge on you.'

'On me? I didn't do anything to them.'

'What did you say? You know what you did. First, you tried to get out of the deal you made with these merchant dogs by running away …'

'I didn't …'

'Then you make all that noise in the forest. You weren't even hiding properly. That man was about to kill you. I had to save your life. If you had hidden like I told you, nothing would have happened. It's your fault he's dead, and it's your fault we're being hunted. You're useless. You can hunt for food tonight. I'm sick of providing for the both of us.'

Boy let him have the last word. He was getting good at keeping quiet.

~

Silvern finished loading Gerard's wrapped-up corpse, his body still leaking liquid. Guards were often buried on the side of the road with a small rock shrine, but Harondi had known Gerard's parents since he was a teenager. He could not let them, in their older years, travel out here when they wanted to spend time near their son.

'Get the rest of the gear packed up. Dawin and Watiti know where to find us,' said Harondi. Peat had never seen such a blank look in Harondi's eyes. He looked as if a fire had taken his caravan full of stock.

'Don't you want to give them more time? They may come back with their heads, and then we can take that beast,' said Peat.

'I have no more interest. I am appalled and angry at this abhorrent act, but we will let the master of arms know. It's their place of work, not ours. Gerard was a working man.'

'Understood.'

In their harbour town's culture, harsher penalties were put to people who commit a crime against a working man: the type of man that would contribute to the society, the docks, and the heart and soul of the town. If a man like this was to suddenly lose his life without fair reason, the full force of the law would hit the perpetrator hard. The criminal, once charged, would have the harshest penalty and usually have to work for years to earn compensation for the victim's family. This law was obeyed and supported by all, and the townsfolk knew it was to protect them.

The faint sound of the horn echoed in the distance – three long sounds – and Peat's head pricked up.

'Did you hear that? They must have them. Sweet revenge for Gerard. You can rest now,' Peat smiled.

'This isn't a time to smile. That's not a victory horn. It's to say they are returning safely, but with nothing. Three long strikes of the horn,' said Harondi. 'You know, there are many different horn calls in warfare. Different tones, notes, and lengths of repetition. The horns vary wherever you are in the world, but the meaning usually stays the same to those trained in their call.'

Harondi went quiet and mounted his horse. His voice was flat and lifeless, like the wind was blowing into his mouth and gathering words just for the sake of it. Peat decided to leave it at that. He let Harondi lead out front alone and rode alongside Silvern and the caravan.

~

Dawin and Watiti led their horses through the forest, picking their way back along their own tracks. They had both respected Gerard immensely. He was the one who had first brought the work to them. They owed him a great debt for starting their employment in the protection business. They would now need to start making their own contacts and find their own work. Dawin and Watiti had slowly become friends, even though they were not alike in anything but hard work ethic and respect for their employer. They reached the road and found the fire, which had recently been washed out with water. It was a short canter before they caught up with the others on the road.

'Did you find them?'

'I'm sorry, Peat. We only found tracks.'

'They just murdered him and ran. Cowards!' Peat spat on the ground.

'Any evidence that we can take to the master of arms? Did you find anything? Weaponry, clothing?'

'No, they didn't leave anything behind. I don't think they knew the forest well from the way the tracks developed.'

'Dawin's right. I had a good look at the tracks. These were not forest men or skilled warriors. One was a man and the other a child. The other strange track was something I'd never seen before.'

'A man, a boy and a giant beetle. Gerard was pierced with an arrow and his head crushed with a rock. If it was those three, it's clear which one of them did it. We will give this evidence to the courts, and the master of arms can take it from here.' Peat felt they'd had a minor win at least, but he would leave this information until later to tell Harondi.

~

Boy set up camp for the night, pushing through the aches and pains. Ahead, the last of the day's hot sun shone gold at the top of the large hill which they would climb tomorrow. Boy busily collected wood, but every few moments he glanced to the horizon as clouds slowly faded from gold to pink to purple: one of the rare beautiful moments in the downward spiral of his life. The moment was over when Tendai returned to camp.

'What are you doing? Leave that. Go and hunt. We need dinner, and you are losing the light.' He kicked the gathered sticks across Boy's bedroll.

'I don't have anything to hunt with.'

'Why do you think everything is so difficult? Is it because you like to complain? There's nothing in your life that's difficult.'

'Listening to you is difficult.'

'Why? Because you don't have the intelligence to understand what I am talking about? You're not as smart as I once believed.'

'Well, I've never thought you intelligent.'

'You're just a child. You don't even know what real life is yet. Now go and hunt – go and learn something.'

'I told you, I don't have anything to hunt with.'

'Figure it out,' yelled Tendai and stormed off into the trees.

Boy gathered various things from his bag, including his small knife, and jogged away into the forest. If only Beetie wasn't so slow. He began to dream again about running away – it was the best option he could think of – but the dreams never lasted long. He had to think about his stomach and how to fill it. *There must be a river or water collecting at the base of that hill.*

He began to run at a slow pace, a burst of energy that came from nowhere, brushing through long spiky branches and thick bushes towards the sound of a bubbling brook. It ran fresh, twisting through smooth rocks then gathered itself to a calm and sheltered pool. A very tranquil place in the darkening day. Boy found a young, healthy sapling and stripped the small shoots clean off the bark. He sharpened the end till it became a reasonably good spear. Boy found an old log nearby and kicked it over with his foot; underneath, the moist soil teemed with grubs and insects. Boy gathered a handful: white and brown grubs, black and pink worms, spiders, and finally a centipede. He placed a few of them on a rock, cut them up into smaller pieces, then tossed them into the water. Then he waited with his spear held ready. In the shadows, the water may as well have been squid ink. Boy couldn't see anything, but when the surface finally splashed, he thrust the spear into the water then pulled it out of the black water. A striped perch writhed on the stick, thick, fleshy, and enough meat for two. In the last of the dying light, he knelt on a flat rock and cleaned out the fish. Then he made a nice little square rack that the fish could sit on over the coals. *Tendai will have to be impressed with this. It should keep him happy for a while. And at least we get to eat, which is all that matters right now.*

Tendai relaxed by the fire, feeding twigs into the flames, while curious creatures of the night looked on from their branches above. Boy's footsteps sounded from the bushes, moving closer, but Tendai didn't turn to look at him. Boy dumped his bag next to his belongings and began to rake out the coals, preparing the makeshift grill. The fish was placed over the coals, and a few of the dried herbs from Glohring were sprinkled over the flesh. Tendai watched and didn't say a thing. They both sat still in silence, staring at the fish over the fire. The aroma soon filled the camp. It smelt like magic. When it was ready, Boy plunged his knife into the fish, breaking easily through the skin as steam burst forth. The sweet taste of fresh fish, with an after taste of smoky charcoal, melted in Boy's mouth. It was the most delicious thing he had ever eaten. Tendai cut a large slice of cheese, which he had kept hidden, and handed it to Boy. By the end of the meal, not one word had been said.

Boy kept rubbing his tongue on the top of his burnt mouth. His belly full, he burped aloud, the echo of the meal returning the welcome flavour to his tastebuds. Then he lay on his back, pulled his blanket over his legs, and fell straight to sleep. He dreamt of wolves and moving bushes that night. When he woke, he did not know how early or late it was. He packed up his things and noticed the leftover fish was gone. *Maybe Tendai wanted to gnaw the remains for breakfast, and I wouldn't blame him.* Boy walked down to the rocky pool again and found Tendai washing his face and filling his water skins.

'Hello, chef. Your great cooking must have affected my sleep for the better,' said Tendai.

'Good morning. Did you sleep well then?'

'Yeah, it was fine. Did you notice the fish was taken in the night?'

'Taken? I thought you'd disposed of it.'

'No, I certainly didn't. I woke up to see it was gone. Probably a jackal or something scavenging around. The smell would have lingered in this valley for a while.'

'But I didn't see any tracks. Maybe it was a bird.'

'A bird? Taking the fish? Don't be so daft. Hurry up down here. I want to set off straight away to get over this hill.'

Tendai strode off towards the camp, and Boy washed himself at the pool. He filled his water skin in no particular hurry and looked around for a creature that could have stolen his fish. His mind jumped and he remembered the wolf on the cliffs – one of the rare creatures he could communicate with. Maybe he did have a special link with certain living things, but that had not been a good interaction. He shivered, remembering the sound of its oily voice, and ran back to the camp. He had a bad feeling about the shadow of this hill and about the wolf who occupied his dreams at night. He strapped his belongings to Beetie's shell and gave him some herbs picked from the riverbank.

'Chicica,' Beetie thanked him.

They set off on the daunting task of climbing the hill that loomed steep to the east. As far as they knew, they did not need to reach the summit, only some part of the southern lower ridge, enough to give them a good view of the layout of the land.

Boy felt the uneasy sensation that something was watching him. The red eyes of the wolf kept appearing in the trees, then instantly disappearing when he looked straight at them. A voice was on the wind, and the hair began to stand up on his head. The giant beetle also seemed to feel his tension, making horrible chirping noises, skittering his feet, and turning his head to look around. Tendai was also uneasy. There was something happening on this hill they were not accustomed to. They both walked on silently in cold dread. Something thick in the air penetrated their minds. Close to midday, Tendai put up his hand to halt.

'We'll cross the river here then rest for a while. The water looks shallow, and that side of the bank isn't very steep at all. If anyone travelled through here regularly, this is where they would cross.'

'What if a predator wants his dinner? Where does he go? He goes where the prey will most certainly go,' Boy whispered to himself.

Tendai crossed the river. 'Yes, I have found the most

perfect place: a safe crossing and a safe way over the hill. Look, the bush isn't even that thick. A perfect path through,' Tendai shouted.

'Glohring once told me that river crossings are ill-omened places. We shouldn't stop,' Boy shouted back, desperately hoping Tendai wouldn't demand to halt, just to oppose his suggestion.

Boy slid down Beetie's shell and started to cross the water, pulling Beetie's reins behind him. They waded through the fresh water and into the thick bushes that lined the riverbank. For once, Tendai seemed to have listened to him; he hadn't stopped to rest and was nowhere to be seen. Boy started up the hill, following Tendai's footprints.

Further up the hill, to their left, was a dark cave: a lair. The beetle stopped chirping and began to flicker his tentacles back and forth. Boy tugged hard on the reins, causing his foothold to slip on the sloping gravel. He thought he saw a red glow coming from the cave, but when he looked directly at the dark entrance, it was gone. He knew in his mind eyes were fixed on him. He knew it, and Beetie seemed to know it. They moved past the black hole opening, fearing the owner. Boy tried walking uphill backwards, pulling hard on the reins, ensuring his back was not to the cave, in case something moved out of the darkness. It felt a long time passed dragging themselves away from the river, but they had made a decent amount of ground. Soon, the entrance to the cave was no longer seen. Beetie settled his twitching and went back to a quiet nervous chirp.

Boy knew then that the wolf had visited them in the night and stolen the fish. *But why not take us in the night? Or why didn't it eat Beetie? Maybe it was because of Beetie that it didn't eat us … could it be scared of him?* The wolf didn't leave Boy's mind all day, but the fear receded, replaced by wonder, curiosity and mystery. *What is this thing to me?* It was nice to have something to ponder besides Tendai's moods.

The path grew less steep, but it was teasing them. Every time it seemed they had reached the ridge, a higher point loomed in the distance. Boy began to keep a lookout for large rocky outcrops or a climbable tree, anything to get an elevated view of the land. He needed to know where they were.

He felt exhausted. His knees hurt. His hip joints hurt. He needed oiling for his creaky limbs; he needed a bath; and he needed his mother. He had battled a long mental fight, but now his body was losing control. He felt weak, and that his body was about to give up. He was going to die, on a hill, in a forest, with rocks all around him, not many birds, and possibly a red-eyed wolf.

'I have to rest. I have to,' panted Boy. He stumbled and collapsed on his side and lay there, breathing weakly. 'Let me rest, let me rest.' He closed his eyes and let his body burn on the hot ground. The air was dry, and the slight wind was hot. Tendai flicked the pack off his shoulder and took a long slug of water. He moved slowly towards Boy, opened his water skin, and poured it into Boy's mouth and over his face. The warm wind began to blow, and the cool water that clung to Boy's forehead quickly evaporated. At the edge of Boy's blurred vision, something dark moved fast from tree to tree, then stopped behind a bush. He gathered some strength to sit up, fearing he was becoming delirious and seeing visions. While his body had stopped, his mind sprinted out of control.

Is something stalking us? I think so, but I am always wrong. Why has everything else gone so wrong? What if I caused everything to go wrong? Maybe it's a curse. Maybe I was cursed by a witch when I was young. Why did mum and dad deserve that? They don't deserve anything bad. I love them. I want to grow old, and I want to be like them.

'What are your parents like, Tendai?' he whispered from a dry mouth.

Tendai seemed too tired and disconnected to care about hiding his past any longer.

'I don't know about my real father,' he said. 'I never met

him, and I never heard about him. Mother never talked about him. She was useless. She had so many different jobs in different towns, but she would always leave with some excuse. She didn't really try. I think she was waiting for someone to take care of her. I just wanted to leave and be a wandering warrior, with battle glory and bards' songs told of me forever.'

'Let's just stay here,' Boy said.

'It's only mid-afternoon,' Tendai said. He suddenly had a burst of energy. 'Get up, come on. Let's go, let's walk. We'll find the top of this damn hill and camp on the other side.'

Boy wrenched himself to his feet. He wondered if he could lie stomach-down on Beetie and just ride him up the hill, but he didn't even have the energy to climb up onto his shell. He forced himself to pick up Beetie's reins and follow Tendai upward. They moved slowly for several more hours, into the late afternoon, until they reached the peak and could view the forest on the other side. Something manmade stood out beyond the tree trunks: an old fort with a wooden climbing tower, possibly an outpost for viewing approaching fires and armies. It clearly hadn't been maintained for hundreds of years. As exhausted as he was, Boy knew he had to climb the decrepit and dangerous tower. He had to see to the horizon, and he couldn't sleep without knowing what he would see. Looking up at the fragile timbers, the fort gave him a hope he hadn't felt since Glohring left. Boy sent a *thank you* to whoever had put this gift in his path and, with a fresh burst of energy, jogged to the fort.

He reached up and placed his hands on the thick support timber that appeared the most stable. The other timbers were blackened with ash from a fire, possibly one that had passed through last summer. He carefully clambered up the weak tower, pivoting around the exterior support logs to take the safest beams that would support his weight. It became a difficult climb, some of the crossbars missing, but he managed to get to the top platform. Boy had reached its peak and gazed over the forest canopy. To the southwest, the distant glimmer of the dying sun mirrored off the sea. To the east, on the far horizon, he recognised the cliffs – there was no mistaking those cliffs – that was where Tree Deep pranced in all its stubborn glory.

Boy's cheek muscles tightened, and his smile unlocked his tired face. He held his hand to his heart in joy and anticipation. He felt energetic again; he felt like riding all night. He estimated the distance, one they could not reach in one day or night. He made a mental note of where the sun was and where it should be rising on the morrow. That would be his compass for the days ahead. As he stood at the top of the tower, he wondered what his family were doing that very sunset. *I will not get this wrong. I will not get this wrong. There is no way I will get lost again, and I will not tire. If I can just reach the cool waters of Tree Deep Trundle, I'll be saved. Nothing can harm me then.*

7

The old flint still worked fine after all these years, and a spark burst forth new flames that began to crawl up the dry kindling. A long fish was carefully lowered onto a wire grill over the fire, then smothered in cows' butter. Leesiele squeezed a lemon, dripping it across the crisping skin of the freshly caught fish. She had not cooked a fish in a long time and had forgotten to pack herbs where its guts had once been.

Leesiele had no more family to cook for, and it made her feel empty inside. Her children were in her heart and her thoughts, but not in her home. Maybe her husband could find them, but she was no longer strong enough for a journey in the wild. She had never been further from herself, waking each morning feeling like she was an unfamiliar person, disconnected from the world and from George. Oh, her sweet George. With him, it was easier to make it through to sunset and even to sleep away the pain and dream of the past forever. She would try so hard not to wake up to reality: no voices, no smells, no laughter, no one to nurture, and no more hugs. She thought about the mornings she had taken for granted, when her babies would curl up at the end of her bed, waiting patiently for her to rise from her slumber.

Leesiele's insurmountable emotions would soon start taking their toll on George and eventually on their marriage. She would pace around the kitchen, searching for things to do. She would pull everything down from the kitchen shelves, meticulously clean and dust, then place the items back on to the shelves. Every day, a new part of the home was taken to this task. She needed the chance to have control over something. George knew her sanity – and his own – would depend on him finding their lost offspring and making them a family again.

Leesiele also felt bitter about the changes to her body. She was growing weaker. She was only thirty-four summers old, but the strain of losing her children was affecting everything. Small lines appeared at the edge of her eyes. Her dark hair had been cropped short to mourn the loss of her babies. She had lost the muscle weight from her once farm-strong body. Her face, once vibrant and almost plump, had withdrawn thinly.

Her husband George still loved her more than the world but was finding it hard to deal with her; she had changed, while he gripped on to the idea of the Leesiele he had always known. But he was losing her more and more with every sunset and every dawn. The days were growing longer on the farm, and the harvest season was almost complete. They had not brought much in this year, without Boy's help and with George absent so much. He had been venturing far and wide to speak to friends and traders, looking for information about his stolen children.

~

George pushed open the creaky door to his home. His sweat-soaked ragged brown hair was streaked with grey from the worry. His skin was dry and tanned from the long heat of the harvest season. His hands were cracked worse than any previous summer, and his once tall stance was now hunched. He kicked his dusty boots to the corner of the room and sat at the table without as much as a kiss or a cuddle for his wife. He waited for her to serve the meal. First, the fish was shovelled into his mouth, then the beans, and then the potato last. He licked the bowl as he always did. Leesiele always told him off about that, but this time she stayed silent.

'I think I'll travel to Gwin's farm tomorrow and see if there is any word on the children. I haven't seen him since we first let him know. He has extended family who live far away, so maybe someone has seen or heard something.' He sipped a warm dark ale from a small cup. George seldom drank – and never in front of the young ones – but that night he felt like it.

'I thought you were going to finish the last paddock? Gwin is a good family man, and I'm sure if they had heard anything, they would have travelled here to let us know. Please stay.'

'Yes, I know. But there is no harm leaving the paddock for a few more days. You know if it wasn't harvest, I would be taking you too.'

'I don't know how my fat old bum would go riding all day on the horse. I might break his back and have to walk.' They both smiled: a rarity.

'That behind of yours is as perfect as the day I met you. I would have let you ride my horse anyway. He's the best, and nothing can break his back. Now, come here.' George slid his chair out from under the table, and Leesiele sat on his lap. They cuddled for a long while, and she cried tears down his shoulder.

~

The summer sun rose slowly above the great river. Tree Deep flowed shallow and long in the shadows of the hills. The birds talked and played in the trees, and the warm wind began for the day. George tossed a leather pack over his mount, a large black mare he had named Reiner. George waved to his wife and, without another word, trotted away from his farm.

He began heading north on a small track through the forest that he only used once every few years. It wound close to the great river at times and moved away deeper into the forest at others. The track crossed winter streams, which were bare and rocky during summer. It resembled no more than a goats' trail, and it was only ever used by him or Gwin when they traded together without the burden of a wagon. They had both been brought up in farmhouses further to the north-east, across the rolling pine forests, and they had both helped their parents cultivate that land before they married.

Gwin and George weren't the best of friends, but they were respectful and loyal to one another. They had known each other since they were young, but long stretches apart between trading and harvests saw these stubborn men as more business acquaintances than friends. They had seen the loss of a busy merchants' trade route, and there was less coordination between the towns. Farmers died without offspring to take over, or merchants finished their careers with no apprentice. This meant that, over time, the trading camps and merchant roads became less known and less used, and the forest started to take them back. Working together with Gwin in recent years had meant they'd been able to bring in a lot more coin than if they traded alone. Knowing he could not provide for his family alone gave George a shallow feeling inside, but not knowing where that family was now made him feel worse. George knew he would never stop searching, asking, hunting, exploring until he found his offspring. He began to think that one day Leesiele would want more children if they never returned home. He didn't want more; he was too old, and his joints would soon be too creaky to have little ones to chase.

The thought vexed him. He wanted everything to go back the way it was, so he could finally rest his head on his pillow.

George camped that night in a large clearing in the middle of a pine forest. The pale glow of the full moon shone down, and he placed his bedroll on a thin layer of pine needles. He decided that he didn't need a fire but, as the shadows at the edge of the pines became harder to see, a sense of foreboding crept into his mind. He accepted that he had chosen a vulnerable place to sleep and hastily built up a fire. He lay perfectly still and finally drifted off to sleep, with his hands clinging to the dagger under his pillow.

~

The early morning sun twinkled through the pines. Both Boy and Tendai rose late, stretching in unison. Boy believed he would be home soon, finally back with the loving family he missed so much. Tendai would then leave to go and do whatever he wanted to do; Boy really didn't care.

Boy admired the beauty of his surroundings; he loved pine forests. His dad had spoken so fondly of their smells and sounds. A thud of a pine cone hit the ground, and its timing felt like a signal: the beginning of a new day and a race for home.

They set off, with Boy leading Beetie by the reins and Tendai following silently behind. Their clay path scattered with pine needles descended through the morning and finally reached swampier terrain with peppermint trees and paperbarks, which was an endless challenge for a cumbersome beetle. It was fertile earth thanks to Tree Deep Trundle's carve across the land.

Could it really only be a day or so more alone with Tendai? But what will his motivations be once I get home? He is not going to leave, I know it. But he can't do anything bad to me once I'm home. My dad would take care of him, and my mum would scream at him. He will have to leave. Or I'll tell my parents everything he did. The sound of the stone crushing that man's skull played again in Boy's head.

'How far?' yelled Tendai from behind him.

The rude tone of Tendai's voice irked Boy, as did the fact he did not even turn and speak to him directly. In Tendai's mind, he was the man who gave up his life to bring this young child home to his family, and his requests must be granted immediately.

'Didn't you hear me? I said how far?'

'Probably just after zenith, so not too far. We just follow the great river when we get there. The hills suggest he's not that far away.'

'What do you mean by *he's* not that far away? Who are you leading me to?'

'You know I call the river Tree Deep Trundle. I guess I always thought of the river as a *he*.'

'You'd better not be lying!'

Boy looked at the ground, and patted Beetie's shell. Tendai had once again drained the energy from him.

8

The sound of rapids echoed ahead as they stopped to rest in a small grassy clearing. Tendai sat down, leaned his back against a tree; he removed his boots and aired his feet out, rubbing his soles on the soft grass. The sound of the river was calming to Boy's ears: it was home, it was familiar, and he knew deep inside it was Tree Deep Trundle. He let Beetie loose to graze around the clearing, which was abundant in herbs and berries. He could feel the constant eye of Tendai on him, watching his every movement while he pretended to rummage through his bag.

'So, you have a little brother and sister? I hope they take care of domestic duties better than you do, for your mother's sake. Go and have a bath in the river. Get clean for your big arrival. Does your water skin need filling? Do it here because we aren't stopping again.'

'This river has the freshest, cleanest water. My dad says it's so good because it comes straight from the northern mountains. Why don't you go fill up your water skin? Have a taste. The river's calm and shallow, so it's easy to get water from there.'

'I'll stay here. Take your time with your bath.'

Boy didn't even want a bath, but he did want to see Tree Deep to get a moment alone. *I suppose he is right though. I am filthy, and I probably stink. I should have a bath.* He tethered Beetie with enough rope for him to be able to graze the wide clearing, then took his spare shirt and belongings down to the river, which was further than it sounded. The noise of the rapids grew louder the closer he drew – Tree Deep was aware of him approaching its shores. He pushed his way through the hanging branches of a willow and finally saw the water flowing hard across the flat boulders. A small sandy beach met smooth flat stones, which he could see through the clear water. He gently placed the balls of his feet into the cool sand that was so familiar to his senses. The water changed direction to greet him, and Boy walked further confidently. The current slowed.

'I'm here, Tree Deep. I'm back home now.' He stepped deeper into the water and dunked himself under. He cleaned himself in the familiar way he had done his entire life, starting from his feet and then scrubbing upwards with his hands. He felt the change, the shedding of old crusty skin. He stood taller and felt stronger, without an ounce of filth embedded in the pores of his memory.

After a few whispers of thank you to Tree Deep, he stepped back onto the sandy beach and stood in the warm wind. He closed his eyes and felt the positive energy flow through him. *I haven't felt this good in such a long time. This feeling is fantastic.* But the thought of Tendai brought him back to the reality of his situation. Frustrated and angry again, he pushed through the branches of the thickest bushes, struggling to button up his shirt. He heard loud chirping and ran in a panic to quickly reach his friend. The giant beetle was flicking his tiny face in spasms left to right as vibrant turquoise and violet colours danced across his shell.

'Calm down, calm down. I'm here. It's okay. What is it, buddy? What happened? Tendai didn't try to ride you or anything, did he?' Boy looked around, assuming Tendai had gone into the woods to do his business or collect new herbs until he noticed the grassy clearing was bare of Tendai's belongings.

'Stay here, Beetie. It's okay; just settle. Tendai! Are you here?' he screamed into the trees, the echo reaching far. Only the sound of water could be heard.

Why would he just leave? Maybe he doesn't want to meet my parents.

Maybe he's scared that I will tell them what he did; turn him in as a murderer. Boy's eyes focused on a snapped sapling deeper in the trees. There were footprints, pushing hard off the balls of his feet. He must have run off in a hurry. The footprints lead south downstream, towards Boy's home. *Why did he run that way?*

'Beetie, we've got to go. We've got to catch up with him. I could get Tree Deep to wash me downstream.' He dismissed the idea – Beetie needed to come with him. Boy tightened the packs, untethered the long lead, and began to pull Beetie along behind him desperately. *Why? Why did I give him the exact location and tell him how long it would take? Why would he be doing this? What is his devious plan?* Beetie was slowing him down, and he had to find Tendai.

'I'm sorry, Beetie, but you'll have to follow my smell, follow my tracks. I have to go, but follow me, follow the sound.'

He ran fast, high on adrenaline and trying not to let his imagination wander to Tendai's dark possibilities. He was an unpredictable man. Boy wanted to get there to protect his mother; he had the feeling his father wasn't there. He didn't know why, but his father came into his head, and he feared for his life more than ever before.

~

Leesiele was busy moving large sacks of grain into a cart and preparing them for her husband's journey to trade them for coin. These days no one came to them. When she'd finished, filth and sweat clung to her old work clothes. She bucketed water from the well to slowly fill up her old iron bathtub. Too tired and overheated, she didn't bother to warm the water first. She was looking forward to a cold, invigorating bath on a hot summer's day. Her hair was dark, her skin was smooth, her hips were wide and her ankles thin. She sank her womanly figure into the cold water and closed her eyes to listen to the wind in the trees, believing her life was crumbling around her.

She stepped out of the water and began to dry herself. The windows were left open for the breeze, and she slipped into a soft cotton dress. She used to love the heat in the afternoons, but now she detested it.

She had dedicated the remainder of that day to finishing George's new shirt. As she gathered up her fabrics and stitching tools, she could hear the river in the distance sounding faster and louder on the rocks. It rumbled like a winter's day. She looked out to the river and noticed something move at the edge of the forest. A figure stepped out from the shadows. At first, she expected it to be George returning with good news, but he had only left the farm the day before. She felt a cold chill run up the back of her spine. The man must have seen her move through the window, and he started to wave. She moved outside to meet the stranger.

'Hello!' The young man with the confident stride and large smile waved.

Leesiele responded with a half-wave. She strode over to meet the man, with her shoulders back and her chin up. The man looked tired. His young skin was tanned from a long time in the sun, and he had big bags under his eyes and scruffy dark hair. He appeared to be smiling too hard; his face muscles were twitching.

'Hello,' the stranger repeated. 'I am finally here. I have travelled long to find this farm.'

'My name is Leesiele. How can I help you?'

'Leesiele. I know. My name is Tendai, and I have been for many days on a mission to bring your son, Boy, home after I saved his life.' Tendai stood smiling, waiting for the praise he had been imagining.

'What?' Leesiele said in surprise. 'Where is he? What's happened? What have you done?' She began shaking and grinding her teeth.

'It's okay, he's coming. He just had to water the pet

companion he has with him. I always ride ahead to make sure the path is safe first. He'll be here any moment now.'

Leesiele started to cry, silent tears that ran down her smooth cheeks dripped off her jaw and landed on her exposed cleavage. Tendai tried hard not to look and moved in for a hug. She stepped back, then suddenly heard Boy's voice for what felt like the first time.

'Mum!' Boy ran fast with his arms spread wide. He launched into her arms and they embraced, their sobbing laughter spreading sweetly across the farm.

'Oh, Boy, my boy. I love you, I love you so much,' Leesiele said through her tears.

Tendai stood next to them, watching, the same weird smile spread across his face. Leesiele held her son's face and ran her hands through his hair. She smothered him with kisses. Boy looked to the house for his dad, Tilly and Armue; he expected they would have heard all the commotion. But the farm stayed quiet. Leesiele clasped her hands on the sides of his face, and the joy in her eyes turned to fear.

'Where's Tilly? Where's Armue?' She was demanding the answers from Boy, but he was shocked at the question.

'What do you mean? I don't know. They aren't with me. Why aren't they here?'

Leesiele burst out crying and dropped to the ground, her head between her knees. She rocked back and forth. Boy had never seen his strong mother like this.

'Where are Tilly and Armue? Where are they? What happened?' Boy began looking around the farm and down to the river.

'We don't know. They never came back. My last hope was that they were with you.' Tears flooded once again as she tried to get the story out of her mouth. 'They never came back from the river. The water must have taken them. With you gone, the wretched water flowed differently, not like when you were here.'

Boy shook his head. 'No, No, Tree Deep wouldn't have done that, even without me here. He knew them.'

'They never came back. Your father searched everywhere downstream for you and then later for Tilly and Armue. There was no sign of them, and their tracks to the river were flooded by the rain that evening. Your dad only found the water bucket in the rocks.' She wiped away the tears, realising that she still had to be strong. *If one can be found, we will find the others.*

'Where's Dad now?'

'He's off again, looking for you kids. He's never stopped looking for all of you. We managed to get a harvest completed. I wish he was here to see you.'

'How long until he gets back?'

'He's gone to Gwin's, so hopefully, only about five more days and he should be home.'

Boy locked eyes with Tendai, and noticed he was no longer smiling. He turned back to his mother.

'I'm so hungry. Is there anything on the stove?'

'I haven't anything on the fire now, but I will for tonight. Would you like some cheese and buttered bread?'

'Yes, please. Yum, I'm so hungry. I've been dreaming of homemade food for so long. Was it baked this morning?'

'Last night, but it's still fresh.'

'I have to tether up Beetie, then I'll come in. You can meet him later.'

Leesiele looked towards the creature who had just appeared in the distance, and her mouth gaped wide open.

'That's your mount?' She looked shocked.

'More than my mount, he's my friend. He's great. Beetie!' Boy called to him.

'I think I'll meet him later. I'll get you some food ready. Come in when you're ready,' said Leesiele, making her way towards the farmhouse.

Beetie occupied himself by rustling around the ground, looking for things that interested him. Boy tethered him to a tree and removed the harness and his own packs. He sprinted to the front door of his house, as he had done so many times before. Inside, it was exactly the way he had left it, but much quieter. Tendai sat at the table, and Boy cursed himself for his stupidity and carelessness; he'd completely forgotten that the viper was hanging around. Now he was in Boy's family home, and there was nothing he could do about it.

Boy tried to ignore the negative thoughts and enjoy the moment. He looked around the room, taking pleasure that things were still in the same spots – the bookshelf his father would look through for tales he had not yet read to them, the kitchen utensils and pots hanging in the corner, the fabrics and yarn piled up in a basket where his mother would work on new shirts. The fire roared, and a wire rack held the sliced bread as it slowly turned golden brown above the flames. Leesiele pulled the bread off the heat, smeared each slice with fresh butter, and served it to the table. She also served a plate of marinated olives, cheese, and a small amount of dried meat. Boy and Tendai ate like they hadn't eaten in years. Leesiele sat down on her regular seat and smiled, watching her son eat. Boy smiled back as he stuffed his face with the warm crusty bread slathered in fresh butter.

'We'll have a vegetable soup tonight. I don't have any fresh meat at the moment.'

'That's more than enough. We most definitely need a good hearty dose of vegetables. I don't mind catching some meat for us tomorrow, and we can then have a roast,' said Tendai.

Leesiele obviously welcomed any hunt of fresh meat, but Boy scrunched his brows in anger. *How dare he just assume he's going to stay? He's telling us the plans for tomorrow, on our farm, in our home. He's not in charge any more.*

Dusk came quickly that day. Boy showed Beetie off to his mother and explained how he saved him. His mother enjoyed their time together and didn't ask many questions. She was just so happy to see him smile, and Boy felt the same. He knew, however, that when his dad got home, they would sit down and he would have to answer all his questions and explain everything in detail.

After a warm bowl of soup, Leesiele showed Tendai to the children's room. She started to make up Armue's bed with spare sheets.

'Thank you so much for your kind generosity, but I am more than happy to sleep in the hayloft with my bedroll. The air is warm enough these nights, so it won't be cold,' said Tendai.

Tendai grabbed his packs from the porch and strolled off to the nearest barn. As Tendai left, Boy thought his mother would ask more questions, but she was content to be silent.

'Is there any chance at all that Dad will be home tomorrow?'

'Like I said before, he usually doesn't sway too much from his travel plans. Possibly four days at the earliest. But we have so much to do around here to keep us busy. We still have a farm to run.'

She pulled him in for a gentle hug, then walked him to his room. Boy felt pleased that Tendai had refused to sleep in the same room: a small win.

'Mum, can I drag my mattress into your room and sleep on the floor? Please?'

Leesiele smiled so sadly, she almost didn't look like his mother, and she agreed. Boy lay down on his mattress and she threw a clean blanket over him and wished him good night. He dreamed of wooded forests, giant bird-like creatures and red-eyed wolves.

~

Boy woke to the sound of his mother laughing and talking boisterously. For a moment, he thought his dad had come home, but then Tendai started to laugh. Boy had never heard the forced tone of this fake laugh. His heart and chest immediately felt heavy; he was pulled down by the weight of Tendai's connection to him. He tried to shake the negative thoughts away and rose to begin his first full day at home. He opened the door to the smell of toast with eggs and herbs, ignored Tendai, and sat down at the head of the small rectangle table.

'It smells good, Mum.'

'I've made some eggs and toast. I thought you would have been up by now, but it should still be warm by the fire. I'll grab it.'

Leesiele picked up the warm plate with a kitchen towel and placed it down for Boy.

'I didn't want to go into detail last night, but we have been struggling this harvest. We were set back further and further each time George went away. It will be an extra surprise for your father if he comes home to see how much work we have done.'

Boy was a little bit shocked. He had never given a single thought to how his disappearance would affect the farm business. He began to feel like the most selfish son in the world.

'I know you're both very tired, and work is probably the last thing on your minds, but I'll show you around anyway, and you can see for yourselves. It's been difficult for your father, although he would never admit that.'

After breakfast, Boy changed into his old work clothes and helped clean up the breakfast dishes. He'd never thought it would be this kind of old habit he'd missed.

Leesiele walked at Boy's side to the old barn to show him the carts of grain. Tendai quietly strolled behind them, pretending to be interested in their casual chatter. She pointed out the estimated delays to the farm's usual schedule as they passed the fields and stock.

'Twenty-two days behind with the packing, nine days behind with the earth airing. We should have been seeding by the time George returns.'

They stood in the barn doorway, and they could see where Tendai had laid out his bedroll the previous night. Beetie was tethered up at the side of the barn and grazed in the shade. They could hear his occasional 'chika chika'.

'I will move my things from the hayloft if we are to get to work today, Leesiele. I don't want to have my things get in the way.'

That's very kind of you, but I know you're just trying to weasel your way into sleeping in Armue's bed, Boy thought.

'That would be good. We will need to get up to the loft today.'

'Mum, there's so much to do. I can start right now. What's the most urgent thing? Maybe even Beetie can help?'

'Well, what can he do? Has he worked on a farm before?'

'No. He was wild, but he can carry packs or something. I can find something for him to do to help.'

'Well, okay. If it makes things quicker.'

'I won't waste too much time trying to teach him, but he is smart.'

Boy, Tendai and Leesiele worked long into the hot afternoon. Every time Leesiele tried to pick up a large grain sack, Tendai jumped to her aid with smiles and politeness. Boy would then jump in between them and lend a hand himself. He worked tirelessly, with one eye on the snake he hated. Tendai kept quiet for most of the day. Boy had seen this behaviour before when Glohring was around, and they had first met.

As the sun lowered to the horizon, they stood together, sweating in their dirty clothes, and admiring what they'd achieved. Another full cart was packed with stock, the chicken pen was cleaned out, and half a paddock was aired and churned.

'If we can do this every day until George returns, we will catch up. He won't believe his eyes.' She looked proudly at Boy, whose face looked so much like her husband's. Tendai turned and walked away, luring her attention to him.

'Is there a stream near here where I can bathe? Or should I just go to the river?'

'No, we have stored irrigation water for a bath, or the stone well towards the forest. We have a second tub in the old shed. It's much nicer.' Leesiele smiled politely at Tendai.

'Well, I'll go down to the river and wash,' said Boy.

'You can have a bath too, Boy,' Leesiele protested.

'No, mum, it's okay. You've worked all day, and we don't need a third bath run. Do you need any herbs from the river bank?'

'Oh yes. I forgot how well they grow down there in summer. I haven't been down there in so long.'

'That's fine. I'll pick whatever I can find.'

'Thank you.' She kissed Boy on the head then gave Tendai directions to the tub.

Boy collected clean clothes from his room and walked down the old path he knew so well to Tree Deep Trundle. The path was overgrown with the tall weeds of spring that had since turned as brown and dry as bush tinder. Where the path ended, there was a beach he knew well; downstream was a natural bath pool. The memories flooded back of playing and laughing with Tilly and Armue on this beach. He wondered if there were more fish stocks in the river now because he hadn't been hunting the banks for so long. He would have to catch some fish for when his dad returned; it was his turn to provide for the family.

'Tree Deep!' he yelled. 'I'm home!' He ran across the sandy beach and up a rock and launched himself into the pool. Tree Deep kept his water quite subdued compared to other times, which Boy appreciated. He climbed into the natural bath, where he floated on his back and watched the trees move from side to side in the warm breeze.

Boy returned home to the sound of his mother's laugh, followed by Tendai's. It made him feel sick. As he approached the house, he could hear Tendai telling her a story about a farmer who would cut out the inside of two pumpkins and place them on his feet to wear as shoes when he came to town on each full moon. Boy didn't believe a word of it, but his mother was lapping it up. He burst through the door to break up the hideous story-time and sat in his father's seat at the head of the table. Leesiele stood up and began stirring the night's pot of soup.

'How was your bath? Were there many herbs along the river track?'

Boy had completely forgotten about looking for herbs.

'The water was calm and warm. It was great. I didn't see any herbs, really. The ground along there is like tinder. Everything is dried out, but I'll find some herbs in the next few days.'

'I can go and collect some,' offered Tendai.

'That's okay. I've still got jars of dried herbs I can use.' She looked at Boy. 'Tomorrow, we'll continue what we didn't finish today, and we'll make a start patching around the fields, so no more weeds begin to grow. Tendai, if you don't mind, you can finish the baling. Whatever doesn't fit on the carts, store in the barn.'

'Your wish is my command.'

Boy cringed, and Leesiele pretended not to hear.

'We can't start ploughing until your father arrives, but we can get everything ready. I'll be repairing the old scarecrow. He's lost a few limbs this season.'

'Oh, I like doing that. It's my favourite job,' Boy complained.

'There's more important things for you to do, and I can stitch quicker. This time I want him to last for a few years and not just one season,' Leesiele replied gently, not wanting to offend her beloved Boy.

~

The next three days were hard work in the summer heat. The morning and afternoon breezes helped keep the air dry and cool, but it was the midday sun they had to fight through. There was little talk or interaction as they worked hard through the searing heat to achieve the results Leesiele wanted for George's return.

At night, when he returned from the river, Boy would catch Tendai entertaining his mother with jokes and smiles. He would burst in the door loudly to catch him off guard and ruin his show. He knew his mother was just being friendly to a guest and farmhand, but he didn't trust Tendai. Maybe he would snap again if he was scorned by Leesiele. His dad would be home soon, and then Tendai could leave.

The next day, Leesiele finished the scarecrow with fresh fabric and colours. Boy had put Beetie to work, pulling a small wooden cart, and he seemed to be handling the work fine and even enjoying it. Boy stopped to inspect how close the wheels were to Beetie's rear legs, concerned the cart could wheel into them if he stopped suddenly. He looked up and saw Tendai carrying the scarecrow and a ladder out into the middle of the vegetable field, his mother at his side.

Leesiele began to climb the ladder to erect the scarecrow, and Tendai watched her hips wiggle with each step. Boy was tempted to throw a rock at him, but was afraid it would hit his mum. A strong gust of wind blew and Leesiele started to lose her balance. The ladder rocked back and forth. She slipped and fell backwards, landing in Tendai's waiting arms.

'Are you okay?' asked Tendai. He continued to hold her in his arms. Leesiele pushed his arms away, stood up, and climbed the ladder again.

'Of course, I'm okay. I'll be fine from here. Go and feed the chickens please.'

She started hammering the post in further and noticed Boy looking at her with a frown. She smiled at him and went back to hammering the scarecrow. Boy tried to push out of his mind the image of Tendai holding his mother and went back to his work. He did not like what was going on and wished his dad would come back quickly.

That afternoon, Boy walked to Tree Deep a little earlier than usual. He didn't always bathe in the river, but he liked his time alone. After he floated in the natural rock bath and talked to Tree Deep about other streams and gullies he had seen on his travels, he packed up his clothes and walked upstream. He felt bad about forgetting to pick herbs before and decided he should gather a bunch or two for his dad's return dinner. He knew that the further he walked upstream, the more herbs there were: sweet basil (his favourite), thyme, dill, lemongrass, bitter tarragon, and oregano. He found only a scant few, cut the stalks, and collected them in a damp pouch. Suddenly, he stopped, sensing a feeling before he heard the clip-clop of a horse. His dad was in the woods and coming his way. A horse neighed out of sight.

'Daaaaaadd!' Boy screamed. The thud of the hooves got louder and quicker.

'Boy?' his father shouted in reply.

Boy ran up the path, crossed a bend, and burst through a bush. Riding a large gelding, his father bounced off the stirrups, swung his leg around and landed gracefully; he swept his son up, wrapping him in a father's warm hug.

'Is it really you?' His father held him up and kissed him on the forehead. 'I thought it was a ghost when I heard you. I can't believe it.'

'It's me!' Boy smiled.

George placed him back on the ground and started to laugh, wheeze, and cough all at the same time. Boy thought he may even start to cry.

'Now, where the hell have you been? Are Tilly and Armue here?'

Boy shook his head no.

'Your mother and I have been beside ourselves with fear. I love you, but I hope you have answers to our questions.'

'I … I … I'll tell you everything later. I'm just happy to be home,' Boy snivelled. 'I only just found out about Tilly and Armue. I have no idea what happened. I have no idea where they could have gone.'

'Okay, we can discuss this later. I would like to know all about where you have been. It will help us know where to search next, although I feel like I've already searched everywhere. Let's go home.'

They strolled along the old track through their beautiful land towards the farmhouse. Boy was asking more questions about where his father had been rather than the other way around. He helped to stable Reiner, then they headed inside for dinner. At first, Boy decided not to mention Tendai; he hoped to catch him in the act, so his dad would kick him out. Then he thought it may make Leesiele look bad, and he did not want that. So, Boy pointed out the work they had been able to complete.

'I can't believe how much work has been done around here. It looks like a different farm, and in only a few days.'

'Well, we had help from a man named Tendai. He kind of helped me get home … in some ways.'

'He helped you get home? Where is this man?'

'Well, kind of, not really. He's probably inside,' Boy sighed.

George strode towards the house and burst through the door. The young man jumped off his chair in surprise. He'd been looking at pictures in an old leather-bound book. Leesiele walked in from the children's room with her head down, flicking through the pages of a book.

'This book has many drawings of the birds found …' She looked up, saw George, and ran to him. They embraced long and deep. Tendai sat back in his chair and shrunk into himself – George reclaimed his home. Boy's father was not a large man, but his eyes had an imposing presence.

'I'm so glad you are home,' said Leesiele, falling into him.

George let go of her and turned to Tendai. His arms were folded across his chest.

'What is your name?'

'Tendai is my name, good sir.'

'And did you help bring my son home to his family?'

'Yes, I did.'

George got down on one knee in front of Tendai. 'Then I am forever in your debt. Thank you from the bottom of my heart. My eldest is now home. And we have a great many things to talk about, don't we, Boy?'

'I only have soup for dinner. If I had known you would be here, I would have plucked a chicken for a roast, my love.'

'Tomorrow then, we will dine with an almighty Leesiele feast. My favourite.' George smiled. 'I'll unpack and join you at the table.'

A short time later, the four dined on vegetable soup, warm buttered bread, and an old jar of pickled onions. George ate fervently, meticulously chopping pickled onions into quarters and pairing them with small crumbling slices of matured cheese.

'What did you have planned to do tomorrow on the farm if I had not returned?' he asked through a half-filled mouth.

Tendai would be lusting over mother, as usual. What if I just blurted that out? What would happen?

'We are almost prepared to air the soil. There is only so much we could plough without a horse. Oh, Dad, I almost forgot … I have to show you my new friend, the beetle.'

'Your new friend, the beetle? Well, be careful not to squash him, wherever he is.'

'No, no, he's tethered up near the chickens. He is a giant beetle. I will show you. He is my friend, and he helped to carry me home. He isn't very good with farm work, but I had him drag the small trailer, just to feel involved.'

'That sounds fine, Boy. I will meet him on the morrow then. Any new pet is always welcome on the farm, you know that.'

'I know, Dad. He's great.'

George smiled, then asked more questions about the farm work. As they discussed Tendai's contribution, George spoke directly to him about his farming background.

'Well, I don't have much experience in farming and agriculture. However, when I have a task, I finish it to the best of my ability. I enjoy hard work.'

'Well, from the little that I saw today, the work was great. Is farming something you wish to pursue? Would you like to make some coin off the land?'

Boy didn't like the sound of where this was going. *Tendai won't succeed at anything, and he should just leave.*

'Well, a small parcel of land would be well-worked if I ever had the opportunity,' smiled Tendai with open eyes. George nodded politely and went back to his soup while Boy and his mother exchanged worried glances.

Later that night, George and Leesiele climbed into bed and under the light covers. George wrapped his arms around his wife, kissed her neck, and whispered a poem into her hair. Silent tears ran down her cheeks, wetting the sheets.

'My white bird flew away from home. My love for him, his love unknown. My heart had sung before that day. To keep me sane, to warm his way.'

'Please stop,' Leesiele closed her eyes and rolled over to sleep at the side of the mattress.

'Okay. Goodnight, my love. We'll talk in the morning. I

love you.'

'I love you more.'

~

The next day, George had Tendai work by his side to test out his mettle. To his credit, Tendai completed everything with an abundance of youthful vigour. The farm was now up-to-date. If they could get ahead of schedule, he could keep searching for his lost children.

George pulled Tendai aside and gave him one last job for the day – a surprise duty, so he could have some time alone with Boy and Leesiele. He set Tendai to task fencing a new paddock for Beetie. The holes had to be dug, and the posts had to be cut and hammered into the ground. George thought Tendai could be the extra help they needed to give them a head start for the season ahead.

As George left him to his duties and walked to the farmhouse, Tendai kept half an eye on him and where he was going. George peered back, doing the same to him – he did not want Tendai interfering in his discussion with Boy.

That bloody kid is going to ruin my chance of getting some land, Tendai thought. *And I'm not happy doing this work for that bloody beetle.*

George found his wife and son repairing part of the old chicken fence.

'Boy, come with us. We are going for a walk.'

Leesiele collected a pack from the veranda that she'd prepared earlier and caught up with them. They walked south, away from their fields, to a clearing ahead where deer would gather to eat the first fresh grass of autumn. Leesiele laid a large rug on the ground in the middle of grassy sward, so no one could easily approach them to listen in. They all sat down and Leesiele passed out a meagre portion of cheese and olive bread.

'Now, Boy, we need you to tell us everything. What

happened? Where did you go? Who took you away? How did you meet this young man, Tendai?'

With his father home, Boy knew these questions were unavoidable, but appreciated that his parents had given him time to settle back in.

Boy recounted the unfortunate tale to his parents: exploring the cliff on the far banks of the river, the flying beast with the basket, saving Beetie's life, and the help that he received from the old man (although he decided to leave out Glohring's tricks of ignition and fire manipulation). He tweaked the story of Tendai leaving the mercenary troop, saying it was down to him not wanting to be in the business of war, that he was looking for a quieter life. The expression on his mother's face changed; she could see the truth wasn't flowing. George had leant forward, listening intently and resisting his usual impulse to ask many questions. Leesiele had ordered him not to interrupt, whatsoever, so he listened impatiently and ate his cheese.

Boy ended the story quickly, skimming through his kidnap and escape, the subsequent journey with Tendai, and seeing the map of the region. Each time he mentioned Tendai, he deflected to what he missed so much about home. He spoke about the land and his need to find Tree Deep Trundle. His parents knew his strange connection to the river, so it was only natural that he was seeking it out.

Boy attempted to race to the end of his story, through shame more than anything else. He wanted to push down the bad feelings and the horrible times; he did not want to relive them. He felt like he was picking the stitches of a recent wound; he did not want his parents to see the raw flesh which Tendai had surely infected. He wanted to spare them his terror.

Boy completed the story of them following Tree Deep to find the farm. He left out why Tendai had arrived first and him further behind.

'Boy, I have to leave the farm again soon, and I want to know everything about the peculiar things that you saw or heard. Is there anything that may give me a clue about where to find Tilly and Armue?'

'Well, I had never seen a flying creature like that. Maybe a similar thing took them? Have any more of those beasts come into our skies?'

'Yes, I have seen one.' George's eyes opened wide. 'But it was injured on one wing. The beastly bird was huge, so I don't want to know what could have injured it.'

Boy disclosed a few extra details, only because he was so desperate for his father to find his Tilly and Armue. He recalled the wolf he'd seen on the clifftop and others that had entered his dreams. He mentioned the travelling merchants, the poachers, the old crone … but there was nothing to go on, no lead, no starting point as to where Tilly and Armue might be.

'What about Tendai?' Leesiele asked.

'What about him?' Boy sat rigid.

'Why do you think he really left his band of warriors? That was his job, his earnings. Why would he go off into the unknown to take a strange boy back to his home? We are so glad that he did, but what did he want?'

Boy gulped. *Here goes.*

'Tendai seemed a bit of a loser, like the weakling of their group. I don't think he was liked at all by the other men. They probably picked on him, bullied him. I overheard him telling Glohring that he was the newest, and he appeared to be one of the youngest. I guess he wanted to get away from his tormentors. If he'd stayed, he wouldn't have had any power, no one to give orders to.'

'Yes, I think so too. From our chats, I guessed that he didn't feel comfortable in that field of work,' said Leesiele.

'When is he going to leave?' asked Boy.

'We were hoping you may know that answer,' said George. 'But we mustn't be too hasty. This young man has done so much for us already, and help is always welcomed.'

'You aren't giving him a parcel of land, are you?'

'It had crossed my mind. I don't have much but land for a reward.'

'Boy, why wouldn't you want him around?' asked his mother, who was peering into his soul. Boy momentarily fell silent. He was facing the farm and, at the edge of the clearing, he noticed some leaves rustle unnaturally. It was Tendai. Now that he had been spotted, he stood up and walked their way.

'I just want things to go back to normal. I don't want change. Why can't everything go back to the way it was before?' Boy whispered through gritted teeth.

'Hello,' shouted Tendai as he strode across the clearing. 'Sorry to interrupt, but I am finished with my duties. I was hoping to go for a walk to pick herbs. I thought I'd just let you know where I was going.'

'That is fine, Tendai. Good luck with your herb hunt,' George shouted back and waved him off.

'Let's go back now.' George stood up and shook the blanket in the wind. 'I need to think about everything you've told us. Your information about the northwest could come in handy, but I have a feeling that's not the direction I need to go in. There is no clear direction, but I think I may have to travel much further than I have done in the past. It sounds like the world has far more humans in the north now. My father's stories never mentioned a castle or so many villages. Let's go back so I can get the maps out.'

They returned to the farm. Leesiele prepared a roast chicken and vegetables for dinner. Boy found clean clothes folded at the end of his bed and headed down to Tree Deep for a bath. George inspected Tendai's work to the new fences, laying on the ground and reaching his long arm into the holes to see if the depth instructions were followed correctly.

Boy paced through the dry trodden grass to the river, calling out to Tree Deep as he approached. Waves began to splash on the sandy shore in greeting. Boy hung his clean shirt on a low branch and sat down on the shore, allowing the unnatural waves to wash over him. Then the river suddenly went quiet, flat and calm, like he wasn't there and it was occupied with its flow at another point. He floated on his back and pondered his parents' reactions to his story. He knew his father's main quest was for something to lead him closer to Boy's siblings. But his mother's stare knew something was wrong and knew that the man who had been with Boy most of the time was not all he seemed to be. Her sixth sense had zoned in on this relationship but knew Boy would only tell her when he was ready.

Tree Deep began to splash over the rocks. Boy sat up straight and looked around, but nothing was there. He dried himself off with a small clean cloth and changed into his clean clothes. The smell of the roast chicken carried itself on the light wind.

Boy wanted to collect more herbs for his mother; it had always been his duty in the past, and only he knew the best places to find them. He no longer wanted Tendai doing things for his mother. He could work for his father on farm duties, but that was it.

Boy walked upstream to a green area that in the past had always had good pickings. He gathered a handful of three types of herbs, all growing in the places he expected, and prepared to head home. The long day of work and the conversation with his parents had made him extremely tired. Tendai stepped out from behind a large tuart tree, holding a handful of herbs.

'I thought I heard something. Looks like you have the same herbs. More the better, I guess,' said Tendai.

Boy went on high alert. His skin tightened, and his knees loosened in readiness to flee an enemy.

'The forest near the clearing earlier … I bet you didn't have any luck findings herbs out that way,' said Boy. 'I know you wouldn't have found anything further out in that direction. Barren rocky dry clay, a few thorny flower trees.'

'Oh, there were some small surprises out that way. But nothing like the soil closer to the river. I'll dry some of these and we can have them with the chicken roast.'

'Can I see the herbs you found? You can't just throw anything green on a roast. We have some poisonous bushes and berries around the farm. There's not many, but they are there, usually with bright flowers.'

'I'm not an idiot. Of course, I wouldn't put those ones on the chicken. So, what was that little discussion about earlier?'

Boy began walking towards the house. 'They just wanted to know if I knew anything about where Tilly and Armue could have gone, anything to help Dad.'

Tendai followed. 'It will be a shame for the farm when your dad has to go away again. Your mother really would like a helping hand around the place. She really would.'

Boy ignored the comment and took longer strides; he was furious all through dinner and could not sleep that night. He kept looking out the window, looking for Tendai. *He has killed before. He could poison my dad … or me … then lie to my mother.* He finally slept, only from the exhaustion of stress. The demons of his mind created by Tendai had their claws even deeper, and each day they would become closer to the things he loved. The hope he had once clung to – that when he reached home these horrible feelings would leave – was now dead.

~

Boy woke extremely thirsty and stumbled out through the door in a daze. Tendai sat at the table with his parents, a bowl of assorted fruit and nuts in its centre.

'Good morning, Boy. You don't appear to have slept very well. Maybe some of my special tea would be good for you? Pull up a chair, young man. We were just discussing my outstanding reward for bringing you home safely.'

A pungent odour filled the kitchen air. Leesiele and George sat with their eyes half open; large black bags had appeared under their eyes that morning.

'Mum, I think I might be coming down with something. You don't look that well either.'

'Yes, I am also feeling slightly woozy,' said Tendai. 'But we have all been working so hard. I think it's just the heat and the exhaustion catching up on us. A good long night's sleep tonight and we'll all be refreshed.'

George and Leesiele nodded in agreement. 'So, are we in agreement then? The parcel of land to the north of the farm will be titled over to me for farming purposes, and you will have a percentage of the profits in exchange for labour?'

'Labour? Whose labour?' asked Boy.

'I think we will work well together, Boy. You need a job. You are not far off being a man, and this way you can stay close to home.'

'We … our family … we have enough work on our farm and our land. Dad, don't make a deal. This is stupid.' Boy struggled not to slur his words.

'I agree with Boy. Land is an important commodity, and we don't want to sell it,' George said slowly and weakly.

'It is unused land that you don't work with,' replied Tendai angrily. 'I thought that bringing home your eldest son would be worth more than that. I saved his life, remember, and protected him. I kept him alive through dangerous lands to bring him back to you.'

Boy felt a burst of rage deep inside him. 'You have no home. You came with me because you have no home and no friends. You can leave now. This is our farm.'

'Boy! Sit down and don't be rude to our guest,' Leesiele slurred, her eyes half-closed.

'Mum, what's wrong with you? You and Dad aren't sick.

I'm not sick. Tendai has poisoned us with his herbs.'

'Boy! Listen to your mother. We don't speak that way to guests. He has done what he said and brought you back to us. You have seen how the young man has helped us getting ready for the season. He shall be compensated. You are right – this will always be our farm and our home. But I need to look for your brother and sister, and the farm will not survive without another man,' said George with extra vigour. His eyelids were almost closed. Boy caught Tendai smiling at his mum, who had since fallen asleep.

'I understand, Dad. But I will only be working on *our* farm.' Boy crossed his arms and felt the drugs wearing off. He was either more resilient to them, or Tendai had given him a smaller dose.

'Well, I'll also need a hand. With the extra percentage of profits going your way, George, you will have more income revenue than ever before,' Tendai said. However, George and Leesiele both had their eyes closed. 'Or maybe Leesiele can help me on my farm.'

'She has a strong back … she is very strong,' slurred George, then he lay his head on the table and began snoring.

'What have you given them? Are they going to be sick? Is it bad for them? Mum! Dad! Wake up!'

Tendai stood and quickly snatched two sheets of paper from the kitchen shelf.

'Dammit! Wake up, George, I need you to sign this.' He grabbed the farmer's shoulders and shook him but, when George didn't respond, Tendai picked up a charcoal quill and ink and began writing George's name, copying the handwriting from a stock trade document he'd found on their bookshelf.

'Don't you touch him! Dad! Wake up!' Boy grabbed the quill and tried to rip it out of Tendai's hand, but Tendai pushed him away with a wide backhand. He fell backwards and landed hard at the base of the door. Tendai rushed him, picked him up by the throat, opened the door, and threw him out onto the hard ground.

'I'll be out in a minute. You are coming with me to stake out the land parcel. Don't go anywhere.'

Tendai strode back inside, and Boy stood up, coughing, and looked around. He grabbed two empty wooden buckets and stepped on them to peer through the glass. He watched Tendai replace the quill, fold the makeshift document, and place it in his shirt pocket. As he passed Leesiele, he rubbed the ink off his hands across her chest.

Boy screamed through the window. Tendai slammed the door behind him and stood calmly on the porch with his arms crossed.

'Stay away from my mum and dad! I will help you mark out your land for those papers but just stay away from them. Let's get on with it. Let's go. We'll need to get river stones for it. Two buckets should be enough.' Boy tossed a bucket Tendai's way.

'River stones? What the hell for? We'll just mark it out.'

'I don't know how the marking of land is done where you come from, but this is how we do it here. My dad taught me. You can't just mark it with stakes and posts. A stone line is how our ancestors have always done it, and it hands over the ownership of the land to a new owner. If the land is ever up for dispute, the new owner would have no right of ownership without the stones. Hear me? No right of ownership. Let's get this done. I have a lot of other work to do today.'

Boy turned his back on Tendai and walked towards the river. He was surprised at how easily he could lie in this dire situation. Tendai didn't say a word; he appeared to be processing the information for any trace of horse dung. He didn't think it sounded like something a kid would make up, but what the hell did he know about land ownership? He had never owned anything in his life. He picked up the bucket and began to follow the path Boy had taken to the river.

Boy stood on the sandy beach at the edge of Tree Deep Trundle's cool morning flow. Tendai strode across the clearing at the end of the track, his chin held high like an arrogant king. Boy took a few steps into the water. He knew what he wanted to do, but he didn't know how to begin.

He placed the bucket on the sand and began picking up small river stones and tossing them into the bucket. He kept one eye on Tendai, who stood high on the bank and just watched Boy work. Boy began to slow down, only grabbing smaller stones.

'What the hell are you doing? Those are all way too small to be markers. Get the bigger ones. You need the long flat ones that can be half buried.' Tendai tossed his wooden bucket towards the beach, but it flew too far and landed on a protruding rock, splintering down one side. Boy knelt in the thigh-deep water, feeling the bottom of the riverbed. He picked up a few good-sized stones and held them in his left hand, submerged just under the surface.

'Protect me, Tree Deep,' he whispered to the river.

He moved one of the stones underwater to his right hand, lifted his arm out of the water, and threw it straight at Tendai's head. Tendai ducked just in time. Boy threw another, this time hitting him in the stomach.

'You little …' he screamed in rage. Tendai picked up a large rock in his right hand, held it over his head, and advanced towards Boy. Frightened, Boy stepped back into the deep water behind him. He began to scramble backward through the water, slipped on the bottom, and fell, only just keeping his head above water.

'Tree Deep!' he screamed for help. He turned and began to swim to the other side to gain distance. A large rock flew past his head; it would have crushed a hole in the back of his skull if it had hit him.

'Help me, Tree Deep!' Boy screamed again. He tried to wade through the deeper water, and Tendai began to follow, then shuffled back into the shallows. He picked up a large long smooth rock and held it above his head.

'Tree Deep! Tree Deep!' Boy screamed one last time before his shoulders dropped below the surface of the water.. Tendai waded into waist-deep water and repositioned the large stone. Unable to outswim an adult, Boy held his breath and ducked beneath the water. Something in the water began to change. The flow slowed, and a partial current swept Boy across to the far side of the river. The bank was steep with boulders and little areas of moss: too steep to climb alone.

Tendai watched from ankle-deep water, his crude weapon still raised for an assault. The water disappeared from below his feet, and large stones were exposed as it receded. Tendai watched the water move in a strange way he had never seen before. The deeper water rose and lifted Boy onto the edge of a boulder, where he could sit safely.

Suddenly, the water rushed around Tendai's feet, and pulled him deeper. Boy's side of the river was now shallow. A massive wave came towards Tendai, knocking him off his feet and dragging his struggling body backwards and forwards across the river. The wave crashed against the rock wall, flung him high, and then smashed his body straight down onto bare stones that had not seen the light of day for a long time. Tree Deep retreated, leaving the area dry with no water flowing around the body. In place of the water, blood now ran through the flat stones. Tree Deep Trundle was no stranger to death. He had taken his fair share of souls to their afterlife over thousands of years. This one was no different to any other he had taken, except he had done it for Boy.

Boy began to choke back tears. He shook as he slid down the boulder into the shallow area Tree Deep had created. Blood ran underneath his feet through the jigsaw of stones. He stood over Tendai, who was coughing up blood. A few teeth and what looked like a chunk of bone came out with his final cough. His eyes were half-open, but he would not live.

'Why didn't you just leave? You should have just left,' said Boy, retrieving the soaking papers from Tendai's blood-stained pocket. Tendai's eyes no longer looked full of rage, but full of sadness. He gargled out a response through his broken and bloodied teeth.

'All I wanted was a part of this world to be my own. I helped you. Why did this happen?'

He died there on the riverbed. Tree Deep Trundle would eventually wash his body downstream, where he would become tangled in the branches of a fallen tree.

Boy retrieved the wooden buckets from the sandy beach, filled the unbroken one with water, and ran with all the speed he could muster back to his parents. His mother and father appeared to have woken up, but they sat in the same place, looking extremely groggy. He helped his mother to her feet and dunked her head in the water a few times. It seemed to do the trick, and she began to come around. Boy did the same to his father, who was not very impressed with his dripping state as he gathered consciousness.

Boy stoked the fire and boiled water to make herbal tea. He helped his mother and father outside to sit in the sun and dry off. They slowly returned to their usual disposition and health.

'What is going on? You'd better explain why I am all wet,' said a dazed Leesiele.

'It was Tendai. He drugged you with some evil herbs. I woke up and you were both at the table, but you were not yourselves, then you fell asleep. Do you not remember?'

'I remember sitting at the table. He was talking about … about something. Soil, was it?' George moved slowly, still drowsy, as if he were trying to remember.

'Where is he now? I want him to answer my questions.'

'I confronted him about drugging you,' Boy explained. 'I felt horrible too. I was dazed, but I don't think the brew I was given was as strong. He was trying to get you to sign away your land to him … well, some of it. You signed something, or he forged your name. He had these papers. See?' Boy pulled out the damp papers run with ink and set them out flat in the warming sunlight.

'Well, where the hell is he now?'

'Let me finish. I was going to the river to get two buckets of water to help wake you up. He chased me down there. He is not a good person, Dad. He is violent. I jumped into the river to get away from him. He tried to follow me, but he couldn't swim, and the river took him. I couldn't save him, so he drowned, and I came back with the water to wake you up. I saw him being washed downstream in a raging torrent, and I think he was already dead. Tree Deep protected me, I guess.'

Boy didn't explain everything to his parents, of course. They would only have been upset. It didn't matter now Tendai was gone. It was over, and he was gone. Gone.

~

Boy's father taught him a lesson that day about his ancestors' traditions when it came to human burial. To respect the dead, the living should find the corpse and bury it – if it was a horrible death, in a place that did not represent the area in which they died – if it was a peaceful death, then near the place they died in.

Later that day, George, Leesiele, Boy and Beetie walked down to the river as the dull haze of the drugs wore thin. The corpse they were looking for could be far away by now, but there were also many branches and rocks that it could be snagged on. The beetle had his leather harness on, ready to transport the corpse of someone he was not fond of.

Several hours into the search, they heard the growling of wolves on the far side of the bank. George held up his hand for his family to stop. They crouched down and peered through the bushes. A black wolf had Tendai by the neck, pulling him out of the water. One albino and two black wolf cubs jumped on the corpse and began tearing at the floppy flesh of Tendai's neck.

'Come on, let's go. There is nothing we can do for him now,' said George.

They began their walk back to the farm, and Boy turned for one last glance. Further down the riverbank, a large black wolf with red eyes was watching him. Boy didn't react and kept walking.

'Dad, where do you think those wolves came from? I have never seen any around our farm before.'

'They come from the north where it's cold. It's too barren and hot for them here. They will soon learn and head back north where there is more food and where the weather is better suited to their furs … or so I hear. They have appeared from time to time over the years.'

George trailed off and walked with his head down. Leesiele's eyes were red and wet. She didn't openly weep on the walk home, but she was visibly distressed. *What has the world become?* she wondered. *My family is my heart, and we have to fight against the world to save our babies.*

When they arrived home, they all slept off the poison that still lingered in their systems. Boy tethered Beetie for the night and told him the story of the day. He thought his beetle needed to know what had happened to Tendai – after all, he had endured the bullying too. Now he knew the end.

9

The air was warm and thick inside the small washroom adjoining the kitchen. The clang of pots and cutlery could be heard from the next room as the cook shouted instructions on dispersing the leftovers from that night's feast.

'Through there. Not here!' the cook ordered the young staff. The door swung open and another armful of bowls was dumped on a bench.

Armue scrubbed old dented steel pots in a deep sink before passing them to his sister on his left. He had to stand on a small crate to reach down to the bottom of the sink, but he made sure he gave Tilly the easier jobs. She was drying and putting away the kitchenware. This was all new to them.

The last of the bowls were unceremoniously dumped on the ground for them to clean.

Tilly had trouble finding where everything had to go. There was shelving on the opposite side of the room for each item, but she always worried she stacked things in the wrong place. Armue would need to dry and stack anything too large for her. They did not understand why the largest and heaviest pots were on the top shelf, but they were told not to move anything and they obeyed that rule. The other rule was not to eat any leftovers from the incoming bowls, but they couldn't obey that one – they would have become so hungry if they did not pick at the leftovers.

'Have you two finished yet?' the cook demanded. 'Clearly not. Get a move on!'

Tilly and Armue rushed to get the cleaning done. The largest pot was left until last. Armue dumped it into the deep sink and, as his arms stretched to scrub the bottom, chunks of old food floated on the surface of the water close to his shoulders.

The door flung open again, and behind the cook stood a tall man.

'That's her. She says her name's Tilly,' said the cook.

The tall man wore a feathered hat and a gold-trimmed cloth vest. His boots were so clean and shiny, they looked as if they'd never been worn before. He had grey streaks through his hair and a thin black moustache. He clicked his fingers and turned around. A young guard of the castle came in and grabbed Tilly by the arm.

'Come on. We are going for a walk. Come with me.'

As the guard dragged Tilly out of the room, she began to cry and scream; she reached for Armue, who pulled his arms out of the water and jumped down from the crate.

'Tilly! Tilly!'

The cook blocked the doorway.

'I have to go with her,' Armue shouted

'No, you don't, young man,' said the cook. 'You're staying right here.'

Other books by this author:

Boy and the Thief

About the Author

Mick J Adams is a writer, screen-writer, musician and voice-actor from Perth, Western Australia. Besides loving spending his free time at the beautiful local beaches, Mick is writing *Boy and the Thief,* the follow-up book to *Boy and the Beetle,* and the second story of the series.